Mercedes Lackey and Rosemary Edghill

Shadow Grail 1

LEGACIES

TOR®

A Tom Doherty Associates Book

New York

SHADOW GRAIL 1: LEGACIES

Copyright © 2010 by Mercedes Lackey and Rosemary Edghill

A Tor Teen Book
Published by Tom Doherty Associates, LLC
175 Fifth Avenue
New York, NY 10010

www.tor-forge.com

Tor® is a registered trademark of Tom Doherty Associates, LLC.

ISBN 978-0-7653-2707-9 (hardcover)
ISBN 978-0-7653-1761-2 (trade paperback)

First Edition: July 2010

Printed in the United States of America

0 9 8 7 6 5 4 3 2 1

Shadow Grail 1

LEGACIES

PROLOGUE

Someone was moaning. Spirit wished whoever it was would be quiet. It sounded horrible, like a dying animal. Why didn't someone do something about it?

And her bed was moving, bouncing, rattling. Was it an earthquake? How could there be an earthquake in Indiana? Her head hurt. She tried to move her arms, but she couldn't, then tried to open her eyes, but she couldn't do that, either. It was like her eyelids were glued shut.

Her head *really* hurt. More every second. And now it hurt to breathe, too.

She wished the person who was moaning would stop. She couldn't think with that horrible sound in her ears. She could hear people around her—why didn't they do something about the person who was moaning?

Everything hurt. Why did everything hurt? She tried to

open her mouth to call for her Mom, and that was when she realized who was moaning.

It was her.

There was a strange taste in her mouth, metallic and nasty, like burned rubber, or plastic mixed with blood. She felt something wet and warm on her face. She tried again to move her arm, to swat whatever it was away, and couldn't. It was all over her eyes, pushing at them, and she tried to move her head away since her arm wouldn't work. But her head wouldn't move either, and the *something* kept swabbing at her eyes until suddenly they came unglued, and she was able to open them.

She regretted that immediately, as bright light stabbed into her brain exactly like a knife, sharp and piercing, and she let out another moan.

A dark shape interposed itself between her eyes and the light. No, not a dark shape. A *person*. Head and shoulders. "Ms. White?" The mouth of the person moved, but the voice seemed to come from far away. "Spirit White?"

Oh, how she hated that name. "Spirit" . . . legacy of parents who just couldn't let the Sixties die. Who named their kid "Spirit" anyway? She was Spirit and her sister was Phoenix and if there had been a third girl she'd have been called Seraphim. All her life that name had been a plague. "Spooky" was the kindest of the nicknames she'd gotten. But the man was waiting for an answer, and she managed to groan out an affirmative.

"Wha— Where?" she asked.

The man looked away, to someone she couldn't see because she couldn't turn her head. "There was an accident," he replied. "You're at St. Francis Hospital."

An accident? But—

They were almost home from the crafts fair, just making that hairpin turn over the ravine with Keller Creek at the bottom of it. Why they had to live back of beyond of everything was just one more instance of the 'rents being holdover hippies. She was already home in her mind, trying to figure out a way to outsmart Phoenix and get to the good computer first so she could keep more than three windows open without it slowing to a crawl. It didn't matter if you had high-speed 'net if the computer had so little memory you couldn't use all that bandwidth! She was trying to think of something she might be doing for school that would mean a lot of research without actually lying about it. What could possibly—

—and then there was a—a flash of dark—all around the car.

It was night, how could there be a flash of dark?

But it had been. It was like a flash, only negative, and before any of them could react with more than a flinch, there was something in the road—right in the middle of the road. It was—

Oh God! It couldn't be— It couldn't be—

And it looked at them and Mom screamed and Dad yanked the wheel sideways—

She opened her mouth to ask where her Mom and Dad and sister were, and all that came out was a moan.

"Spirit, we're going to take you to surgery now. You're going to be fine." There was a sharp pinch at her shoulder, and a moment of burning, then suddenly things stopped hurting. A shot. They'd given her a pain shot. "Don't worry, you're in good hands."

She was all floaty now, and she couldn't keep her eyes open. *Never mind me,* she wanted to say, *where's Mom and Dad and the shrimp?* But she was falling away now, falling into soft, warm blackness, and couldn't get the words out, couldn't even hold onto the thoughts.

Couldn't even beg to be kept safe from that thing that had loomed up in the middle of the road. The thing, the impossible thing that could not exist, with the black, terrible eyes . . .

ONE

Spirit looked listlessly out the window of her room. It wasn't much of a view, just the roof of the next building, part of a parking lot, and some struggling trees beyond. But ever since the accident, there didn't seem to be much point to anything, and one view was as good as another.

Footsteps at the door made her turn her head. It was the orderly, a college guy who was in premed. Neil was cute enough to be a television doctor, not a real one, and spent time with her that he didn't have to. Once Spirit would have welcomed the company. Now, Neil was just one more irritating person who kept wanting her to do things. Like get better. What was the point? Why should she bother to get better? But the people wouldn't leave her alone. Probably they just wanted her out of the nursing home so they could use the bed for someone else.

"Spirit, Oakhurst telephoned. The car is on the way. They'll be picking you up in about half an hour, and I'll bring your chair then." Neil gave her that brown-eyed compassionate look that always made her give up and do or say what he wanted. *He'll make a good doctor someday,* she thought.

"I'm ready," she said, since it was what he wanted to hear. Of course she was ready. She didn't have anything to take with her, anyway. Everything she had now was really Oakhurst's.

When she'd finally woken up after the emergency surgery, the hospital had sent in a social worker and a minister to tell her that Mom and Dad and Phoenix had died in the crash, and that "it was a miracle" she had survived. Who'd want that kind of miracle? She couldn't even go to the funeral. She'd have been the only one there anyway: both Mom and Dad were only children, so no relatives, and, as far as Spirit knew, she didn't have any grandparents. Mom telecommuted—*had* telecommuted—to someplace on the other side of the country, and Dad had worked at home, in the workshop and kiln in back of the house. They'd been coming home from a craft show that night. So, no coworkers. And she and Phoenix had both been homeschooled for the last two years, ever since Dad got into a fight with the school board about the curriculum. So, no classmates.

And then, not three weeks later—like a brick falling on someone who'd been thrown off a building—a sheriff's deputy came to Spirit's hospital room and told her that there'd been another accident, that her parents' empty house had caught fire and burned to the ground. There weren't any neighbors near enough to see and call it in, of course. She'd seen the photos he'd brought her. The only thing left was the chimney and a few heaps of crumpled metal that had been the furnace and major appliances. The fire marshal said he thought "kids" had done it.

She'd been so drugged up the catastrophe really hadn't registered until later, when she'd realized that if she ever got out of there, there was no home to go back to. And why would she want to go home anyway? There was no one there.

That was when the lawyer showed up.

He wasn't her Dad's lawyer, or an insurance company lawyer. He wasn't anybody local at all. He could have been a lawyer on a TV show, all slick and polished and without a hair out of place. He talked to her as if she was six instead of almost sixteen and told her that her parents had set up a "trust" for her, that the trust was administered by this "Oakhurst Foundation," that the Foundation was covering all her bills until the insurance could be sorted out, and that when she was fully recovered, Oakhurst would be sending for her, because she'd be living at "The Oakhurst Complex" until she was twenty-one. And she didn't need to worry about a thing, because she'd have everything she needed.

Never mind that what Spirit needed these people could never give her. Never mind that her parents had never said anything to her about Oakhurst or a trust. Things were already being done, what was left of her life had already been taken over, and Spirit didn't care enough to fight it. Things kept arriving from Oakhurst—both while she was at the hospital and when—six weeks after the accident—she was moved to a "rehabilitation facility." Flowers she told the nurses to take. Books she didn't read. Clothing she didn't bother to wear. Stuffed bears she told the nurses to give to somebody else. She didn't want anything. Why should she? Her parents had always taught her that *people* were important, not *things,* and all of her people—everyone who *counted*—were gone. There was nothing left to fight for.

All Spirit wanted to do was to lie down and go to sleep and never wake up again.

Neil was still standing in the doorway.

She was trying to make up her mind about saying something when he broke the silence. "Look, Spirit. Get mad at me if you want, but this moping around you're doing has got to stop."

She stared at him. "What?" she demanded, lifted out of her apathy by the bite of anger. "I'm not supposed to be *depressed*? In case you hadn't noticed, my whole family is dead, I'm being shipped off to some dumping ground in the middle of nowhere, and nobody cares!"

She felt the tears start then, burning her eyes, burning her cheeks, and she wiped them angrily away. Of course nobody cared! Maybe even Mom and Dad hadn't cared, if this was their idea of what should be done with her—the treacherous thought had been eating at her for weeks, no matter how hard she tried to suppress it. They couldn't have cared, they hadn't told her about any of this, hadn't consulted her—

"Have you got any idea how much your rehab cost, not to mention your surgeries?" Neil asked, scowling. "Did you know the insurance cut off after ninety days, and Oakhurst picked up after that and paid for everything? And all the extras, too—private duty nurses, your physical therapy sessions, your private room at St. Francis and here—trust me, those things don't come cheap. Without that rehab you wouldn't be walking now. So whoever these people are, whatever the school is like, it's not going to be a dumping ground. But that's not why you're being emo—"

"*Emo!* I am not—"

"What would your folks think?" Neil interrupted ruthlessly. "You! Sitting around hoping to die! They went to a lot of trouble, thinking about what might happen if they were gone, planning for it, finding the place they did! You know how many kids with both parents gone end up in the system, tossed around to group homes, foster homes . . . forgotten? No. You don't. And you never will. Your parents took the time and planned ahead, even though they hoped it would never come to this, and now there you sit, wanting to throw away their last gift to you like it was nothing. What do you think they'd think if they saw you like this?" Neil shook his head. "It's not what they'd want for you. And it's not *respectful* to them." With that, before Spirit could think of a retort, before any of the angry replies she wanted to make could actually form into words, Neil turned and left.

It was as if a fire had kindled inside her. How dared he! How dared he say those things! She hated him! But the anger was having a strange effect on her. She began to feel more alive than she had in . . . months. By the time a nurse came to tell her that the car had come for her, Spirit felt almost as if she had awakened from a drugged daze.

The orderly brought her wheelchair—the fancy one that Oakhurst had paid for. She hadn't needed it in weeks, but she knew it was the facility's policy that she wouldn't be let to make the trip from her room to the curb on her own two feet. She'd expected the orderly to be Neil, and had been looking forward to giving him a piece of her mind. Money couldn't make up for the loss of her parents, her little sister, her *life*. But she didn't even see him anywhere on the floor. *Good riddance,* she thought sourly.

She scanned the curb as they emerged into the bright light of a September afternoon, looking for the sort of car she expected would pick her up to take her to an orphanage. She was looking for some kind of van, but all she saw was a limousine—an actual Rolls-Royce in a rich chocolate brown. She frowned; the nurse had been very specific that her car was here.

Her car.

Her—

She took a closer look. On the front door of the car there was a design in gold leaf. She peered at it. She couldn't tell what was in the fake-English coat of arms, but she could read the words *Oakhurst Academy* that were underneath it in Old English letters.

The door opened, the chauffeur—he was even wearing a uniform!—got out and opened the passenger door, then offered her his hand to help her up out of the chair. She blinked at him in disbelief.

"I'm here to take you to the airport, Miss White," the man said with grave formality and a faint trace of an English accent. "Your luggage is already in the boot."

Stunned, Spirit let him take her hand and help her up and into the back of the car.

"It will be a long drive, miss, and the refrigerator is fully stocked. Please help yourself to whatever you'd like," the chauffeur said. "Oakhurst has sent along some orientation literature, if you're interested in perusing it during the drive." And with that, he closed the door behind her.

Feeling out of her depth, Spirit settled back and fastened her seat belt as the chauffeur walked around to the driver's side, got behind the wheel, closed his door, and the limousine pulled smoothly away from the curb.

"Hi, I'm Loch," said a voice from the shadows on the far side of the limousine. "Lachlan Spears, but, you know, call me Loch. I guess you're Spirit White."

She strangled on an *"eep!"* and stared at the corner. Somehow Lachlan Spears had turned off the interior lights on the other side of the limousine's back seat, and the tinted windows made it dark in here, even in daylight. When he leaned forward, though, and Spirit got a good look at him, what she saw was a thin, handsome guy about her age, with the sort of flyaway hair only a good haircut got you, and melting blue eyes. He was holding a big folder—like the kind she had for her school stuff, the kind that had pockets on both sides. He held it out and she took it automatically.

"That's the school stuff," Loch said diffidently.

Spirit made a sour face—because it wasn't a school, it was an *orphanage*—but opened it anyway. It was full of . . . stuff. On one side was a bunch of Chamber of Commerce pamphlets about the area around Oakhurst. She opened one about some-place called Radial, which was apparently "the jewel of McBride County." Spirit wrinkled her nose. According to the facts and statistics in the little pamphlet, Radial had a population of 700 and was four hours away from Billings, which was the largest city in Montana. She gave up and turned to the school litera-ture. It was a very slick booklet that looked more like some-thing you'd get from a pricey private college than an orphanage. On the front was the expected view of the orphanage-slash-school . . . except it didn't look like anything Spirit expected. Oakhurst School looked like one of those big manor houses that got used in movies set in England.

The school's coat of arms had been on the front of the folder, and it was on the cover of the booklet, too, only here it was in color. It was pretty fancy. Spirit bit her lip, thinking of the rude things Phoenix would have said about it. Phoenix had adored every dumb movie about King Arthur and Camelot to come along, from *The Sword in the Stone* to *First Knight* to *A Knight's Tale*.

On top of the shield there was a bear's head on a plate, which was weird just to start with. On one side of the shield was a gold upside-down cup, and on the other was a broken silver sword. She frowned. The design was decidedly unset-tling. On the shield itself, which was mostly red, there was a broad white stripe going from the top right to the bottom left, and on top of that was an oak tree (for Oakhurst, she guessed) in bright green and brown. Only when she looked more closely, there was a gold snake coiled in the branches. Maybe it all made more sense if you were English. She turned the page quickly. More pictures of the manor house. It was *huge*. And unless they'd Photoshopped the heck out of it, there wasn't a chip in the stone or a blade of grass out of place.

She paid no attention to the text . . . it was just a bunch of stuff about the guy who'd built the place back in the early 1900s. Instead she stared at the glossy photographs. They looked like a set for one of the *Harry Potter* movies, not like anything Spirit could imagine being actually *real*. There was the "Great Hall," done up in the kind of grand Art Deco scheme she remembered from visiting the Empire State Building in New York City once. There was a "refectory"—which looked pretty much like a dining room, with white linen tablecloths and enormous chandeliers; a library—which could have been pulled right out of another of those fake British Stately Homes; and a couple of pictures of classrooms. It looked as if there were school uniforms. Spirit frowned. She thought she was going to get pretty tired of brown and gold before she was done with this place, though. She turned the page quickly, intending to skip the rest of the boring stuff (if this was an orphanage, who was this supposed to impress?) but something caught her eye.

"Oakhurst residents will be encouraged to explore information technology in our state-of-the-art facility in order to prepare themselves for the challenges of the future." Spirit knew computers, so she frankly stared at the full-page spread on the computer lab,

because the descriptions of what was available for the students' use was mouth-watering. The whole school had WiFi, and its own servers, and the servers ran on a T1 line to the outside world—a full-duplex circuit transmitting 1.544 megabytes per second concurrently. Uploads, downloads, and net-surfing would take place at the speed of light. And the brochure said that each arriving student was "issued" their own laptop. She turned the page. There were photos of a tennis court and an Olympic-sized *indoor* swimming pool. And there were riding stables! A gymnasium! An exercise room with more equipment than an athletic club! Each picture just made her stare harder. Finally she looked up at Loch.

"What—?"

"I keep thinking it can't be real either, but . . . this is the school's own Rolls." Loch shrugged. "And I can't think of any reason they'd want to fool us. I can't touch a penny of my trust fund until I'm twenty-one, and, uh, it's not like I'm anyone important. All Father's stock and everything just got bought back by the partnership and the money was put into the trust. And neither of us has any place else to go anymore."

She'd thought she was cried out by this time. But that reminder of *why* she was on her way to this place was enough to crack Spirit open all over again. To her dismay, her eyes brimmed up and spilled over, and when she tried to catch her breath, she heard herself give a long shuddering sob. Loch looked helpless as he handed her the box of tissues set into the armrest next to her.

"I . . ." Loch gulped. "I'm sorry, Spirit . . ."

She struggled to get control of herself, and Loch kept talking, stumbling through a long rambling explanation of how he'd ended up here in the back of this limousine with her because he was obviously mortified at having made her cry.

"I don't . . . I mean, my father and I never really got along. I hardly knew him. He was always off on business trips, or working, and my mother died when I was a baby. If Father could have gotten one of his assistants to take me for that interview at Albany Academy he would have, but they said he had to be there, so when the hotel caught fire and he didn't get out, it was . . ."

Loch finally ran down, like a music box running down, his last sentence unfinished. Spirit got control of herself and wiped her eyes and her sore nose. She thought she remembered seeing that hotel fire on the news. It couldn't have happened more than a week ago. Sixty people had died. "How . . . How did you get out?" she asked.

Loch shrugged. "We were in separate rooms. He wanted it that way. I guess he had . . . woman-plans. I went out the window. I free-climb, I do *parkour*. I never even thought about going out the door." He sighed. "I don't know. I mean, he was my father and I should feel something but . . . I know more about *Tom Cruise* than I know about my own father."

Spirit nodded numbly. In a way, she wished it had been the same for her. It wouldn't have hurt so badly.

"I wish I'd had a family like yours," Loch said forlornly. "At least . . . at least I'd have something to miss. I've just got . . . nothing."

He might have said more, except the limousine started to slow, and then took the airport exit. When it entered the airport

21

itself it turned off into what was obviously the private aviation side of the airport. Loch glanced out the window. "I guess there's no direct flight from anywhere to Oakhurst. They sent me a ticket to here from Albany, and the lawyer-dude put me on the plane yesterday."

The limousine pulled up beside a private hanger and the chauffeur came around and opened the doors for them. As Spirit got out, she saw that a couple of men in bright blue jumpsuits were loading what she recognized as her suitcases into a private jet. She blinked at it as Loch got out, just a little relieved to see that it didn't have the same school insignia on it. Suddenly Spirit had the feeling that her entire life had just started a fast downhill run that she had absolutely no control over.

"Master Spears, Miss White, the plane is ready for you to board. If you would please be so good as to follow me?" the chauffeur said discreetly.

With a lump in her throat and a matching one in her stomach, Spirit followed the chauffeur over to the steps, and then climbed them into the cabin and tried not to gawk at the luxurious interior. She might just as well have been dropped into a book. Spirit White, whose parents kept their cars running until they couldn't be repaired anymore, whose house had been filled with furniture her parents had gotten at garage sales and estate auctions and refinished in the garage, who'd learned how to sew so she could finally have clothing her mom didn't get at Walmart or Goodwill, did *not* belong in a private jet that looked like it was owned by Donald Trump!

But Loch just glanced around as if this was all familiar to

him, chose a seat, and buckled himself into it. "This should be pretty fast," he said quietly, as Spirit fumbled with her own seat belt. "Four hours, maybe, with the routing around commercial airspace. This is a Lear."

"Okay," Spirit replied, as someone outside put up the stairs with a heavy *thud*. Immediately the jet's engines began to whine up to speed. It turned in place and taxied to the runway, and before she could ask Loch anything more, suddenly the thing was hurtling down the runway at a speed that pressed her back into her seat. She hardly had time to begin to feel terror at the speed of the tiny thing when it hurtled upward at an angle so steep that she clutched the armrests of her seat and shut her eyes convulsively.

When she opened her eyes again, she saw Loch leaning forward and looking out the tiny window. She forced herself to do the same. The ground seemed impossibly far away, and the plane was still climbing. Loch was saying something.

"What?" she asked, turning back to look at him.

"I said, Lear jets can cruise at about eight miles up," he repeated. "That's probably where we'll level off."

She couldn't tell if it was eight miles or not, but when the jet did ease into level flight, she couldn't even see any roads or buildings on the ground below. She was about to ask Loch if he traveled like this all the time, when suddenly the flatscreen mounted in the front bulkhead came to life. It showed a cool-looking woman, a brunette in a red suit, with an expensive haircut. Was anything associated with Oakhurst *not* expensive? She had a professional TV-newscaster smile.

"Welcome to Oakhurst Academy," the woman said, in a cool clear voice that made her seem even more like a TV announcer. It gave Spirit the sharp scary feeling that she'd somehow wandered into a movie version of Real Life. "And if you had not wondered before this, by this point it has certainly occurred to you to wonder why you are here, and why you have never heard of us before this. Certainly you must be curious about the reasons your parents had for arranging for Oakhurst to become your guardian."

"Well, duh," Spirit muttered, that anger starting to smolder in her again, resentment pushing out the fear.

"The reason is simple. You are a Legacy."

A what? Spirit thought, but Loch clearly understood what that meant, since he stifled a gasp of surprise.

"What this means is that your parents, one or both of them, were also raised at Oakhurst. You might already be aware of that fact. If so, you have some idea of what Oakhurst will be like. But if you were not told, then all this is new information for you. And at this moment, I'm sure you're thinking that they had been remarkably vague about why they had no brothers or sisters, why you had no grandparents." Spirit's resentment grew hotter: this woman, whoever she was, looked unbearably smug to her. "We won't even begin to try to guess why your parent or parents kept this information from you. Perhaps it was a form of rebellion against what they felt was an extremely privileged upbringing. Whatever the cause, we at Oakhurst feel rather proprietary about our graduates. They might sever all ties with us, but we take our guardianship seriously, and keep careful track of their lives. Once they have children of their own, we contact them a single time, to arrange that, should the unthinkable happen, *we* will assume responsibility for their offspring. I am pleased to say this offer has never been rejected."

Oh you are, are you? Spirit wanted to smack the expression right off Ms. TV Personality's recorded face.

"We have no false modesty. Oakhurst graduates are the best of the best. They have the finest educations, and they are of excellent stock. Their children are no less." *Not just smug, but arrogant,* Spirit decided. "You will be given the same education and opportunities. No matter what they become, an Oakhurst alumnus is born to lead."

The television went blank again. Spirit stole a look at Loch. His expression was very thoughtful.

"Well," he finally said. "That explains a lot."

Spirit swallowed. She only wished she could agree.

two

Four hours was a long time to spend in a small space with just one other person. It was long enough for Spirit to decide that she liked Loch a lot. Sure, Loch obviously came from money, but it didn't seem to have turned him into a spoiled brat. She found out that he'd been bounced around a bunch of private schools, but it wasn't because *he* got into trouble, it was because for a while he was bullied a lot, and at the kind of schools he'd been going to, it was easier to take the kid being bullied out of the dorms and send him for a series of "counseling" sessions that accomplished exactly nothing rather than to blame anybody for anything. Each time that started, Loch's father would yank him out of the school and find another one, and nothing really changed.

"It finally stopped when one of the physical culture teachers started teaching me *parkour,* and free-running, and free-climbing." Loch smiled shyly. "I couldn't *fight* back, but if they couldn't catch me, they couldn't hit me, and after a while there wasn't anyone who could catch me."

That was the second time Loch had used those terms, and Spirit *knew* she knew them from somewhere. Then she got it. A documentary about a bunch of guys who did things—*for fun*—that would give Spider-Man a run for his money. "Like in *Jump London*?" she asked. Loch nodded vigorously, looking pleased that she knew.

Once they started really talking, time passed faster for her than it had in months. There was a small pantry at one end of the plane—there was even a sink! Loch got thirsty and went to prowl through it, coming back with sodas and a *covered* (not wrapped) platter of sandwiches, and another platter of fruit and fancy cookies. Spirit nibbled absently while they talked, and Loch inhaled the food like every other guy she'd known. By the time the plane started descending, they pretty much had the major details of each other's life stories. And she decided that aside from the money and the family thing, the two of them were a lot alike. They liked a lot of the same books, same music, same shows—disliked the same kinds of people and attitudes. And for most of the flight she'd been able to *not* think about having lost Mom and Dad and Phoenix.

She'd never particularly wondered about what Montana looked like, but as the plane descended, she quickly realized that she'd been wrong to think Indiana was the butt-end of the universe. *This* was the butt-end of the universe! No cities. No *towns*. At least, not until they got a whole lot lower, and then there was a little bit of a town that looked like it had a main street and maybe four cross streets and that was it. Finally she heard a hum and a thump that must have been the landing gear descending. There still wasn't much outside the windows but miles of Empty.

The plane touched down so softly Spirit didn't even feel it at first, she only saw that there was tarmac on either side. Then the engines reversed, throwing them both forward against their seat belts, and the plane was rolling in a big circle, and coming to a stop, and now there *was* something outside the windows. A line of hangars, and in the distance the tiny town she'd glimpsed from the air. Loch said that this was only a little county airport. Spirit couldn't make up her mind whether to be glad that he was answering her questions before she asked them, or cross that he knew she didn't know these things.

Waiting as the plane rolled to a stop was a *huge* chocolate-colored SUV and another driver in a uniform. The SUV had the same gold-leafed coat of arms on it that the limousine had and the words *Oakhurst Academy* on the side.

The pilot walked back out of the cockpit. Spirit realized in surprise that they hadn't heard the woman say anything during the entire flight. The woman walked back to the hatch and opened it, then lowered the stairs for them, still without saying anything. As Spirit walked carefully down the steps— this was actually the first time she'd been up and down a flight of steps since the accident—she saw that a man in green coveralls was already taking their baggage out of the luggage compartment of the jet and stowing it in the back of the SUV. It was chillier in Montana in September than it was in Indiana, and Spirit wished she had a sweater on.

"Master Spears," said the driver of the SUV, nodding to Loch. "Miss White. Do you need any assistance getting in?"

From here the SUV looked so big it ought to have its own zip code, but Loch was already jumping in, so Spirit shook her head and hauled herself up into it. Inside it was just as plush as the limousine had been, and in the same colors.

She'd thought they'd just be driving to the school, but apparently not. They drove for about half an hour while Spirit looked out the window and tried not to feel like an extra in a Western, until they reached the outskirts of the little town. There was a normal, modern-looking train platform and ticket office on one side of the wide set of tracks—there must have been four sets of them laid side by side—but the SUV drove across the tracks to the other side, where there was a little Victorian-looking platform. The wooden sign hanging over it said "Terry," and Spirit wondered if all the train stations here had girl's names.

"We're taking the train," Loch said in delight.

"Yes, Master Spears," the driver said without turning around. "It will be here in just a few moments."

"Oakdale was originally a private house," Loch said, seeing Spirit's look of bafflement. "It belonged to an old-time railroad tycoon named Arthur Tyniger, and he had a private railway line built that went right to his door. This is Terry—as in *town of* Terry—where you can get the school's private car hooked onto a regular train."

"I can't imagine why I'd want to do that," Spirit said. The

words came out more sarcastically than she'd really intended, and Loch looked hurt.

"Winters here get pretty . . . wintery," Loch said. "I guess it's a lot easier to take the train than it is to fight your way through snow for hours."

Less than five minutes later, their train pulled up. Despite what the train station looked like, the engine and single car that eased into the station were Amtrak-modern.

The driver of the SUV had waited on the platform with them, and as soon as the car's doors opened, he gestured to them to step inside. Spirit thought it was just creepy to have adults waiting on her like she was some kind of *princess* or something, but Loch didn't seem to think it was all that weird. She could see that somebody had stepped out of the door at the far end of the car and was coming to collect their suitcases. Loch had two—a big one and a little one—and they looked just like hers. After a moment Spirit realized why. He would have lost everything in the hotel fire. It looked like Oakhurst had just sent him a new wardrobe rather than having him send for his clothes from home. She supposed that made sense, if there was a school uniform, but what if he'd wanted to bring his personal things?

At least Loch still *had* personal things.

She knew—after the Rolls-Royce and the Lear jet—she ought to be used to the way Oakhurst did things, but the in-side of the train car was still a surprise. Spirit had been on trains several times, but she doubted anybody had *ever* been on a train like this. The whole floor was carpeted. The carpet was chocolate brown, of course. The seats were upholstered like living room furniture, in a plush gold and brown brocade. There were two seats along one aisle and one seat on the other side, so the aisle was twice as wide as normal, and there was plenty of legroom between the seats. The car didn't run the full length of the train, though.

"Probably there's a separate baggage car—or compartment," Loch said, following her look. He dropped down into one of the single seats—on the side of the train facing the station— and Spirit sat down across the aisle.

"What? No dining room? We might starve to death or something," Spirit said, and he laughed.

"I'll check as soon as we get going. It should only be an hour from here to the school, though." As if his words had been a signal, the engine's whistle wailed softly, and the train jerked into motion.

"How come you know so much about this place?" Spirit asked curiously, while a little voice inside her said: *You could have known just as much if you'd bothered to take an interest in anything but yourself any time in the last several weeks.*

"Internet," Loch said. "I don't know much. I just know where it is. I've always been interested in geography, you know? And they weren't exactly trying to hide. I can tell you all about beautiful Radial, Montana. Man, I'd hate to live there. I've gone to schools with a larger student body than their whole population." He shuddered.

The train quickly picked up speed. Soon they were traveling through a lot of vast, green, *empty* landscape. There were roads, but Spirit didn't see any cars on them. Occasionally they'd cross a road—or a road would cross the tracks—and the engine would blow its whistle loudly. After about forty minutes, she was thoroughly bored. She finally turned back to the orientation packet. The folder contained pamphlets from the McBride Chamber of Commerce. Reading them, she found out that McBride County was filled with dinosaur bones, and Radial was known for its winter wheat, its spring wheat, its barley, cattle, lambs, and (apparently) one church per 100 residents. The pamphlets also mentioned that local wildlife included deer, grouse, pheasants, prairie dogs, eagles, and coyotes.

"A hunter's paradise," Loch said.

"You don't approve of hunting?" she asked, because there'd been actual *contempt* in Loch's voice.

"I don't like guns," Loch said flatly. "They're just another way for people to turn themselves into bullies."

"Sometimes they're necessary," Spirit said. Not because she believed it, but because she wanted to see what he'd say.

"Sometimes a lot of things are necessary," Loch said after a pause. "And sometimes people do a lot of things that aren't."

I t was another hour before they reached Oakhurst. It was bigger than it had looked in the brochure—now that they weren't seeing it all cut up into a bunch of photographs they could see that the grand manor house had gotten a couple of wings built onto it. On its right there was a building that had to be the gym because the glass-enclosed pool was clearly visible and it had tennis courts next to it and a track field with covered bleachers beside it. There were some people running on the track, and two people playing tennis. On the left of the manor house (not that close) were the stables, and what looked like a big sandlot in front of them where three people on horseback were doing something. There was an actual road that went past the school, and another road that went through its front gates, but the train went on past it for about a mile as it made a long gentle curve back around in the direction of the school.

But a few moments later the train pulled up about half a mile from the back of the manor house, into a station that made the one in Terry just look cheesy. It was all done in wrought iron and leaded glass—she saw as they approached—and the train pulled into it like it was pulling into a garage. If it happened to be raining that day—or snowing, or whatever—the entire platform would be perfectly dry. Only the ends were open. And of course there was no ticket office.

There were two people already waiting on the platform. One of them was a guy in a blazer with the school crest on the pocket and gold slacks, and the other was the same woman who'd been in the video, only this time she was wearing a black suit, not a red one.

"Here comes trouble," Loch said under his breath.

When the train huffed and shivered to a stop, the two of them got to their feet and walked over to the door.

"Lachlan Spears and Spirit White." The woman nodded at them, but didn't offer her hand. "Please follow me." Without waiting for an answer, she turned and walked off.

The two of them looked at each other and shrugged, but there wasn't really any reason to argue. The man who'd been standing with her had gone straight to the luggage compartment and gone inside; Spirit guessed that they weren't going to be expected to do something as *mundane* as carry their own suitcases.

The woman didn't really seem to care if they kept up with her or not, and at least Spirit didn't have to worry about trying to stay warm. The path from the "train station" to the front of the house was red brick, and it even had streetlights. There was a back entrance—a wide fieldstone terrace with a wall of French doors—but apparently they were going to be entering through the front door.

The front entrance, now that Spirit got a good look at it, looked more like an enormous and expensive "wilderness" hotel than either a house or a school. The architecture was geometric and sort of Art Deco, but it was all done in native stone and peeled logs that had been heavily varnished.

"Arts and Crafts 'Lodge,'" said Loch, with a nod at the front entrance. "I'd bet a lot that Gilbert Stanley Underwood designed this."

"I'd be more impressed if I knew who that was—" began Spirit, when the door was opened by yet another guy in a blazer and they walked into the Entry Hall.

It was impressive in pictures.

It was stunning in real life.

The focal point of the room was the biggest single tree trunk that Spirit had ever seen in person. Probably only one of the giant redwoods could dwarf it. It held up the ceiling, which was crossed with peeled-log beams, but between the beams were panels of wood inlay done in vaguely Egyptian patterns. Behind the tree-pillar a balcony stretched the breadth of the room, and it was embraced by two half-circle staircases with peeled-log banisters and chocolate-colored carpeted steps that led up to the balcony. Seven chandeliers made of what must have been hundreds of deer antlers hung from the ceiling.

The floor was moss green stone, also inlaid with thin strips of brass that outlined more vaguely Egyptian geometric designs in white, cream, gray, and black stone. To the right of the enormous room—it must have been sixty feet across if it was a foot—was a blonde woman behind a reception desk that seemed to fit in perfectly with everything else here, although Spirit was pretty sure there hadn't been a reception desk here originally. To the left there was a fireplace made of rough stone that was more than big enough to park a horse in, with a huge half-log mantelpiece and peeled-log couches with buckskin cushions in front of it. Rugs made up of several sheepskins pieced together were spread around the floor in front of the fireplace, and there was a huge banner with the Oakhurst crest, the red-and-white shield with the oak tree with the gold snake coiled in the branches. It should have looked gaudy at that size. It didn't. If anything, it looked rather sinister.

Everything was as clean as if an entire army of people spent all their time polishing every crevice. There was a faint smell of wood smoke and pine in the air from the fire in the fireplace, and the air was cool, though not as chilly as it was outside.

"He's ready for them, Ms. Corby," the woman at the desk said before Spirit quite got through taking it all in.

The woman with them just nodded, and headed for a pair of huge brass-studded wooden doors next to the reception desk. One of them opened at her touch, and she motioned to Spirit and Loch to go inside. They stepped past her cautiously, and even Loch looked a little daunted by now.

The walls of the room were almost solid floor-to-ceiling bookcases, with books arranged in mathematical precision. Between the books—and along the tops of the bookshelves—there were statues, bits of pottery, things Spirit couldn't even identify, but which looked expensive. The floor was carpeted with thick moss-green carpet that was so plush her feet sank into it. There were two more of those deer-horn chandeliers, and tall bronze floor lamps in the corners of the room. They were all necessary, because it didn't have any windows.

Dominating the room was a huge desk that Spirit decided had to have been built right here, because as wide and tall as the double doors were, there was still no way it could have come in through them. Its top and sides were inlaid with more of those Egyptian-y patterns in different colored woods, and there were two of the peeled-log-and-leather chairs in front of it, set side by side. There was a fireplace behind it, a little smaller than the one in the Entry Hall, with a fire burning in it. And seated behind the desk was a man in a gray double-breasted suit.

His hair was pure silvery white, combed straight back, and long enough to brush his shoulders. His beard was the same color, and it was just a little bit longer than anybody but modern-day hippies wore them these days, but despite that he didn't remind Spirit of any of her parents' friends—or of a kindly, blue-eyed, rosy-cheeked Santa Claus. He looked as if he should have been wearing wizard's robes instead of a modern-day power suit. He regarded them for a moment as Ms. Corby closed the door behind them. Finally he spoke.

"Spirit White. Lachlan Spears." He had a very compelling voice; deep and sonorous, with a faint British accent. Despite his silver hair and beard, his voice didn't sound old at all. "I am Doctor Ambrosius. This is my establishment. Please sit down."

He indicated the two chairs in front of the desk. Gingerly, Spirit took a seat in the right-hand one, leaving Lachlan the left. Doctor Ambrosius regarded them both with the same detached interest that some of the doctors in the hospital had used—as if she and Loch were "interesting cases" and not people. Well, okay. It wasn't as if she had to *like* him. She just had to make sure that from now until she was twenty-one she didn't give him any reason to make things hard for her. So she put on her best poker-face, the one she'd learned over the last few months as she'd fended off social workers and counselors and everyone who'd wanted to "help" her "come to terms" with her "loss."

Doctor Ambrosius leaned forward a little. "What is in the video you saw on the plane," he said, his voice taking on a confidential tone, "was not—quite—the whole truth. Yes, you are Legacies. Yes, we do keep track of our Legacy children. And yes, if something happens to their parents, we see to it that the children are well cared for until they are twenty-one. But"—he held up a finger—"we don't bring all of them here. However *you*—like the rest of the young people here at Oakhurst—are very special."

Spirit exchanged a glance with Loch. Any minute now he was going to tell them they were Jedi Knights, or lost members of an alien race, or . . . something.

"Special how?" Loch asked neutrally.

Doctor Ambrosius smiled slightly. "You, and all the others here, are—or rather, one day *will* be—magicians."

Spirit broke into a disbelieving laugh. "Right," she said, starting to stand up. Mean, she could deal with; crazy was something else. "Thank you, Professor Dumbledore. I hope that train hasn't left yet, because—"

Doctor Ambrosius made a careless gesture, and suddenly Spirit was shoved back into her chair. It felt as if someone had pushed her—hard!—but there was nothing she could see. Before she could react, Doctor Ambrosius crooked his finger, and two of the bookcases slammed together across the door with a hollow *boom*. She could see that Loch was struggling to get up, too, and not having any success.

As the force continued to hold both of them down in their seats, Doctor Ambrosius got to his feet. "You don't believe in magic, of course. And I am sure that in a few moments, you will have convinced yourselves that I am holding you in place with magnets, or some other such nonsense, and that some artifice moved those bookcases in front of the door." Behind him, the fire in the fireplace suddenly flared up, only now the flames were blue and green. "And you will tell yourselves that chemicals—and not the exercise of Power—are the cause of what is happening behind me. But the world, young magicians, is a very, *very* dangerous place for our kind. That danger comes not from discovery by the ordinary, humdrum mortals we live and move among, but from others of our own kind. And I am going to show you just *how* dangerous a place it is for the unwary."

Suddenly he spread his arms wide, and his eyes blazed as the fire behind him roared up, in blues and purples now. In seconds, he and his desk ballooned gigantically, and Spirit squeaked in dismay. And squeaked again in fear, as she realized it was not Doctor Ambrosius who'd grown, but *she* who had *shrunk,* and when she looked over frantically at the other chair where Loch had been, she didn't see Loch—

She saw a small and very terrified white mouse.

He's a mouse! That means I'm a mouse, too! Spirit squeaked again—this time in terror—and leaped without thinking toward the floor. But she wasn't used to having four legs instead of two, or seeing the world this way—flat and with all the colors dimmed down, and seeing almost all the way behind her instead of just straight ahead—and her uncoordinated limbs went out from under her as she landed. She tumbled like a bit of trash, her nose assaulted by a thousand sharp intense smells from the carpet. She looked around in a frenzy of fear, trying to spot Doctor Ambrosius—

And the biggest owl she'd ever seen in her life dropped

down on top of her and seized her in its talons. They were several feet long and sharp as razors. She went limp with terror as pain burned down her—arm?—foreleg. She heard strangled squeaking, and saw that the owl had the other mouse—Loch!—under its other foot.

The bird's beak opened, and a kind of hooting, hissing speech came from it. *"You see, young magicians, just how unprepared you are for the ones that would eat you alive, just as quickly and easily as an owl would eat a mouse."*

The owl flapped its wings, carrying them upward, and as it got over the chair that Spirit had been in, it opened its talons and dropped her into it. She landed on the cushion, bounced once or twice, the breath driven out of her and seeing stars, and then—

Then she was herself again, sprawled over the chair in an awkward and uncomfortable pose, her long blonde hair a tangled mess. She scrambled around into a sitting position, pushing it out of her eyes. Everything hurt.

"Son of a—" Loch held onto one of the arms of his chair with both hands for a moment.

Doctor Ambrosius was standing behind his desk again just as if nothing had happened. He cleared his throat, and they both swiveled their heads to stare at him. "Now you see why you were brought here, and why it is inadvisable for you to leave before you are properly trained." He made another of those little gestures, and the bookcases slid back from the door. The fire in the fireplace shrank, and turned from purple to blue to green and then to the normal yellow. "I trust that now I have your full attention." Doctor Ambrosius sat back in his chair.

Spirit nodded.

"Yes sir," Loch said in a shaky voice.

Doctor Ambrosius did not smile. "There are all manner of magicians," he said. "The power expresses itself in many ways. We won't know just what you can do until we have finished testing you. Once we know, you can begin your training in the Arcane Arts. But regardless of your powers, there is a great, wide world out there into which you must fit and remain undetected—and to that end, Oakhurst is as much the school you saw in the brochure as it is a school of *Grammery*." The way he said that last word made it clear without explanation that he meant magic. "Now, on that note, I shall return you to Ms. Corby's capable hands. She will show you to your rooms and acquaint you with what you can expect from here on. We will have another interview in a few days when you have settled in. Good day."

The doors opened at another of Doctor Ambrosius's gestures. He turned his chair so that it faced the fire, with his back to them. Spirit and Loch slowly got up and walked back out into the Entry Hall. The door closed behind them. The receptionist wasn't at her desk, and Ms. Corby wasn't there either. In the echoing silence, Spirit and Loch looked at each other.

"Did I just have a really vivid hallucination?" Loch asked.

Spirit swallowed hard. "If you did—" she began.

"Hey!" Loch said. "You're bleeding." He nodded at her right arm.

As if him saying the words made it real, suddenly her arm twinged with a sharp pain. "Ow!"

She held out her arm and stared at it. She'd worn a sleeveless blouse to leave the hospital, and had been regretting it ever since she arrived in Montana. *I guess it's just as well,* she thought, half-hysterically, *they say it's impossible to get bloodstains out of a white blouse.* . . . From wrist to elbow her arm was scored with a deep, angry-red scratch. It looked exactly like a cat scratch—if the cat had claws as long as her arm.

Or like an owl's talons—if you were the size of a white mouse.

"Um . . . maybe not a hallucination," she said quietly.

THREE

When Ms. Corby appeared a minute or so later, she had a man in a business suit with her. "Miss White, with me. Master Spears, with Mr. Devon," she said with detached pleasantness. "The Young Ladies' Wing is to the right, the Young Gentlemen's to the left."

For a moment, Spirit felt a flash of panic. Loch was the only person in this whole place she knew! But then she forced herself to be calm. It wasn't as if they were being incarcerated, and after that interview with Doctor Ambrosius, it was pretty clear that being separated from Loch was the least of her worries. The four of them walked back beneath the balcony to where there was a perfectly ordinary set of double doors—a far more ordinary set than those that led into Doctor Ambrosius's sanctum.

"Are you teachers?" Spirit asked, as Mr. Devon held open one door for them.

Ms. Corby looked faintly amused. "Certainly not. Mr. Devon and I assist Doctor Ambrosius directly. He has more to deal with than just this school."

"Are you—" Loch hesitated over the word.

"Magicians?" Ms. Corby asked, sounding more than amused now. "Mr. Devon is, I am not. But everyone here knows what Doctor Ambrosius is, and what you youngsters are." She turned her head slightly, arching her eyebrow at him. "It would be rather silly to try and hide it from the ones who work here."

Spirit felt a little rattled at that. Either everyone here was in on some kind of massive deception, or—

Or it was real. And she couldn't help thinking, with a feeling of icy fear, about what she had seen just before the accident.

They were at an intersection. Ahead were glass doors leading into what could not by any stretch of the imagination be called a "cafeteria." Not when it was full of long wooden tables covered with snowy linen tablecloths, lined by plain, if elegant, chairs. To the right and left were more double doors like the ones they'd just come through.

"As I said," Ms. Corby interrupted her thoughts, "Young Ladies to the right, Young Gentlemen to the left." She walked off—again, without beckoning to Spirit or looking to see if she'd followed—and Spirit hurried after her.

T he hallway was decorated like the Entry Hall. It was the rich man's version of "rustic," lit with deco-Egyptian cast bronze lanterns. It looked like the hallway of an expensive hotel, except that each of the doors had a little engraved plaque with someone's name on it.

"We assumed you would prefer to be on the ground floor," Ms. Corby said, as if she didn't care one way or the other what Spirit preferred. "If not, just e-mail me. There are empty rooms on the second and third floors and we should be able to move you in a day or two." She paused beside one of the last two doors before a staircase.

"Ground is fine," Spirit said vaguely. How many kids were there in this school? There must have been twenty doors on this hallway alone.

Nodding, Ms. Corby opened the door.

Spirit wasn't really expecting a room just like the one in the brochure. And she was right.

This was better.

The color scheme was pretty neutral, and even though the dorm-wings had obviously been built after the house itself, it had still been decorated in the "rich man's rustic" style (and the school colors), with the addition of some pink. Just standing in the doorway she could see a dresser, a desk, a bed (so she'd have a room all to herself!), a huge closet . . .

"Your school uniforms are in the closet," said Ms. Corby, as if she was reading Spirit's mind. "There's a copy of the Oakhurst Code of Conduct in the desk; we expect you to become familiar with it quickly. The uniform for Young Ladies is blazer and skirt during classroom hours; trousers may be worn by special arrangement with your instructor. The computer here is for your personal and academic use. The music library is networked on the school server and other media is available in the library. Attempting to download material from the Internet is in violation of the Code of Conduct. I'll leave you to make yourself comfortable. Dinner is in two hours; you will need to be in uniform. Welcome to Oakhurst."

"Thanks," Spirit said. *I think.*

Ms. Corby turned away and walked briskly off down the hall. Spirit walked carefully into the room, trying not to hold her breath, although she felt as if she should.

Everything since she'd left the hospital this morning seemed utterly unreal, and this might be the most unreal thing of all. This was a huge room, more like an efficiency apartment than a room. It contained a mini-fridge and microwave, a gleaming laptop, and a mini entertainment center with a flat-screen TV.

There was a set of wireless speakers—so she wouldn't be stuck with the tiny tinny ones laptops had if she wanted to listen to the school music library—and a set of high-quality in-ear earphones if she didn't want to use the speakers. And through a door to the right, next to the desk, she could see her bathroom. She'd never had her own bathroom; there'd only been one for the whole family.

She turned away quickly and opened the closet. It was only half full, and it still contained more clothes than she'd ever had in her whole life. And not all of them were in Oakhurst brown and gold—she saw some of the things that she remembered had come to the rehab facility. It looked like someone had brought her stuff to her room and unpacked it while she'd been . . .

. . . being turned into a mouse and told she was a magician whose life was in constant danger.

Spirit walked over to her bed and noted in sheer disbelief that the gold chenille bedspread had the school's coat of arms as its central design. She sat down and looked out her window. From here she could see a vast sweeping expanse of . . . nothing.

Oh it was pretty, and green, but it was like having suddenly been dropped into the middle of Peter Jackson's Middle Earth. Or Narnia. Or some other green weird empty place where the whole world had been turned upside down. This was nothing like Indiana, and the sheer *difference* suddenly made Spirit realize all over again how much of her life was just *gone*. And now she was in a place so strange that she felt completely lost in it. Even the hospital room had been more familiar.

She choked back a sob.

"Don't tell me they set you up with a playlist preloaded with Polka Dance Party. I'd cry over that, too."

She turned, startled. There were two girls about her age in the open doorway, both of them in the school uniform. At least, more or less, because one of them was wearing a lacy black blouse under the brown blazer, black tights, and black boots, while the other looked like she'd stepped out of an English boarding school, with a starched white shirt, chocolate tie, white tights, gold blazer, plaid pleated skirt, and brown Mary Janes.

The Goth-y one had flaming red hair—cut very short and

47

spiked up—and vivid green eyes, and was wearing more makeup than Spirit was willing to bet was allowed in the Oakhurst Code of Conduct. The green-eyed Goth was so skinny she was on the edge of being *too* skinny. She had a sardonic little smile on her face, and something about that face reminded Spirit of a cat.

The other girl was her opposite in every way. Her hair was black—a true black, the kind with blue highlights—and it was completely straight, with straight bangs, and looked really long. Her eyes were a warm brown. If she'd been blonde-haired and blue-eyed, she would have looked just like every picture Spirit had ever seen of Alice In Wonderland, down to that faint little knot of stubbornness at the side of her mouth. She was several inches taller than the redheaded Goth, and sleek to the point of being plump.

"I'm Muirin Shae," said the Goth-girl. "You do not get to call me 'Murray' or 'Rin-Tin-Tin' or any other cute names you can think of, because you will really regret it. This is Adelaide Lake. You can call her Addie, because everyone does. We're supposed to get you oriented, show you around, keep you from slitting your wrists, all that stuff. You aren't going to slit your wrists, are you?"

"Um. No." Spirit eyed Muirin dubiously, unable to tell if the other girl was joking or not.

Muirin let out an exaggerated sigh of relief. "Well good. It makes an awful mess and Addie and me'd get our butts kicked. That's one out of three." She walked into the room, pulled out the chair from behind the desk, and flopped into it. "So what's your sad story? We all have sad stories here. I have a Wicked Stepmother."

Spirit blinked. "You do?"

"She does." Addie rolled her eyes, following Muirin into the room and closing the door behind her. "I just have a trust fund." Addie *did* have a faint accent, too faint for Spirit to tell if it was English or not. "Do you mind if I—?" She gestured at the couch.

There was a couch—a love seat, really—and two chairs, forming a little seating group around a coffee table. "Yes, please," she said, getting up off the bed to join Addie.

Muirin promptly got out of the desk chair to sprawl on the bed, rolling onto her stomach and kicking her feet in the air. "But don't be shy! I know you want to hear all about my *fascinating* life—and that way I can ask you all about yours. Once upon a time I was a normal, happy child—"

Addie snorted rudely and Spirit was startled into a stifled giggle.

"Quiet!" Muirin said imperiously. "Then Mummy Dearest shuffled off this mortal coil—propelled by booze of course. Daddy Darling promptly married the Trophy Wife, then wrapped himself around the nearest tree in his little red sports car, leaving me at the mercy of my Wicked Stepmother."

"It gets better," Addie murmured, as Muirin paused dramatically.

"A little sympathy," Muirin said. "I was only a *baby*."

"Fourteen," Addie explained.

"And had led a very sheltered life—"

"In and out of every progressive warehousing school Mummy and Daddy Dearest could find," Addie footnoted.

"Who's telling this?" Muirin demanded.

"Oh, *you* are," Addie said. "Go on."

Muirin heaved a theatrical sigh. "All right then! My Wicked Stepmother planned to *lock me up* in yet another boarding school while she took off for Europe to spend Daddy Darling's fortune. Too bad—how sad—that Daddy Darling wasn't as well-fixed as he'd looked." Muirin smiled sweetly, but there was a wicked glint in her eye.

"First Wicked Stepmother tried to hand me off to a relative. Only neither Mummy Dearest or Daddy Darling *had* any. Then she figured she'd save money and keep me in public school instead of sending me off to another facility for troubled teens. Except that meant I was *around*, and by then I'd been . . . learning things, so whenever she tried to pretend she was in charge, I'd just show her who was *really* the boss." Muirin sighed dreamily. "So of course when Oakhurst offered to take me off her hands, no charge, she couldn't sign the papers fast enough."

Muirin rolled over on her back and stretched herself like a cat, then held out her hand, palm-up. In rapid succession, a glowing ball of blue light, then a flame, then a tiny human figure appeared on it, before she closed it again. "I do illusions. Adelaide's a Water Witch. What do you do?"

"Nothing," Spirit said, still staring at Muirin in shock. "I mean, I don't know, I—"

"Don't let her tease you. Most of us aren't as precocious as Murr-cat," Adelaide said kindly. "You should get into a uniform though. They don't like us to be out of uniform until after supper—no matter how many demerits *some people* want to collect."

"Oh Addie! What are they going to do—send me home?" Muirin said mockingly.

"You know they won't. But you wouldn't like to be locked out of the music subdirectory, or lose your library privileges, or be restricted to your room when you aren't in class," Addie said reasonably. "So I'd consider being a little more careful in the future. And I think Spirit should be here at least a week before she starts collecting points. Where are you from?" she asked.

"Indiana," Spirit said.

Addie nodded. "So you're probably freezing." Without waiting for either Spirit or Muirin to reply, she walked into Spirit's closet and began rummaging through it. When she came out, she was holding a brown wool blazer with the school crest on the pocket, and a pair of matching wool pants. She handed them to Spirit and went over to her dresser, coming up with an ivory-colored turtleneck and a gold-colored pullover sweater.

"There," she said, holding them out. "You should be warm enough in these. It's after class so it doesn't have to be a skirt."

Feeling as if things were getting away from her, Spirit took the clothes and went into the bathroom. She was about to put them on when she glanced at the long, deep, bloody scratch on her arm again. Why hadn't Addie or Muirin mentioned it? She didn't want to think it was because injuries like this were too familiar to them.

She ran water in the sink and dabbed at it gingerly with the washcloth from the rack. It mopped up the blood, but it stung a lot, and she didn't want to get blood on the ivory turtleneck. Without thinking, she opened the medicine cabinet over the sink. In addition to toothbrush, toothpaste, and all that sort of thing—all new, not the half-used items from the hospital— there were Band-Aids, gauze squares, a roll of gauze, adhesive tape, antibiotic cream, spray antiseptic, and bandage scissors. It only took Spirit a minute or two to squeeze salve along the scratch, cover it with squares, wrap that in gauze, and tape the gauze into place. It looked much worse than it actually was when she was done, but she was confident the bandages would hold.

Then she put on her new clothes, and she had to admit that she finally felt warm for the first time today. And she had to admit, even the blazer didn't look nearly as dorky on as it did on the hanger. It was actually kind of cute, if you went in for that sort of thing. She brushed out her hair with the hairbrush and put it back in the drawer of the vanity, and when (on a hunch) she opened the top drawer on the other side, she saw a selection of barrettes, headbands, and hair-ties. *Stupid place thinks of everything,* Spirit grumbled to herself, before selecting a hair-tie and whipping her hair back into a quick ponytail. When she came out, Addie was getting a pair of brown loafers out of a box.

"Here," she said, handing Spirit the shoes. "Socks are in

your top drawer, but the ones you have on will do fine. As uniforms go, these aren't bad—as long as you like brown, gold, and white."

"Makes me feel like a box of caramels," Muirin said with a snort.

Spirit stepped into the shoes. Everything fit perfectly, but that was hardly a surprise, since Oakhurst had bought all of the clothing she'd worn in the hospital and rehab. They ought to know her sizes by now.

While Spirit had been in the bathroom getting dressed, Muirin had gone to Spirit's laptop and turned it on. The Oakhurst crest was on the screen, surrounded by icons. Spirit walked over and looked over her shoulder.

"You're always connected to the intraweb, but assume the nannies are watching, because they always are. You can put on anything you want as wallpaper"—Muirin moused over the icons, talking as she went—"anything you can download, anyway. This goes to the school e-mail. Your default password's your birthday—six numbers, so if your birth month's before October it's zero-something, and ditto if you're born before the tenth of whatever. If it's blinking you better check it, because it might be from a teacher or the admin. This is our school intraweb portal."

She clicked on the small copy of the Oakhurst coat of arms, and another page of icons sprang open. "IMs, music library, electronic library, class stuff, yadda. You can reserve physical stuff at the bricks-and-mortar library from here if it's not on the server. Some Oakhurst weirdness. This is the gateway to the *real* Internet, but don't get your hopes up: we're not allowed to have Facebook or LiveJournal or a Hotmail account or anything like that. If they find out about it—and they will—it'll get nuked and your ass will be grass."

Spirit blinked at that. "But—why?"

"Because they're fascist pigs," Muirin said.

"It's a school rule," Addie said, shrugging. "Murr-cat knows perfectly well there are a lot worse rules Oakhurst could have."

"They made me *cut my hair*," Muirin said darkly.

"It was blue," Addie explained to Spirit. "And it looked really awful. They did their best with it, but it was *cooked*—you know darn well it was, darling Murr, don't glare at *me*—and the Code says you can't have dyed hair or extensions. So all they could do was cut it really short and keep cutting it until they got all the dyed bits out. I don't see why you ever dyed it, really. It's such a gorgeous color."

"Easy for you to say," Muirin said sulkily. "Anyway, Addie's going to say we should give you the tour now, so let's go." She bounced to her feet and strode toward the door. "Well, come on! What are you waiting for?"

Spirit shrugged. Addie had already gotten to her feet, so Spirit followed the two of them out into the hall, and found herself whisked around a tour of the grounds and school buildings.

Behind the original mansion—she'd thought it was part of it until Addie said it was an addition—was the classroom building. While on the outside it was the same architecture, on the inside it was completely modern. Clearly no expense had been spared. Spirit wondered why they'd gone inside at all—Muirin and even Addie didn't strike her as being the type to go into raptures over homework. Then they reached the end of the hall, and instead of going up, they went down.

"All the good stuff is down," Muirin said, and laughed.

One side of the basement had doors just like on the floor above (except that these didn't have panes of glass in them so you could see what was inside); but the other had doors spaced much closer together, as if the rooms were much smaller. Each of those doors had little lights above them, and about half of those lights were glowing red.

"These are the magic practice rooms," Addie explained. "People aren't always good at control." A muffled thud from inside one of the rooms emphasized what she had just said. Spirit felt her eyes widening.

The rest of the tour included what she had seen from the train—the gym, the theater, the indoor pool, the stables, the tennis courts, the athletics field. It also included something she hadn't seen from the train—an indoor and outdoor shooting range. That also made her eyes widen a little. She thought of Loch's opinion of guns and hoped that shooting wasn't mandatory.

"Why all the sports stuff?" she asked, as they headed back to the main building.

"Well, it's not like we have the usual sort of teams that play against other schools," Muirin replied with a smirk. "That's partly because we're kind of too *isolated* to play any other private schools, and I think the public school over in Radial doesn't want to play against us. Doctor Ambrosius is serious about being fit and about encouraging competition though, so we play against ourselves."

Spirit could well imagine why the Radial public school wouldn't want to play against a school like Oakhurst. Oakhurst even taught *fencing*! There'd been four people in white outfits and disturbingly android-looking masks fighting in there when they'd passed the door. It was the first time Spirit had ever seen a fencer in person.

In between bits of explanation, Addie and Muirin filled her in on most of the rules. Except in the worst winter weather, uniforms were mandatory during school hours except for sports. For sports you either wore the special gear—like fencing stuff, or riding stuff—or sweats in Oakhurst colors. For most classes, skirts and blazer were required for girls, but there were several different styles and colors of skirts—including the plaid-with-pleats that Addie was wearing—and if you were doing something where you might end up rolling around on the floor or getting dirty, you wore trousers. On any day you were studying *Grammery,* you wore trousers.

"And that's *at least* two days a week, so the Dress Code doesn't suck as much as it could," Muirin said. "They hate you wearing makeup, though."

"That isn't true," Addie said. "*Light* makeup is okay. They just don't want you Gothing out during school hours. Now. Breakfast is seven to eight, lunch is noon to one, dinner is six to seven. You can have food in your room, but not junk food, of course."

"They check," said Muirin mournfully. "You can kiss any idea of privacy you ever had good-bye, so if you used to keep a diary? Don't. The only thing they let you get away with is soda, but they ration it. You can have all the bottled tea and juice and water and health drinks you want, but they only let you have seven cans of soda a week."

Seven cans a week? Spirit made a face. She had the feeling she was going to go through serious Diet Pepsi withdrawal.

"Well, popcorn," Adelaide amended. "You can have popcorn."

"Lights out at eleven," Muirin said, taking over from Addie. You weren't supposed to be outside the dorm after ten, but the way that Muirin said "supposed to" made Spirit pretty sure that there were ways around that. Like, if you wanted to meet a boy.

No more than two people (besides you) in a dorm room except by special arrangement. "We're supposed to use the lounges for more than two, so people in their rooms can study," Addie said. "Otherwise, there might be too much noise. But the lounges are really nice."

And apparently there was a lot to study—magic stuff (*Grammery,* Spirit tried to remember they called it here) along with the regular high school courses. And everyone was supposed to have at least one sport they did regularly.

"Don't you have time for any fun?" she asked, feeling desperate.

Adelaide and Muirin exchanged amused looks. "You'll get used to it," said Adelaide, as they reached the dining room.

People were already filing in the now-open doors. "Oh, is that the guy you came in with?"

With a feeling of relief, Spirit saw Loch standing with a tall, broad-shouldered guy who practically looked like two of him. Loch spotted her at the same time and lifted a hand.

"Yeah—" she began, when Muirin interrupted.

"Oh good, he's with Burke! We can all sit together and you can introduce us." She grinned. "He's cute. And *new*. We can keep him to ourselves."

So Spirit found herself sitting between the tall guy—whose name was Burke Hallows, and who was brown-haired, brown-eyed, and cute in a Boy Scout way—and Muirin, feeling just a bit intimidated. There hadn't been more than a handful of times in her whole life that she'd sat at a table with a white linen tablecloth, white linen napkins, porcelain plates, and real silverware made of real silver. And never had she had as many kinds of silverware as there were here. Her folks' idea of a restaurant generally involved a buffet.

Burke saw her confusion. "You work from the outside in," he said, kindly. "Don't worry too much about it."

Spirit said, frustrated, "Only rich people eat like this. . . ."

Burke shrugged. "You aren't the only one here who's not rich," he replied. "We're supposed to get used to this, though. Doctor Ambrosius expects us to be movers and shakers out there." He waved his hand vaguely as if to indicate the world outside the walls. "Just relax, nobody's grading you on eating. It's probably the only thing they don't grade us on," he added in an undertone, and Spirit wondered if she'd been meant to hear that.

It was hard to relax when people in uniforms were serving you. She felt awkward and uncomfortable, and very out of place. It didn't help her feel any better that Loch was casual and comfortable, asking questions, even making jokes. Still, it was hard not to notice that the food, like the snacks in the plane, was light-years beyond any school cafeteria or even family-night-out restaurant food she'd ever had. It was all so fancy, though, that she found the meal exhausting. Nothing was familiar: the lettuce in the salad wasn't regular lettuce and tasted odd, the mashed potatoes weren't exactly mashed potatoes, she had no idea what kind of roast bird she'd been served—except that it wasn't either turkey or chicken—and even dessert had *looked* like chocolate pudding but turned out not to be.

She would have been perfectly ready to go back to her room and just collapse after that, but the other four insisted she come along to the lounge to get acquainted. They were like a wave that washed her along with them, where she sat in a big comfortable chair next to a fireplace and listened to the others talk. A bunch of the other kids from the dining room had followed them to introduce themselves and find out who they were, but names and faces were kind of a blur. There was Seth Morris—who Muirin seemed to know well—and Nick and Marc and Andrew and Troy. Everyone's names and faces seemed to run together—she couldn't for the life of her remember whether Camilla or Jenny had the short curly hair, and if it was Claire or Kristi who had the long braids and carried the sketchbook. She just curled up in the chair and listened to Muirin and Loch and Burke talk. Now that she wasn't running interference between

Muirin and Spirit, Addie didn't talk much, but she listened so intently you felt as if she was saying more than she did.

Loch wanted to know what sorts of magic they all did, and Muirin demonstrated again, this time with a larger illusion, a copy of herself that she made do some gymnastic flips. Addie poured a glass of water from the pitcher on the sideboard and made a fountain in it. One of the other boys took the glass when she was done—Spirit wasn't sure whether it was Nick or Troy—and the clear glass turned opaque and sort of grayish brown.

"Transmutation," Muirin said, and he grinned and tossed it at her.

Some of the others had kinds of magic that you couldn't show off easily or safely—one of the girls said she was learning Transformation, which apparently wasn't the same as Transmutation, and one of the other boys said he was a Fire Witch. Burke just shrugged.

"Combat magic," he said, with the smallest of grimaces. "Give me a weapon and I can use it right away; give me a couple weeks with it, and I'm an expert. Takes me about two months to get pretty good at about any martial art. Already got a black belt in three. Right now I'm learning sword stuff."

Spirit's jaw dropped. "That's—amazing!" she blurted.

Burke snorted dismissively, but his smile was kind. "Yeah, but it's not like I can compete at it. It'd be cheating. It's the magic doing it, not me."

Muirin laughed up at him. "You and your ethics!" she said mockingly. "No one would ever know!"

"*I'd* know," Burke said stubbornly. "And it'd be cheating

people who worked for years and years out of the reward they earned."

Muirin made a face when she saw Addie, Loch, Spirit, and a couple of the other kids nodding in agreement with him. "Doctor Ambrosius says that it's no different than a genius competing with ordinary people in college, or in business," she answered, sounding certain of her ground. "Really, why should it be? For that matter, we'll be using our magic to compete with them in things like business. So how is that any different?"

Burke set his jaw. He seemed to struggle for a moment for words, then said, "It just *is*."

"I'm not all that impressed with Doctor Ambrosius anyway," Spirit said softly, and winced a little when half a dozen people turned to stare at her, including all four of her new friends. Then she decided to stand her ground. "I'm *not*," she repeated more firmly. "Especially not if he says things like that." She held Loch's gaze and spoke directly to him. "I think he could have showed us that magic was real today without attacking us and hurting me. That's just bullying, and just because he owns this school and has magic powers, it doesn't make it less like bullying. And how about all of you? Don't you think you should have been allowed a choice in whether you came here or not? Was that fair?"

Muirin laughed sharply. "Since when is life fair?"

"The only people that say that are people who don't want it to be." It was Spirit's turn to set her chin stubbornly. "And I don't think that because we can do things, it always means we should."

Muirin rolled her eyes, but Addie smiled, Burke beamed at her with approval, and Loch winked at her. She immediately felt better.

"I suppose you'll all tell me we should all rush out to save the world or something," Muirin said, and wiggled her fingers. "Buh-*bye*! You do that, kids. I'll be over here, trying to pass algebra."

"Of course not, goofus," Burke retorted good-naturedly. "Weren't you listening to Spirit? Just because we *can* do something, that doesn't mean we *should*." He rubbed the back of his head broodingly. "Besides, all that would happen to me if I went out and became Captain America or something is that the Army'd probably grab me and try to figure out how to make more guys like me. Which isn't going to happen, but I'd never see the light of day again."

"I knew you weren't as dumb as you look, Burkesey," Muirin replied, mollified. "Hey. Did anyone hear anything more about whether we're having a Halloween dance or not?"

In a lot of ways, the change of subject was a tremendous relief. Spirit didn't particularly like thinking about this magical power she was supposed to have. It made her feel as if everything in the world was just a thin skin stretched over a reality that was too scary to contemplate for very long.

The discussion of a Halloween dance—Halloween was a little less than two months from now—occupied everyone until one of the older students showed up to tell them the lounges were closing. He wore an armband with a badge on it that Burke said made him something called a "proctor." You could become a proctor once you were eighteen, and they did a lot of stuff that had to do with running the school, and when they were wearing their armbands you had to do what they said the same as if they were one of the teachers.

In the hallway outside the Refectory—Spirit had finally remembered what it was called—they split up, boys going one way, girls going the other. Apparently the lounges closed half an hour before you had to be back in your room—she didn't have a wristwatch, and she wondered if she could get one here—so there were a lot of kids drifting back to their rooms. Addie and Muirin had rooms on the second floor, so they took the stairs to the second floor, leaving Spirit to make her way back to her room on her own.

"It'll be the one without a nameplate on it," Muirin told her helpfully. "Just keep opening doors until you find it."

"Check your computer," Addie added. "Your class schedule will be on it."

Spirit nodded, and walked off down the hall. One of the other girls from the lounge—Camilla, Spirit remembered, the girl who said her power was Transformation—was on the first floor, too.

She said she'd lived at Oakhurst for three years, and that it was a lot nicer than the place she'd come from. "You grow up in a Florida trailer park sharing a beat-up doublewide with half a dozen sproggs and your Mom and your no-account brother and his girlfriend and their brats, and a place like this is going to look damned good to you, even if they are a little touched in the head," Camilla said, setting her jaw. "Didn't help none that they was—*were* always trying to beat the Devil out of me either." She smiled a little sadly.

"I'm sorry," Spirit said. What else could she say?

"Not that I'm not sorry they've passed," Camilla said. "But I was sure as heck glad that Oakhurst came along before I ended up going on the county. And here you are," she added, pushing open the door. "You'll have a nameplate on it by tomorrow, and then you won't get lost anymore. Mine's right down the hall. Camilla Patterson, if you need anything. Don't worry too much about the demerits—they go easy on you the first week."

"Thanks," Spirit said. She pushed open her door and stepped inside, closing the door behind her.

Following Adelaide's advice, the first thing she did was check her computer. A tap on the spacebar cleared the screensaver—it was the school coat of arms again, only now it was rotating—and sure enough, the e-mail icon was blinking. She sat down in her chair and clicked on it. It prompted her for her password, and she had a moment of panic before she remembered what Muirin had said, and typed in her birthdate: 070895.

There were only two e-mails. One was pretty much the same orientation that Muirin and Adelaide had walked her through, with a reminder to read through the Oakhurst Code of Conduct for more information. The other was her class schedule. It looked pretty standard: Science and Math and English and History and Physical Education—and (of course, since this was apparently Hogwarts West) *Grammery*. Her schedule was organized like a calendar, so it took her a moment to make out that her classes didn't start tomorrow, they started the day after. Tomorrow—tomorrow she was scheduled for just one thing.

Testing.

FOUR

Spirit was jolted awake by loud unfamiliar music—something bouncy and upbeat that sounded like the soundtrack of a movie she didn't ever want to see. She thrashed upright in her bed and forced her eyes open, and the shock of seeing an unfamiliar room made her realize where she was. Oakhurst. *Montana.*

It took Spirit almost two minutes to discover where the music was coming from. Her laptop. By the time she managed to make it *shut up* (in the process discovering that the horrible movie music was the Oakhurst School Song) she was thoroughly awake. It was a few minutes after six. Spirit shuddered. She wondered what the penalties for missing breakfast were. She'd give anything for another hour of sleep in her nice warm bed. . . .

Suddenly she remembered that today wouldn't be an introduction to her classes here at the Orphan Asylum, but some

66

kind of mysterious "testing." After her extremely unpleasant interview with Doctor Ambrosius yesterday, just the thought of that made her stomach knot. In just twenty-four hours, everything she knew about the world had been turned inside-out.

And worse than that.

When she'd walked out of Doctor Ambrosius's office yesterday, she would have happily run away from Oakhurst. But there wasn't anywhere for her to run *to*. She was fifteen years old, she was completely alone in the world, and she had nothing except what Oakhurst Academy was willing to give her: no money, no home, nobody willing to take her in.

Dad had always told her that it was smart to keep your options open and to know where your escape routes were. Mom had said a Smith & Wesson beat five aces. Phoenix had said she planned to grow up to be an Evil Overlord. Spirit took a deep breath. Right now she was out of options and escape routes, and Oakhurst was holding all the cards. All she could do was hang in there until she grew up. Or maybe until some other option presented itself. Maybe something would turn up.

She grabbed her robe off the back of the closet door (plaid, flannel, quilted, in the school colors) and went into the bathroom to shower.

※

At least she didn't need to guess what to wear to find out if you were a wizard. She remembered she had to wear a skirt, and by investigating her dresser drawers, she discovered she had a choice of nylons, tights in any of the three school colors, knee socks, or ankle socks. She decided on brown tights (since she couldn't wear jeans) and another sweater and turtle-neck combo. By the time she got out of here, Spirit thought darkly, she was going to be desperate to wear something in some other color. Bright green, or fire-engine red, or pink with purple polka-dots and orange stripes . . .

D espite the fact that getting ready was so easy, she was al-most late for breakfast—she got lost on the way from her room to the Refectory—and the room was full by the time she got there. The servers were already going around to the ta-bles, and Spirit hesitated in the doorway. Maybe she should just leave . . .

But Burke saw her and stood up, and Muirin waved enthu-siastically, so Spirit hurried across the room toward them and slid into the empty seat between Loch and Burke. There was already a glass of orange juice by her plate.

"You get a choice of juice in the morning," Loch said qui-etly, "but you weren't here, and almost everybody likes or-ange juice, so—"

"It's fine," Spirit said quickly. She was relieved to see that Loch looked just as nervous as she felt.

"You don't get a choice of breakfast," Muirin said darkly. "It's all healthy. Ugh. Unless you can prove you have a horrible allergy."

"To bacon and eggs?" Burke asked, sounding amused. "I suppose it's possible."

"Well, what if you're Jewish?" Addie said. "You couldn't eat bacon then."

"I guess you'd eat eggs and . . . eggs," Burke said. "I know Troy's allergic to peanuts, and the kitchen's careful not to poison him. That doesn't mean you're going to talk them into letting you have your Froot Loops, Muir."

"Though God knows I try." Muirin sighed theatrically.

The good-natured bickering among the others was actually soothing, and when one of the servers placed a bowl of oatmeal in front of her, Spirit realized she actually had a little appetite. There were bowls of fruit and brown sugar on the table, and pitchers of honey and maple syrup and milk and cream. She put a little brown sugar and milk on her cereal, while Muirin poured so much sugar *and* syrup onto hers that Spirit wondered if she could even taste the oatmeal.

Burke plucked the pitcher out of Muirin's hand. "Leave some for the rest of us, greediguts."

Muirin squealed in outrage. Addie sighed. "Every morning," she said to Spirit, in an aside.

Spirit tried to smile back, but it was hard. "What do you think's going to happen today?" she asked Loch in a low voice.

"I don't know," he answered. He was stirring his oatmeal around but not eating much of it. "When I checked my e-mail this morning, all it said was to report to the Front Desk after breakfast. You?"

"I forgot to check mine," Spirit admitted. "My computer woke me up at six this morning with some horrible song."

"'Oakhurst We Shall Not Forget Thee,'" Loch said, his

mouth twisting wryly. "It was composed by one of the first students here," he added, and Spirit made a rude noise. That just figured. "You can actually set your computer to wake you up with any song in the library. Or just a .wav file if you prefer. I can walk you through that later, or I think there's a tutorial somewhere in the library files," he added, as if it was an afterthought.

"If I can't find it, I'll ping you," Spirit said. *If we're both still alive later,* she thought, and grimaced, reminding herself that, as weird and awful as the interview had been, the worst she had gotten was a scratch. What could be so hard about a few tests? If Dr. Ambrosius didn't want them here, he wouldn't have worked so hard to get them here.

Oatmeal was followed by bacon and eggs and toast. Apparently it was okay to ask for seconds, because Burke did. Spirit couldn't even finish her first helping. She noticed that a lot of kids were leaving as soon as they finished eating, and Camilla said that you didn't have to stay in the Refectory after you'd finished breakfast if you wanted to get a head start on studying.

"Me, I'd rather put it off as long as possible," she said, grinning.

There wasn't any coffee, but there was tea if you wanted it, even if it was herbal, and despite Muirin's constant complaints about the lack of "junk food," there was cocoa if you asked for it, and you could even get marshmallows in it. Of course Muirin did, and tried to get Spirit to order some, too, but Spirit refused. Her stomach was already rebelling.

"On Sundays there's pancakes," Muirin said longingly, licking marshmallow off her upper lip. "I guess it's supposed to make up for having to go to church."

"Church?" Spirit said, alarmed. There hadn't been anything in the brochure about church.

"Mandatory spiritual education," Muirin sighed. "It's kind of Unitarian, I guess. Dr. Ambrosius gives a sermon, and then reads a passage out of the Bible and then out of another holy book so we can see how they're all actually alike. So it's more like a class. But there's a choir."

From Muirin's tone, Spirit couldn't tell whether she thought the choir was a good thing or a bad thing, and she was about to ask if there was any way to get out of it—because her parents hadn't exactly been religious, at least not in that way—when she was distracted by someone sitting down in the empty seat on the other side of Loch.

"Hi," the new girl said, leaning forward and making it clear she was talking more to Spirit than to Loch. "I didn't get to introduce myself last night. I'm Kelly Langley. I'm one of the 'Young Ladies'' proctors, so if you need anything and you don't want to ask one of the teachers, I can help you out."

Kelly looked as if she was maybe three years older than Spirit. She had hazel eyes and dark brown hair cut even shorter than Muirin's, and she looked frankly amused at the idea of having to refer to them as "Young Ladies."

"Do you know who the, uh, 'Young Gentlemen's' proctor is?" Loch asked. "We saw him last night, but . . ."

"Actually, there are five of them right now," Kelly said

briskly. "And we're hoping to get a waiver to grab Burke next year when he's seventeen because Gareth graduates then, damn him. What a slacker. But there's one proctor for each ten students, so right now there are ten of us. I'll tell Gareth to find you after you've finished your tests and make sure you know who the proctors are for your side."

"Thanks," Loch said.

"I know the first few months here can be rough," Kelly said, and now she was talking to both of them, "but there isn't anybody here who hasn't been through at least some of what you have. If you don't want to talk to the teachers, talk to somebody, m'm kay? Okay, end of lecture." She got to her feet.

"Wait," Spirit said. "Are you—? I mean—"

Kelly smiled at her. "One of those wizard guys?" She snapped her fingers, and suddenly a flame was burning on the end of her thumb. She folded her thumb into her fist, and the flame was gone. "Fire Witch. It's the commonest Gift; nobody really knows why. Gotta go. I'll see you later."

Spirit watched her as she strode—she already had the idea that Kelly strode everywhere—from the Refectory. Loch's touch on her arm made her jump.

"I think we'd better go," he said when she looked at him.

❧

It was strange how the Entry Room already seemed like a familiar place. There was still a fire burning in the fireplace—or maybe that was "again"—and Spirit wondered if they kept a fire burning there 24/7. Then another thought struck her. *Maybe there isn't any fire there at all. Maybe it's just an illusion.* The thought was so sudden and so disturbing—this time yesterday she hadn't even known that real magic existed—that she tripped on the perfectly smooth tile floor.

"Steady," Loch said. "How bad can it be?"

"I don't know," Spirit said, keeping her voice level with an effort. "What if we flunk?"

From the look on Loch's face, the thought hadn't even occurred to him.

⁂

There was a different blonde woman behind the Front Desk this morning. She was just as glossy and groomed as Ms. Corby had been, and wearing a Bluetooth headset; when Spirit peered over the edge of the vintage-looking counter, everything behind it was twenty-first-century modern, with enough keyboards, touchpads, and display screens that she ought to be able to launch the whole school into space.

"Ms. Smith will be with you in just a few moments," the blonde woman said. She regarded them with the same distant haughtiness that Ms. Corby had yesterday, as if she couldn't imagine why they were here at Oakhurst at all. Spirit was tempted to offer to leave, but fortunately Ms. Smith arrived before she could.

"Hi. I hope you weren't waiting long," she said, glancing at her watch. "I'm Jane Smith. Come on, I'll take you to the testing rooms."

In contrast to the blonde receptionist, Ms. Smith looked

friendly and like an actual human being. She was wearing the school uniform, but with pants, not a skirt, and her long brown hair was pulled back into a casual ponytail. She was holding a clipboard cradled in one arm, and she had a pen tucked behind her ear.

Spirit and Loch followed her through a doorway and along a corridor. The corridor was carpeted, and the framed pictures on the walls were all old-time photographs of railroad things that had probably belonged to the house's original owner. Spirit hadn't been here long enough to get a real sense of the layout of the main house, so she was lost very quickly. Ms. Smith stopped in front of a door and opened it.

"Go right in and take a seat, Mr. Spears. Doctor Ambrosius will be right with you," Ms. Smith said with an encouraging smile. "Relax. This isn't the kind of test anybody flunks."

Loch gave her an unconvinced smile in return and walked into the room. Spirit wanted to see what was in there, but Ms. Smith was already moving down the corridor. They passed a few more closed doors, then she stopped and opened another one. "And here we are," she said brightly.

Spirit walked in hesitantly. The room was surprisingly small—a little smaller than Spirit's new bedroom—and gave her the feeling of an old-time schoolroom. The ceiling was high for the room's size, at least twenty feet. There were windows, but they were completely covered by blackout shades made of black fabric, and the light came from lights in the ceiling.

There was nothing in the room but a large heavy wooden

table and two heavy wooden chairs. Spirit walked over to the table and looked down at it. Arranged on the surface were a stone, some kind of plant in an ordinary red clay pot full of dirt, a clear glass bowl filled with water, a copper bowl filled with charcoal briquettes, a tall white pillar candle, and several feathers. The surface of the table had several burn scars on it.

"Sit down and make yourself comfortable," Ms. Smith said. "I'll explain what you're going to do here today." She settled herself into one of the chairs and set her clipboard on the table. Spirit sat warily in the seat on the other side.

"I know that all of this has to seem very strange to you," Ms. Smith said. "But we won't ask you to take any of it on faith. What today's test is for is to determine which elements you have a particular affinity for, in order for us to determine what your Mage Gift is."

"Kelly said Fire was the most common one," Spirit said hesitantly.

"Right," Ms. Smith said, nodding. "Now, scientifically, there are one hundred seventeen elements, but the ancient world believed there were only four: Earth, Air, Fire, and Water, which aren't really elements at all. But for the purposes of magic, we treat them as if they are, and your Mage Gift will probably fall into one of what we call these 'Elemental Schools.'"

"Probably?" Spirit asked.

"It's possible that you might have Gifts from two different Schools," Ms. Smith said, "though in that case, they're less likely to be strong Gifts. While a Mage can have an entirely elemental Gift—such as being a Fire Witch—they can also have a power that belongs to an Elemental School without controlling its underlying element. For example, I know you've met Burke Hallows. His Mage Gift is Combat Magic, which has an affinity with the School of Earth. Knowing the supporting School to which your Mage Gift belongs will be important when you go on to study magical theory. And you're wishing I'd stop nattering on at you and get to the testing part of things, aren't you?"

Spirit glanced up, guilty and a little alarmed.

"Oh, I'm no mind reader," Ms. Smith said gently. "But I've administered a great number of these tests. This is how it works: the items here on the table symbolize the Four Elements. You should feel a resonance—an *affinity*—with one more than another. Take your time. And remember, there aren't any wrong answers here. This isn't a test you can fail. We already know you're a magician, or you wouldn't be here."

Two hours later, Spirit wanted to be anywhere but there. She didn't have the least "affinity" for any of the objects on the table: not the stone or the potted plant that symbolized Earth, nor the bowl of water that symbolized (of course) Water, nor the candle and the bowl of charcoal that symbolized Fire, nor the feathers that were the symbol for Air. Despite the fact that Ms. Smith said Spirit had magic, nothing she could do seemed to be able to get its attention. While Ms. Smith hadn't stopped being kind and supportive—something Spirit instinctively mistrusted after all those weeks of social workers and nurses at the hospital and in rehab—Spirit could tell she'd been getting more and more frustrated.

But as far as Spirit could tell, the stuff on the table was just a bunch of tacky New Age decorations. She couldn't set the candle on fire with the power of her mind. She didn't even *want* to. Ditto for making the water swirl around in the bowl, or suddenly wanting to cuddle up to the rock, and she wasn't really sure what she was supposed to do with the feathers.

"What's the problem here?"

Spirit was sitting with her back to the door; she jumped as it flew open and hit the wall with a bang. Doctor Ambrosius came storming into the room.

"I'm sorry, Doctor Ambrosius," Ms. Smith said, getting to her feet. "Miss White hasn't been able to manifest an Affinity yet."

"Not able? Not willing, you mean," Doctor Ambrosius said contemptuously. "The child is a natural magician! This is no time for tantrums or games, my young woman," he added, glaring at Spirit sternly. "Hiding what you are will gain you nothing."

Up until that moment, Spirit had been frustrated and even a little intimidated by what was happening, but now she was just angry.

"In the first place, how am I supposed to hide something I

barely believe in?" she demanded hotly. "In the second place, why would I do something like that?"

Doctor Ambrosius's frown became even more thunderous, if that was possible. "Ms. Smith, go and finish up with young Master Spears. I shall get to the bottom of the situation here."

Ms. Smith didn't glance at Spirit as she walked quickly from the room. When the door closed behind her, Spirit swallowed hard, trying not to feel as if she'd just been trapped.

Doctor Ambrosius began to pace. "I am certain Ms. Smith explained to you that magicians' powers are linked to the elements. It is from these we draw our power. It is these that shape our essential natures. Denying what you are will accomplish nothing. It will only leave you defenseless—helpless—in the battles to come. Dark times are coming, Spirit White. Do not doubt that for an instant. Do not allow fear—or anger—or weakness to stand in the way of embracing what you were meant to be."

Listening to him talk was like listening to a Shakespeare play. Only creepier. She wished he'd stop pacing around. It was making her nervous.

Suddenly he turned back to the table and slapped both hands down on it. "Here are your choices! One of them is your chosen path!" he all-but-shouted at her. "You must try again! Now!"

Spirit reached out and grabbed the first thing her hands touched, mostly because she was afraid not to. She was *trying*, but this wasn't like her math homework or learning to sew or climbing trees or anything else she'd ever done in her life. It wasn't even like choosing which flavor of ice cream you wanted. What was she supposed to do with a candle? Maybe it was the wrong candle.

Her hands shook as she set it back on the table and reached for the stone. She'd done this over and over in the last two hours. Ms. Smith had said she'd *know* when she reached the right one, that these were just symbols but that was okay, that magic worked in symbols and this was just the first step to discovering what her Gift was.

But the stone was just an ordinary stone in her hands, and now her head was starting to hurt, and the room seemed hot and airless. She could feel her heart thumping in her chest; she had the panicky throat-closed feeling of being about to cry, and the thought of crying in front of Doctor Ambrosius simply made her angrier.

"Try harder," he barked at her.

Spirit's hands curled into fists, and she glared at the objects on the table, feeling a combination of anger and frustration and panic. The lights in the room seemed too bright. What should she try next? What would make him stop *glaring* at her? All she really wanted to do was pick up the little potted plant and hurl it to the floor. The glass bowl of water, too. She wrapped her arms around herself and gritted her teeth, squinting her eyes against the glare. There was no point in handling any of the things again—nothing would be any different than it had been the last dozen times—

"How dare you defy me?" Doctor Ambrosius shouted.

The sudden sound of his voice made Spirit jump, but it also cleared her head a little. Enough to let her know how horribly sick she felt. *Enough is enough.* This place had to have a school nurse somewhere.

Anything to get out of this room.

She pushed herself to her feet. The room seemed to spin crazily around her, and she felt a drop of moisture spatter onto the back of her hand. Her first thought was that—somehow—she'd started crying without having noticed, but when she looked down—forcing her eyes open, because they were almost completely closed now—it wasn't water on the back of her hand.

It was blood.

❋

What a strange dream. Spirit was so convinced that she was still in the hospital back in Indiana—the drugs they gave her made her have really weird vivid dreams sometimes—that it was a horrible wrenching shock to open her eyes and see Loch sitting beside her bed.

"Oh, you're awake!" he said, sounding relieved. "Are you okay?"

Spirit stared at him, breathless, knowing she must look more than a little wild-eyed, still trying to get over the shock of all this being *real*. As she did, a woman in a white nurse uniform with a cardigan over it folded back the privacy screen around her bed. Once it was gone, Spirit could see she was in a large, airy, open room. There were two beds along one wall and three on the other, with a desk in the corner.

"How are you feeling?" the nurse asked, sitting down on the opposite side of the bed. Of course the next thing she did was stick a thermometer into Spirit's mouth so she couldn't answer the question. That was strangely reassuring—at least some things were normal here! She took Spirit's wrist in her hand, counting her pulse, and then took her blood pressure before removing the thermometer. "Well, everything seems to be in order," she said cheerfully. "I'm Ms. Bradford, the school nurse. You're in the Infirmary. Apparently you fainted during Testing."

Spirit could hear the capital letter in Ms. Bradford's voice when she said "Testing." Ms. Smith had said it wasn't possible to flunk. Apparently she had.

"I want you to stay here and rest for another half hour, then you can dress and get up. You've missed lunch, but I can call the kitchen and get a sandwich sent over," Ms. Bradford said.

"I'm not hungry," Spirit said hastily. How long had she been passed out for? There wasn't a clock anywhere she could see.

"Skipping meals never did anybody any good," Ms. Bradford said darkly. She got to her feet. "Just yell if you need something. I'll let your friends come in now. Is that all right?"

"Yeah. Sure." She looked at Loch, frowning a little.

"It's after three," he said, glancing at his watch. "When I didn't see you at lunch, I started asking around, and found out you were here. But they wouldn't let me come and see you until after I was finished with Orientation."

"I guess you—" Spirit began.

"I thought you promised no emo suicide attempts!" Muirin said, bouncing in through the open doorway. Addie and Burke followed. Both of them looked worried about her.

"I didn't—" Spirit protested, struggling to sit up.

"Ignore the cat; she's just trying to make trouble," Burke said.

Loch got to his feet politely, and Muirin promptly sat down in the chair he'd vacated. Addie tsked and went to get her own chair. Loch came around the bed and sat down on the other side.

"Everybody knows you didn't do anything stupid," Burke went on. "You just ran into some problems during Testing."

"She fell on her face," Muirin said flatly. "I've never heard of that happening to anyone before—and before anyone says anything, no, I have *not* been here since Oakhurst was founded in 1973. But people talk. Trust me. Nobody's *ever* fainted during Testing."

"That makes me feel great," Spirit muttered, sitting back against the headboard. She felt better than she thought she should: everyone kept saying she'd fainted, but she didn't know of any "faints" that lasted four or five hours. She glanced at Loch. "I guess yours went okay?"

Loch shrugged. "Pretty much. I've got minor Gifts from two Schools—you got that far, right?" he asked, and, when

82

Spirit nodded, "—Kenning and Shadewalking—that's School of Air—and Pathfinding—that's School of Earth. It's supposed to be kind of rare to get Earth and Air gifts together, even when you *do* get Gifts from two Schools. Ms. Smith says they really all kind of go together, though." He shrugged. "I guess I'll find out more about them later."

"Well, Pathfinding's a good one to have," Burke said, smiling at Loch. "A Pathfinder always knows exactly where they are and can find their way from place to place without a map, whether they've been to where they want to go before or not. When you get really good with it, you'll even be able to describe the place you want to go before you've seen it."

"Cool," Loch said, looking impressed.

"Shadewalking's better," Muirin said. "I wish I'd gotten that. You can make yourself just about invisible—and move silently, too." She frowned. "I'm not sure what Kenning is, though. Nobody I know has it, even if it *is* an Air Gift."

"Well, in Old English, 'to ken' something was to know it," Addie said. "Maybe it has something to do with that."

"Maybe," Loch said, looking excited. "It was so strange—I was nervous about the whole thing, and at first I couldn't decide which of the things on the table to pick. But I kept going back to the feathers, and I picked them, but it didn't seem as if I was *done,* and Doctor Ambrosius said I should see if one of the other elements resonated with me, too, and, so, well, there was a cachepot of begonias on the table, and I sort of liked that." He shrugged, looking a little embarrassed. "Then all there was to do was figure out exactly what my Gifts in those Schools *were*. I guess that must have been when you, uh, ran into trouble, because he left and Ms. Smith came in and finished up with me. I didn't even know you'd had a problem until later."

Spirit opened her mouth to tell him—all of them—that she hadn't had a problem until *after* Doctor Ambrosius came in to see what was going wrong with her Testing, and stopped. Sure, he'd been pretty out of control. But Loch obviously didn't have any complaints about him. And Mom had yelled at her plenty of times when Spirit did things that she later realized had been stupid dangerous. If what Doctor Ambrosius had said yesterday about the world being a dangerous place for untrained magicians was true, maybe he'd just been angry at her for refusing to protect herself. She was already pretty clear on the fact that he didn't have the hottest people skills on the block.

It didn't change the fact that, despite the fact that both Doctor Ambrosius and Ms. Smith had said she was a magician, she hadn't been able to do what Loch had done so easily.

Maybe they were wrong. Maybe she didn't have any magic at all.

"Hey, if you guys don't mind clearing out of here, I could get dressed," she said.

⁕

She had to admit that a lot of things about this place didn't completely suck, Spirit decided. Of course, a lot of them did. Every time she thought of something she wanted to share with Mom and Dad—and especially Phoenix—she had to re-member they were dead all over again. And then she'd feel uneasily guilty about having all this *because* they were dead.

But if a week's time wasn't long enough to make deep friend-ships, she'd certainly started to make friends. And Kelly had been right when she said that Spirit's situation wasn't unique. There was Camilla, who'd lost her whole family down to her youngest nieces and nephews. And Addie, who'd been at sum-mer camp when her parents died in a light plane crash. Burke had managed to lose three families: He'd been left as a month-old foundling in a church with nothing but his birth certificate tucked into his blanket with him. Three months later they'd traced his parents—to the city morgue—and he'd been put up for adoption, since they'd never found any other relatives. When he was eight, his house caught on fire. He managed to get to the baby's room and get out with her, but their parents died in the fire. She'd gone to relatives, but they hadn't wanted a boy who was "no relation to them." He'd been quickly taken in by a nice couple, the Martins—though as a foster child this time—and been happy enough for the next few years, until Oakhurst came forward and offered him a place.

"It only made sense to come," he'd told Spirit quietly. *"Ma— Mrs. Martin—wasn't getting any younger, and her health wasn't so good, and I already knew there wouldn't be any money for college or anything. Couldn't ask it of them. Oakhurst was offering me every-thing. And maybe—when I get out—I can look them up again and see about paying back some of their kindness."*

No, she didn't have it as bad as she possibly could.

But Oakhurst was still . . . frustrating. Weird, in a way Spirit couldn't quite put her finger on. As if she was always trying to put her foot on a step that wasn't there, or banging her nose against invisible walls.

Maybe it was the whole magic thing.

In all the days that followed, nobody had even so much as *suggested* that she do the test over. Because she'd spent most of the day in the infirmary, she'd missed her orientation tour, which would have been a walk-through of her classrooms, meeting her teachers, and getting signed up for her "extracurricular" activities, so she'd had to make do with a "virtual" tour online and the slightly scattershot rundown she got from the others. So Spirit had been more than a little surprised to walk into her Science class to find that Ms. Smith was the teacher.

She hadn't had the nerve to bring up being retested, though—either there or in her magic classes.

Because this was a school for magicians. Of course they got lessons in magic.

⋆

Spirit stared down at her notebook and pretended she was taking notes. She was doing her best not to fidget, but it was hard, and they had that harpy Ms. Groves today, and if Ms. Groves thought you weren't paying attention to her lecture she'd bring everything to a screeching halt, bring up the room lights, and make you stand beside your desk and explain just what it was she was doing that was so terribly *boring*. From the way the others teased her, Spirit got the impression that Muirin got to do a lot of explaining in class whenever Ms. Groves lectured.

The trouble with going to a small exclusive private school was that the classes were small and exclusive, too. There were only four other kids in the room with Spirit: Loch; a boy named Taylor Parker who'd gotten here about four months ago; and two girls, Zoey Young and Jillian Marshall, who'd both arrived about a week before Taylor did.

There were two periods slotted in for Magic Theory. One was right before lunch, and the other was the last class of the day. All the before-lunch periods were for Advanced students, and two of the end-of-day periods were, too, so they only had M-Theory three times a week, which was more than enough. It generated more homework than the rest of her courses put together: history and theory and what went with which. It was like a whacko mix of *The X-Files* and cooking school.

Maybe it would have made more sense if she was actually *using* all of this stuff for something. Why did she need to memorize the subcategories of magician in each of the four Schools—and what the powers and weaknesses of each were—if she didn't even know which Elemental School she belonged to and probably never would? Why did *anybody* need to know about the entire history of magic dating back to the Year Zero, when Ms. Groves (and Ms. Smith, and Mr. Bowman, and Ms. Holland) said most of it was wrong? What was the point in learning the details of the spells all the old-time magicians cast, when Muirin said that you either had the

Mage Gift or you didn't, and if you didn't you could boil up bat's blood and snake fins for ever and ever and not get any results? At least the others got to go off after their classroom hours and practice actual magic, though Spirit felt really sorry for whoever had Ms. Groves as a coach.

Ms. Groves clicked a button and another slide appeared on the screen behind her. "If we aren't *boring* her too much, perhaps Ms. White can tell me what this symbol is on the screen behind me."

"It's the Greater Seal of Solomon, Ms. Groves," Spirit said, making very sure she didn't sigh aloud—much as she wished to.

❧

Spirit was lucky enough to escape having to explain to Ms. Groves why M-Theory wasn't boring (a good thing, because with the mood she was in today, she might have snapped and told Ms. Groves that no, it really *was* boring), but not lucky enough to escape another brutal homework assignment: showing the correlation between the Greater Key of Solomon and the Lesser Key of Solomon, and indicating where the so-called "powers conferred by demons" matched up with the Mage Gifts of the Elemental Schools. Spirit *did* sigh then; it was a good thing that Oakhurst had such a good library, both on- and off-line, or she wouldn't have a prayer. She got to her feet gratefully when the bell rang. She'd have the library practically to herself until dinner. Everybody would either be in their M-labs or off doing their extracurricular stuff.

But when she walked out of the classroom, Muirin was leaning against the wall waiting for her.

Spirit had been at Oakhurst two weeks now. She knew that you weren't allowed to shop online (even if you had any money), that incoming mail was searched by the school before you got it (even if you had someone to send things to you), and that violations of the Dress Code were practically punishable by death. Since all these things were true, she had no idea of where Muirin managed to find the stuff she kept showing up in.

Granted, it was after class. But Spirit thought it would probably have to be *after the Apocalypse* before the length of Muirin's skirt wouldn't give some of the more conservative teachers chest pains. The fact that it was one of their regular plaid pleated ones just added insult to injury—as did the fact that she was wearing brown cabled socks that would have fit the dress-code perfectly—if they didn't come up to mid-thigh.

"You look like an escapee from an animé," Spirit told her, "one that ends up with things with tentacles in it."

Muirin dropped into a mocking curtsy.

"What are you doing here?" Spirit added. "Don't you have somewhere to be?"

"I lead such a busy social life," Muirin said ironically. "Come on. I decided to take a mental health day."

"Yours or your teacher's?" Spirit asked. Muirin only snorted.

❊

Aren't you blowing off your practice hours?" Spirit asked as they walked down the hall. Everybody was leaving their classrooms at the same time, but the halls weren't crowded; there were only about a hundred students at Oakhurst right now, though the school was obviously built to accommodate at least twice that many.

"You're obviously forgetting I'm precocious," Muirin said pertly. "Besides, it's not like I'm ever going to blow something up with an illusion. I can practice anywhere." She glanced at Spirit speculatively. "So I usually like to hit the gym right after class."

"Oh my God, don't start," Spirit groaned. Muirin was on the fencing team, and she'd been bugging Spirit since Day One to pick a sport—or several—to get involved with.

"Why not?" Muirin asked. "We start the first round of competitions in October. If you don't want to join the fencing team, there's lacrosse, basketball, swimming, track, gymnastics, boxing—"

"Oh, like I want someone to punch me in the head!" Spirit replied.

"I've heard the idea is to *not* get punched in the head," Muirin said drily. "Camilla's pretty good at it—but I think I'd rather leave boxing and football to the guys."

"I have a sport. I ride," Spirit said. She'd signed up for the stables within a few days of arriving and was taking lessons three times a week.

"Doesn't count. Isn't competitive," Muirin answered. "At least come over to the gym with me and watch Burke hit things. It'll be fun."

Spirit wasn't sure about how much fun it would be, but she

was already sure that when Muirin got an idea in her head, it was less trouble to go along with it than to try to talk her out of it.

❦

Spirit had actually been in the Oakhurst Gymnasium several times already: sports might be optional, but calisthenics weren't, and Addie had insisted they all come to a basketball game last week because a friend of hers, Cadence Morgan—Spirit had winced in sympathy, knowing what it was like to grow up with an "exotic" name—was playing, and Addie had wanted to go and cheer her on. The gym was huge; Muirin said it was tournament-sized. And today one end of the enormous gym was set up as a dojo with heavy padded mats on the floor, and about a dozen kids in karate *gi* and different-colored belts were practicing.

Burke was easy to spot; he was about twice the size of the other boys here. He was facing off against a blond man in a black *gi* who almost made him look small. They circled each other for a moment, watching intently, then there was a flurry of blows—all blocked—then they stepped back and bowed. But to Spirit's shock, even as Burke bowed, the instructor aimed another blow at him. Burke straightened up—not seeming to hurry—and blocked it easily.

"That's cheating!" Spirit said, outraged. The noise of the basketball players masked the sound of her voice.

"That's Brett Wallis," Muirin replied, as if that was any kind of explanation. "He coaches karate and kendo. Mr. Gail coaches everything else but the fencing; and that's Ms. Groves, so trust me: Mr. Wallis is the nicest, the youngest, and the cutest of the sports coaches. I'm thinking about taking kendo in the spring, because you actually get to hit something sometimes."

Now Mr. Wallis was moving around the other students, correcting a stance here, offering encouragement there, demonstrating a move in the third place. Burke had picked up a long wooden rod and begun performing a slow precise series of movements with it. He saw them and smiled, but didn't stop what he was doing.

Even in those few moments with Mr. Wallis, Spirit had been able to see how good Burke was, and it was obvious, when she looked at the other kids, that he was much better at this than they were. *Combat magic,* she thought. "Can't he ever just turn it off?" she asked Muirin. She didn't have to say who she meant; they were both watching Burke.

Muirin snorted. "It's painfully obvious you haven't figured out your magic yet or you wouldn't ask such a dumb question. But I'm magnanimous, so I'll take pity on you and explain. No."

"That's your explanation?" Spirit asked, trying not to feel hurt.

Muirin shook her head in wordless annoyance. "Look. I make illusions, and I can choose to make them or not. But because I'm an Illusion Mage, I can never choose to be fooled by an illusion, because I'll always see the spell. With Combat Magic, Burke doesn't even cast a spell. It's what he *is.*"

Suddenly Spirit was very grateful that her magic hadn't been awakened. She'd been thinking of it as a kind of add-on, something she might like or hate, but an *extra*. What Muirin was describing was something that might change what she was completely, whether she wanted it to or not.

After a few more minutes—a couple more sets of kids sparred, but Mr. Wallis was always right there watching—he called for a five-minute break. Some of the students knelt down on the mats, others began doing stretches. Mr. Wallis walked over to them.

"You must be Spirit White," he said, holding out his hand. "Brett Wallis. Have you studied any of the martial arts before?"

Spirit was in the middle of shaking his hand politely (and wondering why he was introducing himself) when she realized what he must be thinking. "Oh I, uh—"

"No, she really hasn't yet," Muirin interrupted brightly.

Spirit flashed Muirin a suspicious glance. Muirin was looking much too innocent. Spirit was pretty sure that Muirin had told Mr. Wallis that Spirit was interested in signing up for his class. She was about to protest more firmly, when she gave a mental shrug. Why not? It wasn't as if she had anything better to do with her afternoons. "I'm looking forward to it," she said. "If you still have room."

He smiled at her. "Sure. Just get a uniform and be here for class on Friday. I'll make sure it's added to your schedule."

"Actually . . . she's already got a uniform," Muirin said. "It's in her locker."

"Well, go get changed, then," Mr. Wallis said. "You'll be in time for the second half of the class."

⁂

I do not," Spirit said, as she and Muirin headed for the Girl's Locker Room.

"Do, too," Muirin said. "I've spent enough time in your closet to know your sizes. I picked one up from Housekeeping yesterday and stashed it in the locker room this morning."

"I hope it's still there, in that case," Spirit muttered, because nobody had a permanent locker in the Gymnasium. They were just there for whichever class was using the gym to leave their school clothes while they worked out.

"You have to learn to trust me," Muirin said irrepressibly. "And I bet you're gonna like hitting things, too. I'm never wrong about stuff like that, you know."

Actually, after the last two weeks, Spirit thought Muirin might be right.

⁂

FİVE

He'd always been a survivor. Last man standing. Everybody always said fast food would kill you, but it wasn't fast food that'd killed Seth Morris's parents, it'd been a crazy Realtor depressed over the housing market who opened fire in the Micky D's. Like that would change anything.

He hadn't even wanted to go, because Dad had been out of work for a year and a half and all he and Mom did (back then) was argue about money. Seth didn't even *like* Micky D's, and he knew that Dad would order too much food and then complain about how much it cost until Mom started snapping back at him.

Helluva last memory to have of your folks, Seth thought. He remembered seeing the ice and Coke from his drink hanging in the air, sparkling, even before he heard the sound of the first shot. He'd thrown himself to the floor and gone squirming across it on his belly, so tunnel-focused on getting behind the order counter to safety that he hadn't thought about anything else.

There'd been eighteen people in the place when the shooter opened up. Twelve of them died, including his parents. Seth Morris had been the only one who wasn't even wounded.

And that had been almost two years ago, and for a long time after he'd gotten to Oakhurst it had just been a relief that everybody wasn't yelling all the time. There were a lot of rules, but Seth had always been good at getting around the rules. And when there was a place like this that was rolling in velvet (like Dad would've said), nobody was going to notice if he boosted a few things and traded them off. By the time he'd been at Oakhurst a year, he'd had a sweet arrangement going with the kids in Radial. Everything from clothes and magazines to downloaded MP3s went out, and anything Oakhurst didn't want them to have came in: extra chocolate, extra soda, mail that hadn't been censored . . .

The handoff place was an old boxcar out in the middle of nowhere, about halfway between Oakhurst and Radial. There were a bunch of them scattered all over the place out here; the locals used them to store feed hay in for the cows stranded in the winter blizzards. They were never all the way full. He'd leave his stuff when he could, and go back when he could and pick up what the townies left. He'd never gotten burned, and he'd never actually worried about it. Hey, it wasn't like he was playing with his own money.

But in the words of Master Yoda: *"It's all good until somebody loses an eye."*

No deal was sweet enough to risk your ass for.

He hadn't been sure at first. He still wasn't entirely sure. Even at a school full of magicians, the idea that people really were trying to kill you because you did magic was just too weird. He was uneasy enough about it now, though, that he'd decided leaving Oakhurst was a really good idea. It would be a lot easier to hide what he was when he wasn't sitting in the middle of nowhere surrounded by other people with targets taped to their backs.

It would be nice if he had one of the bigger, flashier Mage Gifts. But even a minor Earth Gift meant he'd always know when magic was around him. And this way might be safer. Nobody'd ever actually said so outright, but Seth suspected that the more power you had, the easier it was for *Them* to find you.

He stopped, looking back at the school. The whole place was still lit up. He was too smart to wait until after curfew to leave, or to go too early. Half an hour before curfew, if nobody saw him in the lounge or the library they'd just figure he was in his room. And if he wasn't in any of the online chatrooms, people'd figure he'd either turned in early, or was even (shock) studying. They wouldn't miss him until morning. He figured he could make it to Radial tonight—it was about ten miles, a long hike, and a cold one, but possible—and find some truck to hide in the back of. Once he was far enough away from Radial, it'd be safe to hitchhike until he got to a big city. And then—?

He didn't know.

Better than here, though.

✦

An hour later, Seth was most of the way to the boxcar. It was a good thing he was a Pathfinder: there was no moon tonight and he wasn't stupid enough to use his flashlight out here. But having Pathfinder Gift meant you *couldn't* get lost: he could find his way to any place he'd ever been—and for that matter, to any place he'd *never* been. And that was a good thing, because he'd never actually been to Radial. Being sure where he was going didn't keep it from being creepy out here, though. Seth had grown up in San Francisco's East Bay; he was a city kid, and all this open country without a shopping mall or a freeway or a skate park anywhere in sight was just unnatural. He'd never even seen snow until he'd come to Oakhurst, and it had been great—for the first month. Then it was depressing: too cold, too white, and too much of it. Then it was a stone drag and he wished it would go away. Which it hadn't, not for another three months.

It was too quiet out here, and too loud, both at the same time. He stopped, thinking he'd heard voices, but it was only something howling off in the distance. Wolves or coyotes, whatever they had out here. He stuffed his hands deeper into his blazer pockets and kept walking. He had a coat stashed for his getaway, but it was at the boxcar; he hadn't dared leave to-night looking as if he was going anywhere, in case somebody

saw him. He'd be there soon. Another hour, tops. It was almost eleven, and once—before Oakhurst, back when he'd still
had parents—that wouldn't have seemed late, but being out
here where streetlights (and streets) were an optional extra
made it seem like it was a thousand o'clock already.

He stopped again, because the wolves (he was pretty sure
now it was wolves) were making a lot of noise. Brendan, who
could talk to animals (and who couldn't be convinced that didn't
mean all the little fuzzy creatures loved him) said that wolves
howled either before or after a hunt, and usually at twilight or
when the moon was full. Brendan was a dork, but he was a nice
dork, and he'd come to Oakhurst about the same time Seth had,
and he'd tutored Seth on his English Comp for the last two
years, so Seth knew a lot about wolves by now.

Whatever was howling out here tonight, it wasn't wolves.

He stood for what seemed like far too long, listening, as
the chorus of wolf *(not-wolf)* howls crescendoed and died away.
The silence seemed to echo afterward. And in it, faintly . . .

He heard the sound of engines. What the— Were the local
rednecks doing some kind of creepy night-hunting? Or was
someone missing, so they sent out the sheriff's department
with bloodhounds?

Seth didn't wait to hear more. He took off for the boxcar at
a lope, just hoping he remembered the ground well enough
and there was nothing that would trip him. If the ground was
smooth he was sure he could reach the boxcar before the drivers of the vehicles saw him—he was on the Oakhurst Track

Team; he had both speed and stamina. For now, he'd just hope they weren't heading right this way. He'd get to the boxcar, duck inside, hide out for an hour or two . . .

But a few seconds later he had to admit that the crawling feeling between his shoulder blades wasn't fear, but magic, and the sound of the engines was louder. And there was something very *wrong* with the sound.

He remembered his first day at Oakhurst, the first time he ever saw Doctor Ambrosius, when Old Doc A. told him the world was filled with good witches and bad witches, just like *The Wizard of Oz,* and back then Seth had figured Doc A. had been playing too much D&D in his spare time.

Later Seth had decided the Doc was speaking from personal experience.

That the Doc wasn't training all of them out of pure unselfishness, but because someday they might need to fight the evil magicians. And Seth hadn't wanted to be drafted to fight in somebody else's war the way his grampa had. As the months passed, he'd kept his eyes open, put a few things together, and figured out that Doctor Ambrosius's war wasn't something that was going to happen "someday." It was something going on *right now,* and the people involved—at least the ones on the Other Side—didn't have any intention of letting anybody just sit on the sidelines.

Oakhurst should have been safe. But Seth didn't think it was. He thought one of the enemies Doctor Ambrosius knew about had found it and gotten inside, secretly. He thought that whoever it was, they were making sure that when Doctor

Ambrosius decided it was time to take on Emperor Palpatine and the Sith Lords, there weren't going to be any Jedi Knights left.

His breath rasped in his throat as he ran; the night air was dry enough to burn. The motor noises were louder now. Not just one engine, but too many to count. They were coming closer, but he still didn't see any sign of headlights, and that was just crazy. There weren't any roads along here—he was heading on a straight "crow flies" path from Oakhurst to Radial, and both the county road and the railway line were south of here (at least until the tracks swung north onto the Oakhurst campus)—but the engine sounds were to the north of him. When he'd just been learning his magic, Seth had trained with maps of the area. There wasn't anything to the north except miles of open range. *Rocky* open range. Even if whoever was out here was driving off-road vehicles and trusting to night-sight gear instead of headlights to show them where to go, they had a better than even chance of busting an axle.

Except they weren't using night-sight gear. Seth knew that. The magic he could feel was strong enough to make his skin crawl. He could see the boxcar up ahead, a dark shadow against the sky.

Almost there. Almost safe. He put on a final burst of speed.

And suddenly the boxcar was lit in a dazzling wash of brilliance as his pursuers turned on their headlights all in unison.

And Seth Morris realized that he'd run out of time.

❧

Spirit bounced into the Refectory with just minutes to spare, but Addie, Cadence, and Camilla were holding her a seat. There weren't assigned seats in the Refectory—you could sit in a different place for every meal if you liked—but certain groups of kids just tended to sit together, like her and Muirin and Addie and Cadence and Camilla. And the boys, of course.

In any other school Spirit could imagine, Burke would be going around with his football hero nose in the air, refusing to even *notice* ordinary mortals. And while Oakhurst technically had a football team (two of them really, since they never played against any other schools) and Burke was on it (Burke was on *all* the Oakhurst sports teams), and Burke was its star player, he was as far from being dazzled by his own wonderfulness as it was possible to be. In fact, he and Loch had quickly become best friends, although Loch was the star of the Oakhurst chess team and had only taken up fencing because he'd done it at one of his other schools. Addie had talked him into adding swimming to his list of sports; they liked it here if you had what most places would call "a lot of extracurricular activities." There really wasn't much else to do.

Despite her early misgivings, Spirit had found herself settling in to life at Oakhurst. Burke was sweet, and Loch had a sly sense of humor once he got to know you. And Seth and Brendan and Nicholas were all kind of nice, although Nick was tongue-tied to the point of total silence except with Camilla, and Brendan seemed to believe absolutely everything anybody told him, no matter how ridiculous. Muirin (of course) teased Nick until he practically choked and told Brendan the most outrageous lies as if they were absolute fact, but Spirit was pretty sure that Muirin had a kind of *thing* for Seth, even though both of them would probably have died rather than admit it. So if Spirit thought that sometimes Seth's sense of humor crossed the line into rudeness or even cruelty, she kept her opinions to herself. She didn't think Muirin had that many friends.

Spirit slid into her seat and kicked her book bag under it. You could leave the Refectory early enough to go back to your room to get your books for your morning classes, but she preferred to save herself the hike. She reached for her juice glass.

"Where's Muirin?" she asked, looking around.

Addie shrugged. "I haven't seen her since last night. You know Muirin."

Burke laughed. "You mean, you *never* know Muirin. She'll probably stroll in here just before—"

The doors burst open. Muirin stood between them, out of breath, her face flushed. "He's gone!" she yelled, her voice breaking on the second word. "Seth! He's gone!"

Pandemonium inevitably erupted. Mr. Gail and Mr. Bowman came out of nowhere, seized Muirin by the elbows, and hustled her out of the Refectory before she could say anything else.

The others at Muirin's usual table stared at each other over their plates, speechless. The room had erupted with speculation, students chattering so loudly it would have been impossible to speak, anyway.

And that was when Ms. Corby walked in, just as dramatically as Muirin had. Silence immediately fell. She looked around the room through narrowed eyes.

"Doctor Ambrosius wishes you to remain calm, finish your meals, and proceed to your classes in an orderly fashion," she said, in tones that made it very clear that This Was An Order. "There will be no speculation regarding Mr. Morris until we have determined precisely what has occurred. If Doctor Ambrosius deems it necessary at that time, you will proceed to your rooms in an orderly fashion and remain there until you are released. Is this understood?"

One of the proctors stood up, somehow managing to do so subserviently. "Yes, Ms. Corby."

He sat down. Ms. Corby cast her gaze over them again. Spirit tried not to squirm. "Very good. Breakfast will end at the usual time. That is all."

She swept out, but the silence remained.

❋

Halfway through First Period, the word came that they were all to go to their rooms. Spirit went back to her room like everyone else, but no sooner had Spirit closed the door of her room than she got the bird-chirp of an IM. Although the school had forbidden "speculation," they'd forgotten to shut down the e-mail and Instant Message system. She ran over to her computer and opened IM.

ADDIE4: WTFs going on?!?!?!?!?

SPIRIT: Idunno!!!11!!

Brendan pinged her.

BRENDAN9: S ws out last nite, didn com back. M say NEthing?

SPIRIT: Not 2 me.

She kept repeating what Brendan had told her to everyone who pinged her until Addie opened up a chatroom for everyone to join. There were fifty people in it and the number was climbing when she finally saw Muirin's icon flashing in her taskbar.

SPIRIT: ??? ??? ?

IMTOXIC: Double plus ungood

Of all the people Spirit knew here, Muirin was the *only* one besides her who not only had read *1984,* but used terms from it. And the only reason she would be using *that* phrase now had to be because she was warning Spirit that "Big Brother was watching." The first day Spirit had arrived at Oakhurst, Muirin had warned her that they monitored everyone's computer use. So Spirit replied in kind.

SPIRIT: Dept of Hist B sez S wnt out, didn come back

IMTOXIC: MG sez S ran away. We have always been at war with Eastasia

Spirit considered that for a moment. *"Mr. Gail says Seth ran away."* The fact that Muirin had phrased it just that way—followed by more *1984*—told Spirit that whatever Mr. Gail thought, Muirin thought it was a cover story. She'd have to wait to talk to Muirin in person to find out what *she* thought.

SPIRIT: Wut naow cops?

IMTOXIC: Probly Y we're N jail.

Spirit fidgeted; she had the feeling, no, the certainty, that there were a hundred things Muirin couldn't tell her over IM. Unfortunately . . . they were all going to have to wait.

About ten minutes after that, someone in Admin—or maybe one of the proctors—bought a clue and figured out everyone was on IM, so the whole intraweb was shut down: no IM, no e-mail, no access to the online libraries. Spirit didn't think the cops would want to talk to her; she didn't really know Seth and she was new in the school. Meanwhile, she might as well take the chance to curl up with her music downloads and a good dead-tree book.

In theory, anyway. In practice, she kept thinking about how Muirin had looked at breakfast: upset, almost in a panic. Would she be that upset if Seth really had just run away?

It was almost noon before the intraweb came back up again. Her in-box icon was flashing and beeping, which meant a priority e-mail from the Administration. Two of them, actually. The first one simply said that they were all now free to leave their rooms. They were to proceed to the Refectory for lunch as usual, then go on with their regular afternoon schedules.

The second one was about Seth. It was short and to the point, and if any of them still had parents, Spirit thought wistfully, it would probably have gotten the school a few brusque phone calls once it got forwarded.

Dear Students: As you are aware, as of this morning, Seth Morris has left Oakhurst Academy. We regret to inform you that Mr. Morris has elected to pursue opportunities elsewhere. We know that you will share our regret in his unfortunate life choices and will learn from this experience. Regards, The Staff of Oakhurst Academy

Spirit stared at the e-mail incredulously. *"Unfortunate life choices"? "Pursue opportunities elsewhere"?* They made it sound like he'd quit some middle management job to go into rehab. *"Learn from this experience"?* She sure would. She'd learn that if anybody here had ever seen a real live teenager before they'd taken their shiny new jobs, she'd eat her entire new wardrobe.

She hurried back to the Refectory. Everyone in their group was already there, and Muirin was almost in tears, she was so angry. ". . . and of course they don't give a damn! We're just the freak-kids! It's not like we're real human beings or anything!" she was saying.

She had her arms wrapped around herself, and Spirit immediately put an arm around her. "Muirin, what happened?" she asked, feeling Muirin's tense muscles trembling.

"What happened? Nothing! I talked to the cops, but they didn't take notes, they didn't even listen to half of what I said! They aren't even sending out people to search for him! I asked! And he didn't run away! Ask Brendan!"

But when Spirit glanced toward Brendan, he wouldn't look

at her or Muirin. "He didn't take a coat," Brendan muttered awkwardly, staring at the floor.

He thinks Seth did run away, Spirit realized in surprise.

"And why would he?" Muirin continued obliviously. "Where would he go? He hasn't got anyone either! If any of us had any place that wanted us we wouldn't have gotten dumped here! OK, he didn't really like it here, but he didn't hate it enough to make a run!"

Together, Addie and Spirit managed to coax her to sit down and eat something, though not even a PBJ with bacon tempted her much, which just showed how upset she was, since a PBJ was as close as Oakhurst got to allowing junk food most of the time.

❧

On the way out of the Refectory, Spirit cornered Brendan. "You think he did *run* away," she said without preamble.

Brendan looked as if he didn't want to answer her. "You know I won't tell anything you tell me to Muirin," she coaxed.

Brendan sighed. "Well, you know, I don't know for sure, Spirit. But one or two kids always do every semester. They just take off. I figure, we've all got magic, right? And I guess they think with a Mage Gift like oh, Healing or Transmutation or Weather, they can make it on the outside. All I know is the deputies come around and go off again and nothing ever happens." He shrugged. "I'm gonna be late to class."

Spirit stepped back, and Brendan hurried away. She didn't think he really believed the e-mail, and she knew Muirin didn't. But it really didn't matter what the e-mail said, or how badly it said it. Seth was gone, and there wasn't anything any of them could do about it.

※

I said block—you aren't paying attention!" Mr. Wallis snapped.

Spirit heard the clonk of the *bokuto*—the wooden kendo practice sword—against the *shinai*. *Bokuto* were solid wood and were only supposed to be used to practice *kata*—not to hit anything—but Mr. Wallis didn't seem to care. She winced, flinching back, and smiled apologetically at her partner. Kylee smiled back a little nervously.

"I'm sorry, sir. I'll do better next time," Burke answered softly.

It wasn't fair, Spirit thought. Burke *had* blocked. If he weren't a Combat Mage, Mr. Wallis could have broken his arm—or worse. This was supposed to be a sport, not war. But no matter how well Burke did—and he was better than all the rest of them put together—Mr. Wallis never let up on him once. And Burke just took it all without complaint, the way he put up with Mr. Gail and even Ms. Groves.

And if Mr. Wallis seemed to be trying to raise bruises on them, well, Mr. Gail seemed to be trying to get his football teams killed outright. More than once, during the games, Spirit had seen players carried off the field on *stretchers*. Of course, Oakhurst had an advantage that most schools didn't: When the stretcher got to the sidelines, there was a Healing

Mage waiting there to put the player back together again so Mr. Gail could put him back into the game. But all the Healing Mages were students—healing the players was part of their spell-practice—and sometimes if the game was particularly rough they'd get too tired to keep casting spells, so the players with minor injuries wouldn't ask for help—they'd just play injured.

There'd been a game yesterday, and Spirit knew that Burke had really taken a beating. Mr. Wallis knew it, too. He ought to lighten up.

"Pay attention," Kylee hissed, and Spirit nodded, raising her bamboo sword and circling the other girl. They were paired off today to practice forms. Burke, of course, was paired up with Mr. Wallis.

She'd thought several times about dropping her martial arts class and switching to something else. But Mr. Gail coached all the other sports, not just the football—except for fencing—and Spirit honestly couldn't imagine how Muirin could stand Ms. Groves. And—much to her surprise—Spirit had discovered that she liked both karate and kendo. When she could tune Mr. Wallis out and just concentrate on her practicing, it was actually fun. And she was good at it, too. She'd only been in the class for three weeks, and while she hadn't caught up to the kids who'd been taking it for three or four semesters, she wasn't the worst student in the class.

And it wasn't like she was sluffing off taking only one sport, because Ms. Wood, who gave the riding lessons, said the Riding School (she called it an *ecolé,* which was French for "school") would be giving an exhibition in the spring, which would include jumping and precision riding. On the afternoons Spirit wasn't in the dojo area of the gym (because the *kendoka* and the karate students were both going to be competing at the end of November, not just exhibiting), she was down at the stables. Only Sundays were free.

But only in a way.

Mr. Wallis called for a five-minute break before they changed partners. Spirit gratefully lowered her sword, stepped back, and bowed to Kylee before going over to the mat to rest. Karate was done on mats, kendo on the bare wood floor. She pulled off her mask and ran her hands through her hair, scraping it back into her ponytail again, and thought about Sunday.

※

Every Sunday at Oakhurst began the same way, with a pancake breakfast that was just as good as Muirin had said it was. And after breakfast, they all had half an hour to go back to their rooms and get their coats for the walk across the campus to the Chapel.

The Chapel was a freestanding stone building that looked as old as the main house. It even had a bell tower with an actual bell, not a recording of a bell, that Mr. Gail rang for Sunday service. It was one of those "neutral" kinds of places that didn't really look as if it belonged to any denomination—or any religion—at all. There were pews, and a pipe organ, and a pulpit, but the stained glass windows all showed odd pictures of knights in armor.

Spirit thought it was kind of odd for somebody to build themselves their own church; Loch said he didn't think that Arthur Tyniger *had* built it when he built Oakhurst, but that Doctor Ambrosius built it later when he turned the place into a school, maybe even putting it together out of bits and pieces of other buildings that were as old as the main house, because it certainly *looked* as if it matched.

Just as Muirin had said, Sunday service wasn't exactly church, although there were songbooks and a choir—that Addie sang in—and all the students sang along with the choir. But in the last six weeks, Doctor Ambrosius had read to them out of the Diamond Sutra, the Yasna, the Rig Veda, the Qur'an, the Bhagavad Gita, and the Tanakh as well as out of what he said were several different translations of the Bible. Spirit couldn't make up her mind whether Doctor Ambrosius was trying to convince them that all religions shared an underlying spiritual truth—or that they were all equally false. But at least after the service, the rest of Sunday was free.

Only last Sunday when the service was over, Spirit had been stopped on her way out the door by Ms. Smith, who told her she'd be having *afternoon tea* with Doctor Ambrosius. When she'd caught up to Muirin and the others and asked about it, Burke said that Doctor Ambrosius took afternoon tea every Sunday with four boys and four girls chosen at random from the student body. Once you'd been to an Afternoon Tea, you couldn't be picked again until everyone else at the school had been picked. *("Kind of like jury duty," Muirin said.)* Spirit knew that one of the things Oakhurst was supposed to be teaching them was what that section of the Oakhurst intraweb that talked about their curriculum called "genteel deportment" and Camilla called "fancy manners," and Spirit guessed that the Afternoon Tea thing meant that Doctor Ambrosius got to spend Quality Time with all of the students at least once a year.

When he wasn't turning them into mice, that was.

At least she didn't have to worry about what to wear.

The Afternoon Tea was held in the Senior Teachers' Parlor, a place Spirit hadn't been until now. It was one of the rooms on the second floor of the original house, and Spirit couldn't imagine what it had been originally. Bedroom? Library? Roller-skating rink? Whatever it had been, it was an enormous room. The walls were paneled in golden oak, except for the outside wall, which was all windows (with window seats, or at least padded benches, although nobody sat on them). There were a bunch of oil paintings on the walls: some of them landscapes, but one of them—a huge one—was a portrait of an annoyed-looking man in old-fashioned clothes, who Spirit guessed must be Arthur Tyniger.

The other kids looked just as nervous about being here as she felt, and it didn't make Spirit feel any better about this Tea that there were half a dozen teachers here, including

Ms. Smith and Dr. Mackenzie, the Oakhurst psychological counselor.

Back when she'd still gone to regular school, Spirit had liked some of her teachers a lot and suffered through others, and the ones she hadn't liked, she and her friends had all complained about together. But here at Oakhurst, nobody would complain outright about any of the teachers—even Muirin—and in Spirit's opinion, there was plenty to complain about. The teachers like Ms. Groves actually weren't the worst ones—Ms. Groves made no secret of the fact that she didn't ever expect you to ever do anything that satisfied her. And nobody really expected a school shrink to be anything but a loser.

But then there were teachers like Ms. Smith.

Ms. Smith was always smiling and friendly and so interested in you and everything you were doing, and all the time she was asking a lot of prying questions about your life that none of the other teachers asked, like what were you thinking and how were you feeling and how were you doing, and Spirit had even fallen for all this friendly "concern" for a week or so—right up until Ms. Smith started asking her about just how depressed was she not to be a magician like everybody else here at Oakhurst. And over the last six months Spirit had too many people trying to climb inside her head trying to figure out where her switches were so they could flip them. She recognized the signs. If Ms. Smith wanted to flip somebody's switches, she could look elsewhere. So Spirit had started keeping her mouth shut, and just saying she was fine, everything was fine, no matter what Ms. Smith asked her, and finally Ms. Smith had started to leave her alone.

At first the tea party had gone okay. There weren't too many ways to screw up holding a glass of cider and a plate of cookies, after all, and Spirit knew better than to take more than one or two cookies. If she wanted to pig out later, she could go see Muirin, because Muirin always had some chocolate she could be talked into sharing. And there was always popcorn. Or apples. It wasn't like they starved you here.

Thanks to Loch's obsession with Oakhurst history, she'd been able to make mindless small talk with the teachers (she tried not to think of Phoenix, who'd always called it Spirit's Stepford-Robot-Barbie act) while assuring them that she loved Oakhurst, loved her riding lessons, loved her karate lessons, loved her classes, loved the school, loved, loved, *loved* . . .

All the while she'd been constantly aware of Doctor Ambrosius, who was moving around the room making sure he talked to everyone, teachers and students alike. She'd never seen him wearing the flashy power suit he'd worn for her first interview again; he always wore a black suit in church, but now he was wearing a tweed suit with a vest that made him look like he probably ought to be talking with an English accent and riding around in a carriage. On television.

Since Doctor Ambrosius hadn't turned anybody into anything this afternoon, Spirit was pretty much unruffled when he wandered over and sat down next to her on the couch. She'd picked it as a nice safe location because she could stare out the window at the (non-lethal) touch football game going on, or into the fireplace (where of course a fire was burning—and it was a real one, she could feel the heat) and not look as if she was as paralyzed with mind-numbing boredom as she actually was.

"And how are you finding Oakhurst, my dear? Spirit White, isn't it?" Doctor Ambrosius asked.

"Yes sir," Spirit answered obediently. *Don't you remember turning me into a* mouse *last month?* she thought. "I'm very happy to be here," she said, for what seemed like the ten thousandth time this afternoon. She knew Muirin said Afternoon Tea only ran ninety minutes tops, but that was starting to seem like a very long time. And just what would somebody here do if she said she was miserable? Give her some happy pills? Or worse—cast a spell on her to *make* her happy?

"Good, good. Very good," Doctor Ambrosius said. Spirit thought for a horrified moment that he might pat her knee, but he didn't. "And how are you coming with your magical studies? Your spellwork?"

Spirit stared at him, mouth open in surprise, caught in the middle of starting to say she was doing just fine, because she'd been sure that the next question was about her schoolwork, not her *spellwork*. "Um . . . I flunked my magician test," she finally said. "You remember?" *You practically had an entire cow right there and I woke up in the Infirmary? Hello?*

He stared at her for a long moment in silence, and Spirit had the crazy feeling that he was about to tell her that she was mistaken, and even the thought that he might struck her as so unreasonably funny that she had to take a deep breath to keep from laughing.

"Well, don't worry about it, my dear. I'm sure it will all sort itself out eventually," Doctor Ambrosius said with grave politeness. "You just . . . continue to apply yourself to your studies like a good child."

This time he *did* pat her, but on the arm, and he might have meant it to be consoling, but it just raised goose bumps. How could he have forgotten? He'd known her name, after all.

Maybe he was twins.

Maybe he was several fries short of a Happy Meal.

Maybe being a magician drives you crazy eventually. Oh hey. Something for everyone here to look forward to. Insanity. Once again she fought back the demented urge to laugh out loud.

Maybe that explained why all the teachers were so weird.

All right you slackers, playtime's over." Mr. Wallis's voice jerked Spirit out of her reverie. His tone was contemptuous. He almost seemed to be taunting them.

She rose to her feet again and walked out onto the practice floor, pulling on her mask as she went. This time Mr. Wallis paired her with a boy named Dylan Williams. Spirit winced inwardly. Dylan was a year older than she was and had been taking kendo for three semesters. He was good and he was fast. And he liked to hurt people.

Normally she'd just complain about him to the instructor.

But normally the instructor would see what Dylan was doing and stop it. She knew that wouldn't happen here.

Maybe Mr. Wallis expects me to stop him myself?

It was a new idea, and one she didn't like very much. It made it seem as if Oakhurst was some kind of cage-match, and only the strongest would survive to graduate. But it made sense—in a warped kind of way—if what Doctor Ambrosius had told her and Loch when they arrived about being at risk from evil magicians was true. If she could believe anything he'd said that day. If he wasn't crazy.

Mr. Wallis gave them the order to begin, and Dylan raised his sword and began to circle her, his teeth bared in a predatory smile.

She couldn't stop him—not today. She wasn't good enough yet. But she was learning fast. And for now she'd count it a victory just to stay out of his way.

To stay out of *everybody's* way.

SIX

This was her third year at Oakhurst, and like her Dad always used to call Wednesday "Hump Day"—because you were halfway through the week and over the hump and it was all downhill from there and the weekend was on its way—Camilla thought of the Halloween Dance as the "Hump Dance," because it meant they were almost all the way through the year. Halloween meant there'd be the cold weather that she loved after growing up in Florida, and it would start snowing soon so they couldn't do most of the outdoor sports, and there'd be a whole week of no classes at Christmas, and for Christmas they all got something from their Wish Lists in addition to some candy.

Yeah, okay, maybe it was lame. But it was also better than home. The one time she'd called the Halloween Dance the "Hump Dance" out loud, though, she'd gotten laughed at, so she'd never done it again. Sometimes she just wasn't as good at making the words come out right as everyone else was—Camilla knew what she meant, but between her brain and her mouth, it just ended up sounding stupid. Sometimes she thought that when she got her powers working all the way right and could take on her animal shape, she'd just turn into something—a wolf, maybe, or an eagle—and just never turn back.

Having Transformation was a really cool Mage Gift, and she'd been excited when Mr. Bowman explained to her that someday she'd be able to turn into any animal she wanted to. But it was also dangerous, because if you got stuck halfway you could die, so she still had a lot of practicing to do before she did it for the first time. Right now she had what he called "the perks"—sharper senses, faster reflexes, being just a little stronger than somebody else her age.

And one of the advantages of that was it made it easier to sneak around.

The gym had started to fill up right around eight. The dance was going to run from eight to midnight, and the Dance Committee had been fighting in their chatroom for weeks over the playlist (which they did *every dance*), but they'd finally locked it down, and now the songs they'd picked were blasting out through the monster speakers in the corners of the ceiling.

There were tables along the walls with soda, and candy apples, and cupcakes, and enough sweets and junk food—chips and pretzels and soda and candy—to send everybody in the entire school into a white-sugar-coma. Everybody always rushed the snack tables during the first hour of a dance, but Camilla didn't bother; she knew better. When Oakhurst relaxed the junk food ban, it didn't do it by halves. The only rule was that you couldn't take anything back to your room for later, but the tables would be full all evening.

She slipped out the side door of the gym, flicking a glance at her watch. Eight-thirty. Perfect. Nick would wait ten minutes and follow her out so nobody saw them sneak out together, and they could probably have at least twenty minutes out here together before somebody came looking. She knew the teachers practically patrolled the grounds during the dances.

But this was too good a chance to pass up.

She ducked around the corner of the gym, into the shadows, and dug into her vest pocket. The vest was patchwork velvet, the pieces stitched together in metallic thread, and it was the prettiest thing she owned. She'd added the inside pocket herself. She'd always been handy with a needle and thread.

She pulled out the half-empty pack of cigarettes and the lighter, fumbled a cigarette into her mouth, and lit it. She took a cautious drag, and coughed slightly. She wasn't used to smoking anymore. She wasn't supposed to be smoking at all (*Hello? Sixteen?*) but she'd always used to back home. When she'd come here she'd had to go cold turkey until she'd hooked up with Seth Morris and started swapping her weekly soda ration for cigarettes. She didn't really crave them by that point, but they were kind of a link with home. The good parts. Now that Seth was gone, it looked like she'd be giving up smoking again—for good this time. This was her last pack.

She took another drag on her cigarette—and then nearly strangled as she heard a noise coming from the direction of the Sunken Garden. For a few seconds she was scrambling to figure out whether to throw the cigarette away, swallow it, or just try not to cough herself to death. Then she blew out a mouthful of smoke on a shaky silent laugh. She could hear them, but whoever was making the noise was too far away to even *see* her.

Camilla frowned as the sounds continued. But what was it? It sounded like leaves rustling, and it couldn't be—the only things that were still green this time of year were the pine trees, and they didn't make sounds like that. Plus, it was a little early for any of the make-out artists to have snuck away from the gym—and if they did, they'd pick someplace warmer. Like the Greenhouse, or the swimming pool, or even the train station.

And those noises didn't sound . . . right. She couldn't quite put her finger on it. They just didn't.

She carefully ground her cigarette out and picked up the remains, tucking it into her pack and tucking her pack into her vest. Best not to leave any evidence. Then she trotted off to investigate. She had a good five minutes before Nick showed up. He'd wait for her.

Every time Camilla stopped to listen, the noises stopped just a beat later. Scuffling. Giggling. It didn't sound like any of the kids from here, and she wondered if some of the townies from Radial had decided to play a Halloween prank on the school. She passed the Sunken Garden. The noises weren't coming from there. Maybe the train station?

If they'd just keep making noise when she stopped to listen, she'd know where they were. And then they'd see who gave who the fright of their life!

Camilla was standing on the railroad tracks, wondering how she'd come so far without realizing it, when she heard the sound of engines. Car motors, but bigger, like a truck or an SUV—a bunch of them—but the school only had two SUVs, and they were locked up in the garage. And the motor noises weren't coming from the direction of the road, and she didn't see any headlights.

This is wrong. This is all wrong.

She didn't know what was going on out here, and she didn't want to know. The only thing Camilla wanted was to be back in the gym, back where there was noise and light and *people.*

The engines got louder.

She turned around and began to run as fast as she could. She could see the lights of the gym in the distance.

She didn't get far.

Spirit hadn't been sure whether the dance was going to be fun or awful. It wasn't the kind of thing she'd used to do in her old life. She couldn't keep from thinking of it that way, because going and standing around some sweaty gym somewhere waiting for a guy you probably didn't even really like that much to ask you to dance had never been her idea of a good time. But at Oakhurst, at least it was something different to do.

The whole day had been a little strange. She wasn't really used to seeing her friends and classmates out of their school uniforms. Everyone looked so different. Of course, Muirin had taken shameless advantage of the "No Dress Code" day to show up in all of her classes looking like a vampire version of Hello Kitty, but most of the students just wore band t-shirts, or sweatshirts, or jeans and some color that wasn't gold or brown. Addie had come to class wearing a powder blue turtleneck, and she'd loaned Spirit a green sweater so at least Spirit had something nonregulation to wear with her jeans. For a change.

She didn't know if her friends would have paired off more if Seth were still here, but since he wasn't, they'd all sort of decided without talking about it to go as a group. It meant Spirit didn't know if Loch would have asked her to "go" with him—but on the other hand, it meant she didn't have to find out that he wouldn't have.

The gym had been decorated for the dance, but they hadn't tried to make it look as if it wasn't the gym. The Theater Department and the Art Students had gotten together and designed some scenery flats that were painted up to look like old graveyards, and the inside of Dracula's castle, and spooky forests, which was kind of babyish, but it was traditional, too. There were black and orange crepe streamers hung from the walls, and one set of bleachers had been opened out so everyone would have a place to sit, and there were tables full of food and drinks.

Everything might have been awkward, except that Addie announced that she was going to dance with Burke and Spirit was going to dance with Nicholas and Loch was going to dance with Muirin and Camilla was going to dance with Brendan and then they'd all go get cupcakes and punch. Spirit was too busy keeping Brendan from dying of shyness to think about how she felt, and after that, everything didn't seem as weird. Addie was on the Dance Committee—there was a dance roughly every other month—and they'd picked some good music. No matter what you liked to dance to or listen to, it wouldn't be too long before something you liked came up. She was a little surprised, though, when Burke asked her to dance during one of the slow ones.

"It's like this," he said, smiling at her and holding out his hand. "Addie won't let me hear the end of it if I don't dance with everybody we came with—I mean, all the girls—and I'm kind of the world's worst dancer. I figure a slow dance gives you a better chance of getting out of my way."

"Doesn't your—?" Spirit asked, trying to take his hand and gesture inarticulately at the same time.

He shook his head, still smiling. "Combat Mage," he said.

"Dancing isn't fighting. Unless, of course, you're dancing with the Murr-cat."

Spirit laughed, because Muirin had been showing off, dancing the last fast dance with herself, an illusion that had mirrored her moves exactly. She'd been in a strange kind of mood ever since Seth had . . . done whatever he'd done, withdrawing more from the rest of them all the time and not hanging out in the lounge as much in the evening. Spirit knew that Addie felt hurt by it, because she and Muirin had been best friends, but there wasn't a lot anyone could say to Muirin without setting her off, which no one, least of all Addie, wanted to do. Spirit just hoped that Muirin wouldn't do something stupid. Really stupid, like running away.

Meanwhile, even if it was a school dance, there were a lot of things about it that made it different from any other school dance *ever*. A lot of the kids were showing off: the Ice Mages freezing cups of soda into slushies, the Jaunting Mages apporting food across the room, the Air Mages conjuring up little wind-devils that picked up dust and twisted the streamers around themselves and whirled across the floor like the baby sisters of Dorothy's tornado. And Muirin wasn't the only Illusion Mage here.

"You shouldn't let it get to you," Burke said, under cover of the music. "Everybody's magic doesn't show up at the same time. Muirin got hers when she was twelve. Some kids come here and they're older than either of us, and they don't know they're magicians yet."

Spirit looked up at him, startled. And relieved, too, because she didn't think she actually wanted to be a magician, but everyone else was, and it was hard to be left out. "I don't—" she began.

"Don't sweat it," he said. Despite his claims of clumsiness, Burke wasn't that bad a dancer. Just careful and a little nervous. "Give it a few months and you can—"

He broke off in the middle of a sentence, taking a half-step away from Spirit and looking toward the back of the gym. The dance floor was pretty crowded, but Spirit could see that the door was open, and Nicholas was in the doorway talking to Kelly. He looked really upset.

"C'mon," Burke said.

"—gone! I was supposed to meet her outside and I waited for ten minutes then I went looking for her," Nicholas was saying. "She wouldn't have just gone wandering off!"

"It's not that warm outside," Kelly pointed out reasonably. "Maybe she came back in here and you missed her."

But Nicholas was shaking his head frantically, and Spirit was looking around and couldn't see Camilla anywhere.

Within ten minutes, everyone knew Camilla wasn't in the gym and wasn't in her room. The five of them knew something Nicholas hadn't wanted to mention around the proctors or the teachers, too: the reason he was sure that Camilla was in trouble was that he'd found her cigarette lighter outside on the ground. It had belonged to her father—a brass Zippo with the Navy world-and-anchor and the initials "CMP" engraved on the lid—and it wasn't something she'd just drop and not notice. It proved she'd been outside, and it proved—at least to Nicholas—that she was in trouble.

"Let me have it," Loch said quietly, holding out his hand. "One of my Gifts is Kenning," he said, when Nicholas just stared at him. "I might be able to learn something." Loch closed his hand around it, and for a second or two nothing happened. Then he winced, gasping, and forced his fingers open with an effort. He shook his head. "I'm not very good yet," he said apologetically. "All I got from it was cold and darkness. You don't need Kenning to know it's cold and dark out there."

"I'm going to look for her," Nicholas said determinedly.

"Not by yourself," Burke said firmly. "We'll all go."

"Coats," Addie said. "I'll get ours. Brendan, you get the guys'. Come on."

"Before the teachers say we can't," Muirin muttered under her breath.

🌟

But the teachers were out searching, too—at least some of them were. It was a storybook kind of Halloween night—clouds, a full moon, the wind whistling through whatever wind whistled through. There weren't any fallen leaves to kick through—Burke said the Air Mages got together in the fall and swirled them all up into a cyclone and dumped them twenty or thirty miles away—but aside from that it could have been a Halloween in a movie.

Right down to the missing coed.

Don't think like that! Spirit told herself fiercely. Camilla was here somewhere, she was fine, they'd find her and everything would be okay. She hadn't run away. Camilla was one of the few kids Spirit had talked to who actually liked being at Oakhurst better than she'd liked being at home.

But Spirit couldn't help but think about what Brendan had told her. About how a couple kids went missing every year. And when you put that together with what Doctor Ambrosius said about them having enemies somewhere out here—

Well, maybe the school isn't that safe a place after all.

And it wasn't like the teachers or Doctor Ambrosius would actually *tell* you that kids were being grabbed by the Bad Guys right off the campus! That would just start a panic, which wasn't what the faculty would want. She stopped where she was and looked around. She could see the beams of flashlights flickering off in the distance, and could hear people calling Camilla's name.

No, no, that was stupid. Really, that was *stupid*, Spirit insisted to herself. Camilla was just—maybe she heard something and fell in a hole and twisted an ankle. Maybe someone else was trying to play a prank on them all. She shook her head and kept walking. Maybe—

Maybe it's the townies. Spirit didn't know much about Radial, but once in a while some of the kids that had been at Oakhurst for a while got to go there, and from what they said, there was a lot of resentment from the town about the kids here. The townies seemed to think that everyone here was living some kind of Rich and Famous lifestyle, where they all lounged around in mink bathrobes, didn't actually ever do any work, and got handed top grades just for showing up for class. Which was stupid, of course, but even if Doctor Ambrosius let people from Radial on the campus, they'd probably still believe stupid stories like that, just because the place *did* look like a resort. And if Radial was anything like the rural towns where Spirit came from, the schools were getting by on shoestrings, and what Oakhurst spent in one year just on computers would probably equal the entire district budget.

She was almost to the Chapel, and the five of them had agreed to meet there when they'd finished checking their search areas. Burke was already there, standing on the steps; she didn't need to ask him if Camilla had been found, because she could still hear other people searching.

"What if someone from Radial decided to play a prank on us?" she blurted out as soon as she reached him.

Burke shook his head. "They might want to. But if you don't belong here—or aren't wanted here—you run into a bunch of big-time protection spells. The teachers call them 'wards.' Mr. Wallis told me they just lead anybody who doesn't belong here straight to the front door, no matter where they think they're going."

"Mr. Wallis?" Spirit said in surprise.

"Well, yeah," Burke said. "He's my magic coach. Doesn't make sense for a Combat Mage to have a magic coach who can't do martial arts."

By now the other three had arrived—Addie and Muirin together, Loch by himself. "We checked the whole Sunken Garden," Addie said. "Nothing."

The Oakhurst campus was what Loch called "extensively landscaped." But at this time of year, what the campus mostly had was bare-limbed trees and bushes and flowerbeds already in their winter protection. The Sunken Garden was a couple of acres where the ground had been dug out to a couple of feet below ground level, then shored up along the edge with a brick wall. Ms. Holland, who taught the art classes, said it was partly for beauty and partly for warmth for the more delicate plants. There was a fountain in the middle (drained for the winter), and trees planted along the walls, and flower beds covered in burlap for the winter so that they looked like giant pincushions. Even so, it was one of the best places on the campus to hide—or to be hidden.

"I took the main path all the way down to the train station. I even looked inside," Loch said. He shrugged, not needing to say he hadn't had any better luck than Addie and Muirin had. "Maybe she's in the stables. Or the greenhouse."

"Maybe she's just *disappeared*," Muirin said angrily. "Like Seth. Like all the other kids who've just vanished."

"How many kids?" Spirit asked, looking at Burke, Addie,

and Muirin. None of them said anything. "Which of you've been here the longest?" she asked.

"Me," Burke said quietly.

"And?" Spirit demanded. "How many?" she repeated, when Burke didn't answer.

"Not many," he said at last. "Three or four or . . . six . . . or so a year. But sometimes, uh, kids just leave early, like if Oakhurst sends them off to a regular college or something."

But that doesn't make sense! Spirit thought. *Not if we're all here to be trained as magicians! And the prospectus said we were all going to stay here until we were twenty-one . . .*

But as she glanced at the others, none of them looked really suspicious. Even Loch only looked puzzled.

"Whoops," Muirin said bitterly. "Here come Mulder and Scully."

Spirit glanced over her shoulder. A sheriff's car was coming around the side of the Main Building. Its blue and red crashbar was flashing, and the searchlight on its door was lit. Suddenly there was a click and a grating squeal as its bullhorn woke to life.

"*Attention Oakhurst students! Please return to the Gymnasium immediately! This is an order! Return to the Gymnasium at once! Attention Oakhurst students—*"

"Ow, my ears," Addie said. "I guess we'd better go."

"Yeah," Burke said. He forced a smile. "If Camilla's out here anywhere, she's sure to hear that."

None of them answered him. They didn't think—any

more than Burke did—that Camilla Patterson was anywhere on the Oakhurst campus.

❧

When they got back to the gym, somebody had already shut down the music and everybody was standing around talking at once. The sound was deafening. There were two McBride County sheriff's deputies standing next to a man and a woman who weren't part of the faculty by the other door to the gym, the one that led in through the classrooms. Two of the teachers—Ms. Holland and Mr. Bridges—were with them, and so was Ms. Corby. Spirit could see a couple of the other teachers and several of the proctors moving among the students, separating them out into groups.

As the five of them walked in, Kelly Langley came over to them.

"Doctor Ambrosius called the Sheriff's Office as soon as Nick said Camilla was missing. They sent some detectives over to talk to us and a K-9 unit to search the grounds. They want to start with everyone who knew her best," she said. Her expression was solemn. "That would be you."

"It won't—" Muirin began angrily. *It won't do any good.*

"We have to try," Addie said quietly.

"Go on," Kelly said. "I see Nick and Brendan. I'd better go round them up."

They walked toward the waiting adults. Ms. Corby was holding a clipboard and talking to the two detectives— probably telling them there wasn't anything to detect, Spirit thought ungenerously. "These are some of Ms. Patterson's friends," she said, when they got there. "Ms. Carson has opened two of the classrooms for you to use. Right this way."

Spirit had thought it would be done like it was on television, with the cops interviewing them one by one in private, but it wasn't like that at all. The police brought all five of them into the same room—one of the English classrooms—and dragged chairs around and told them they could sit anywhere they wanted. While they were doing that, Kelly arrived with Brendan, Nicholas, and Cadence Morgan and Sarah Ellis. Sarah was on the boxing team with Camilla, and Cadence was another member of "their" group.

Ms. Corby hadn't stayed, and Kelly left once she'd brought the other four in. Spirit wondered if the detectives were going to talk to anyone else—Camilla had been here for two years; she knew most of the students.

"I'm Detective Beth Mitchell and this is my partner Tom Carter," the woman said, perching on the edge of the desk. "We're with the McBride County Sheriff's Department. We understand that you think that a friend of yours has gone missing tonight. We'd like to ask each of you a few questions to help us find her. Who wants to go first?"

There was a moment where they all stared at each other in stunned disbelief. Burke beat Nick and Muirin to volunteering to be first by half a second, and walked up to the front of the room.

Neither Mitchell or Carter bothered to keep their voices down, so the eight of them could hear every question they asked. Had Camilla been happy? Had she been doing well in school? Had she ever talked about leaving? Had she been corresponding with anyone outside the school? Did she have a boyfriend? Had she broken up with him recently? Did she do drugs?

Spirit thought that Burke really had an awful lot of patience, because he answered all their questions as if they were actually serious. Nicholas was sitting behind her, and Addie was holding his hand and Brendan was kicking him in order to keep him quiet. As soon as Burke got to his feet, though, Nicholas jumped up.

"Camilla didn't do drugs!" Nicholas said furiously. "I mean, look around—this is *Oakhurst*! It's not like she could *get* any even if she wanted to do drugs—and she didn't!"

"Mr. Bilderback?" Detective Carter asked. "Would you like to go next?"

By the time they'd worked their way through Nick, Sarah, Brendan, and Muirin, the questions the two detectives asked had started to change. Now they seemed to think that somebody might have abducted Camilla from the school grounds, maybe somebody she'd met in some Internet chatroom somewhere and arranged to go off with, or at least to meet.

And the horrible thing was, none of them could explain the real reason why that was impossible, even though Addie and Spirit both explained that none of them were just allowed to *hang out* in random Internet chatrooms. Access to

the actual Internet—as opposed to the Oakhurst intraweb—
was closely monitored and net-nannied, and all of the social
media and chat sites were blocked.

And if Burke was right, the only stranger who could have
gotten onto the campus without permission was another magician.

But they couldn't say that.

"She wouldn't have run away—and she wouldn't have
made arrangements to leave," Loch said. "She's an orphan.
This is an orphanage. And she's happy here."

"Thank you, Mr. Spears," Detective Mitchell said, getting
to her feet. "You've all been very helpful. We have a few more
people to talk to. We'd appreciate it if you don't talk to anyone
else, okay?"

Even if they'd wanted to, they didn't have the chance.
Gareth Stevenson—another of the proctors—was waiting for
them outside the door. "C'mon guys. I'm supposed to take you
back to your rooms. There's a consolation prize, though."

He led them through the Refectory on the way back to
their rooms. Laid out on one of the tables were bowls of candy,
trays of cupcakes, and cases of soda. The same treats they'd
been supposed to get at the dance.

"I know it doesn't make up for Camilla being gone," he
said, looking at them. "I'm not saying it does. But it would really suck for you to miss out on the goodies, too."

Muirin was the first one to move toward the table. "Hey,"
she said. "If we get cake every time somebody disappears
around here, this place is going to start being livable!"

❋

It was eleven-thirty by the time Spirit got back to her room. Oakhurst locked the students out of e-mail and IM at eleven sharp—lights out—though you could still get into the virtual libraries if you wanted to flout curfew and pull an all-night study session. She tried it tonight on the chance the Administration might have something else on its tiny minds, and she was right: IM and e-mail were still live—and best of all, none of the proctors were anywhere near a computer.

I wonder why they've never figured out what we do with this? Spirit thought in disbelief, as she flipped back and forth between half a dozen different chatrooms. About two-thirds of the students had just been held in the gym for an hour and then sent back to their rooms without being questioned. The cops were only talking to about thirty of them, and from what Spirit had seen when they questioned her, they'd already pretty much made up their minds. They were going to go chasing off after a mythical kidnapper, and ignore whatever had really happened to Camilla.

Despite the warning he'd gotten from the two detectives to not talk to anyone, Nicholas was telling everybody on IM everything that had happened when they'd been interviewed, and there was nobody online stopping him. Considering the draconian way Oakhurst ran things, it was hard to believe they let the students get around the rules this easily. Then Spirit remembered what Muirin had said when Seth vanished: *Big Brother is watching you.* How easy would it be for somebody with superuser privileges—that would probably be most of the faculty—to just pull the chat-logs off the servers and use them to figure out who their malcontents and troublemakers were? You didn't need a network of spies among the student body. They were spying on themselves.

She shuddered at the thought. Just what were the penalties for being an online discipline problem—and how much of a problem did you have to be before you were punished?

Suddenly flouting this particular rule didn't seem like so much fun anymore. She logged out of IM and e-mail. Now the only notifications of incoming messages she'd get would be from "Staff."

She turned off the overhead lights and walked over to her window. She turned off the light beside her bed and opened the curtains. As her eyes adjusted she could see clearly. Her windows didn't overlook any of Oakhurst's outbuildings. All there was outside her window was earth and sky and darkness and stars . . . a vast dark emptiness that made Spirit feel very alone.

She stood staring out the window for a long time, wondering where Camilla was, and what had happened to her, before drawing her curtains again, and switching on her light, and getting ready for bed.

⁂

In the morning, Spirit checked her e-mail before she did anything else. She was hoping for an announcement that Camilla had been found, and half-expecting an announcement from "Staff" that they were under house arrest today. There was neither one.

She dressed in her uniform, as usual, giving her lacy blouse a wistful glance. She hadn't gotten much chance to show it off last night, and not a lot of time to enjoy wearing it, either. She made a mental note to remember to return Addie's sweater to her sometime today, and headed off to breakfast.

The mood in the Refectory wasn't much different than usual. *Of course it isn't,* Spirit thought. *This is Oakhurst Academy. Kids disappear here all the time.* She didn't like thinking that way, but it was hard to stop.

She slid into her usual place at their table—in between Burke and Loch—and reached for her juice. She wondered what time the others had finally gotten to sleep last night, because Muirin looked completely wrecked—she wasn't even up for her usual morning rant against healthy breakfasts—and Addie looked positively grim. Spirit exchanged subdued "good mornings" with the others as the clock over the door ticked over to seven o'clock and the servers began setting out bowls of hot cereal.

Nicholas wasn't here.

"Hey, guys? . . ." Spirit said hesitantly, her voice almost a whisper.

"You might as well tell everyone, Murr," Addie said darkly.

"Is it something about Camilla?" Loch asked, his voice as low as theirs.

"Nick," Muirin said. She was so distracted this morning

she was actually eating her oatmeal plain. "He PM'd me last night to meet him, and I figured it was something he didn't want to say on the intraweb, so I did. He said he knew the cops weren't going to really look for Camilla, so he would."

"And she didn't tell me until this morning," Addie said, sounding disgusted.

"You'd just have tried to talk him out of it, Ads," Muirin said, and Addie made a face at the hated nickname.

"You should have stopped him," Burke said fiercely. "You know damned well it's dangerous out there. And Nick only has a minor Air Gift. Being able to predict the weather isn't going to do much to save him if he gets into trouble."

"Nobody else is going to look for Camilla!" Muirin whispered back, just as fiercely. "You were there last night—the cops had their minds made up even before they talked to us. They just wanted to know what we knew to make their story sound good."

"They must know something they aren't saying," Addie said slowly. "But what?"

"I'll tell you something else," Muirin said. "If Seth really did run away like Oakhurst says, he'd have written to me by now. A long time ago he set up a deal with the kids in town: He brought them stuff from the school and traded it for contraband—and uncensored mail. Where do you think Camilla got her cigs? Or where I get all those Hershey bars? A lot of the kids at Oakhurst showed up with some fancy stuff—clothes and iPods and stuff—and they're willing to trade it off for candy and soda and magazines. And . . ."

Her eyes shifted a little. ". . . and there's stuff that you can do. Keep fried memory chips and motherboards and video cards around, wait for a storm, put 'em in and say your computer got hit with an overvolt from a ground strike. Then you've got hardware to trade. Report you lost something. Burn MP3 disks. Seth had a drop, partway between here and Radial. I took it over when he left. It's been a month. He'd have sent a postcard. Something."

The others did their best to calm her, to offer other explanations for Seth not having written, but Muirin wasn't hysterical this time, she was coldly angry—and she had facts to back her up. Her explanation was delivered in whispered half-sentences over breakfast, but the picture it painted was a chilling one.

As Burke had told Spirit the night before, a few kids vanished every semester, and (so they were told) a few kids graduated early. But none of the "graduates" were ever heard from again. They didn't write to any of their friends still at Oakhurst, even though their letters ought to have been let past the school gatekeepers and delivered to their recipients.

"And Tabby Johnson and Ryan Miller graduated last year—supposedly—and both of them knew about the thing Seth had. They could have sent a letter through the post office box in Radial and it would have gotten here. They never did," Muirin added. "If we weren't a bunch of orphans—if Oakhurst didn't have so much money—any other school would be *investigated* if so many kids kept running off and vanishing. I mean, I don't have any money, and I know Burke doesn't—and neither do you, Spirit—but Loch isn't hurting—and Addie, you're stinking rich. What happens to your inheritances if you just vanish?"

Addie blinked slowly. "I . . . really don't know. Loch?"

"My father's estate is set up as a trust that I can draw on once I'm twenty-one. I get full control of it when I'm twenty-five," Loch said. "I guess if I . . . vanish . . . it goes to some charity."

"Like Oakhurst. An orphanage that takes in a bunch of poor kids would qualify, right?" Muirin said.

From the stricken look on Loch's face, Spirit guessed it would. And Muirin wasn't finished yet. She said that for a week during the summer, Oakhurst held "Alumni Days," during which a number of former students returned to visit. Most of the students were kept completely out of the way of the visitors and barely saw them at all—but a few of the kids, and even some of the teachers, disappeared from their classes for that whole week, and the kids who were involved in Alumni Days refused to talk about what they'd been doing when they came back.

"But everybody knows about that," Burke said slowly. "It's just . . . I always figured . . . Doctor Ambrosius always says we're going to be important people someday. So I kind of thought . . . it might be kind of like a job interview. You know, they might be going to go to work in their companies after they graduated."

"You are too good to live, Burke," Muirin said disgustedly.

"Have you forgotten we're all *magicians*? And why wouldn't they talk about it afterward?"

"A secret society," Loch said. Everybody looked at him. He shrugged slightly. "They have them in colleges. They're like fraternities, most of them, except one of the rules is that you can't talk about being a member."

"So what kind of an exclusive club like that would Oakhurst have?" Spirit asked. "Who's in it—and what's it for?"

No one had an answer for her. And the clock had ticked over to eight o'clock and they were out of time to wonder about it.

The four hours of Spirit's morning classes seemed to drag on forever, and she had difficulty concentrating, even though they were fairly mindless: English, History (regular History, not History of Magic), and Art. Everyone was restless, but most of Spirit's fellow students seemed to be more pissed-off at Camilla picking the night of the dance to run off—and ruining it for them—than worried about her. She was surprised, after what had happened when Seth disappeared, that the school hadn't even seemed to notice that Nicholas was gone at all.

Had Muirin's love of gossip and drama made her blow up a collection of unrelated incidents into a huge conspiracy? Was this Muirin's way of grieving for Seth—making his disappearance into part of an enormous persecution of the Oakhurst student body?

Or was Muirin right? When you looked at the cold, hard facts of it . . . how could she *not* be right?

※

Spirit was on her way to the Refectory at the end of Third Period when Loch showed up in the hallway. They didn't have any morning classes together—he was in a different "module" for History and English, and he had Science while she had Art—so she was a little surprised to see him. She was even more surprised when he put a hand on her arm and drew her toward the wall.

"Skip lunch," he said. "Come on. We're taking a meeting."

She'd thought Loch would be one of the last people to flout the Code of Conduct, so if he was willing to do it, it had to be important. She slipped out the side door with him and hurried down the brick walkway, wrapping her arms around herself against the bite of the wind. November in Montana was a lot colder than November in Indiana.

"Yeah," Loch said, seeing her shiver. "Sorry. This is important."

Their destination was the little railway station. When she and Loch arrived, Spirit saw that Addie and Muirin were already there, and Burke arrived a couple of minutes later. Spirit could practically have *kissed* him when she saw he had two blankets with him—big heavy wool ones, the kind they used down in the stables.

The five of them huddled together under the platform with the blankets wrapped around them. Loch had brought bottles of juice, and granola bars, and apples, and Muirin had several Hershey bars and a Coke, and Burke had some PowerBars and bottled water, and Addie and Spirit both had granola bars tucked down into the bottom of their book bags; they shared out the food as Loch explained why they were all here breaking the rules and missing lunch.

"Nicholas is back," he said, looking grim. "The police brought him into the Infirmary today. They found him down in Radial this morning—wandering down the street like a zombie."

"*What?*" Burke said, stunned.

"How do you know?" Muirin asked suspiciously.

Loch glanced toward Addie. "I've been in prep schools all my life, you know? So a lot of the time I'm doing 'Special Projects' in my English class, because I've pretty much got English Comp covered and they want to keep us busy. So today I started in the Library as a page. It's pretty cool, actually—"

"Get to the point," Muirin snapped.

"The *point*," Loch said, an edge to his voice, "is that library pages shelve books, and they also run all over the school getting them back from wherever the teachers have left them. All the library books are RFID-chipped, and the school computer can find them. What that means is, A: I have the run of the school during my English class, and B: the library has a great view of the driveway."

Muirin opened her mouth to say something else, and Addie poked her.

"So I was in the Library when I saw the ambulance from

Radial drive up, followed by a sheriff's car, so I waited about ten minutes, then I snuck down to the Infirmary to see what was going on."

"But—didn't you worry about being caught?" Spirit asked.

Loch smiled at her unhappily. "Hey. Shadewalker here, remember? That means invisible and stealthy, and I probably couldn't fool a magician, but I'm pretty sure Ms. Bradford isn't a magician, and the cops and the EMTs from Radial sure aren't. I was able to stand right outside the doorway and hear everything.

"They told Ms. Bradford that they found Nick wandering around the center of town right around dawn. They said he was barefoot and in shirtsleeves, so they took him over to the local hospital for a couple of hours to make sure he was going to be okay. Which he is—physically. The cops are calling it a drug overdose, and now they're saying that Camilla was involved with drug dealers, and she disappeared because of a drug deal gone wrong."

"No. No. Absolutely not." Burke was shaking his head. "Nick's mom was a junkie. He wouldn't even touch aspirin. He thought *Coca-Cola* was the hard stuff."

"Camilla smoked," Spirit pointed out.

"Yeah, sure," Burke said. "And cigarettes will kill you, but they aren't exactly heroin. Murr, Seth wasn't bringing anything like that in, was he?"

"Not even pot," Muirin said, making a face. "He said even beer was too risky, because what if the proctors or the teachers caught someone 'faced? Junk food, mail, some clothes, magazines, software, cigs, condoms—that was it. I'd know."

"And Seth was the 'dealer,' not Camilla, anyway," Addie pointed out. "Camilla was supposed to meet Nick outside the gym last night. She disappeared off the school grounds. Nick went looking for her—and I don't care *what* the police are saying, he would have worn a coat and shoes when he went," she finished angrily.

"So . . . what are we saying?" Loch asked, looking around at the others.

"That there's something going on here at Oakhurst," Spirit said into the silence. "It's something that makes kids disappear. And either the authorities in Radial are in on it—or they're being bribed to look the other way—or they're being . . ." She hesitated. "*Bespelled.* Bespelled to not notice what's going on. No matter what it is."

"That's ridiculous," Muirin said instantly.

"Ridiculous?" Spirit shot back in disbelief. "*Spells* are ridiculous?"

"Mind-control spells," Addie said, frowning. "Telepathy, or . . ."

"Or *glamourie?*" Spirit asked. All those mind-numbing lessons with Ms. Groves were finally coming in useful. "How is controlling what somebody thinks and feels any different from controlling what they see? Muirin?"

"I don't know," Muirin said thoughtfully. "But it isn't an

Air Gift. Or Water or Earth or Fire. We get taught every Gift that every School can have—you know that, Spirit. It's in case, you know, we show up with a secondary one later. Right?" she said, looking at the others.

Or any Gift at all, Spirit thought. "But everything we know about magic—*real* magic—we know because Oakhurst has taught it to us, and told us it's the truth. If they aren't telling us the truth about how our classmates are disappearing, what else aren't they telling us?"

"If you're right," Loch said slowly, "then I think we may have a real problem."

"Just the one?" Burke said, rolling his eyes. "That's a relief. For a minute there, I was worried."

"First things first," Addie said. "We need to find out what happened to Nick. Somebody has to talk to him."

"Loch, you're up again," Muirin said. "Time to work those magic ninja powers."

"Yeah," Loch said, glancing at his watch. "But now we have to get back to class. I don't know what they'd do if they noticed us going off to talk like this, but I don't want to find out, either. So lets just keep this here. No Cadence, no Brendan. Nobody else—and especially none of the proctors. Just us."

The five of them exchanged glances, their faces serious as they nodded agreement. Spirit had known this was serious when Loch told all of them about Nick, but making this a se-cret only the five of them shared seemed to underscore that fact.

"Yeah, and I don't think I have to remind any of you orphan geniuses to keep this off the intraweb, right?" Muirin said.

Nobody said anything. Even Burke didn't protest.

SEVEΠ

If Spirit had found it difficult to concentrate that morning just knowing Nick was gone, it was a hundred times harder that afternoon, knowing he'd run into something last night that had fried his brain. And whatever it was, it seemed like the administration didn't think a Healing spell would do any good. Were Healing spells no use on someone who'd been traumatized so badly that he'd completely flipped out?

Maybe they thought whatever had happened to Nick might be contagious. Was that even possible? Spirit didn't know.

Or maybe there wasn't anyone here who could Heal him? That didn't seem right, either.

It couldn't just be that they wanted to conceal what had happened from the students, because with so many magicians among the teachers, the odds were that one of them must be a Healer as well. Had to be. How could they not have a Healer? It had to be Doctor Ambrosius, if nobody else.

Or . . . maybe not Ambrosius. Transformation was a Water Gift, and Healing was a Fire Gift. Even if somebody had Gifts from two Schools, it was usually from Schools of compatible Elements, so maybe Doctor Ambrosius was out of the running for School Healer.

True, Loch had three Gifts, but Kenning and Shadewalking were both from the School of Air, and apparently Pathfinding—School of Earth—wasn't that incompatible.

On the other hand, you were only supposed to be able to Transform yourself, not somebody else; and he'd certainly turned her and Loch into mice. So what School did that make Doctor Ambrosius?

Could you have Gifts from several Schools? Or was there a secret School that let you do things they didn't talk about in class?

She chewed on the end of her pen. Why hadn't anybody ever thought about these things before? (*Maybe they had,* a little voice inside her suggested. *Maybe the kids who think about things like this are the ones who vanish.*) The more Spirit thought about Oakhurst, the more she realized there were so many things none of them knew, and more things that just didn't make sense.

She was so distracted that Ms. Groves caught her not paying attention in Magic Class, and as a result she got an extra assignment—write a ten-page paper on how the traditional folklore practices of Wiltshire were adapted when the English emigrated to the New World, due Monday. There went every scrap of free time over the weekend, not that there was much to begin with. And last Sunday Doctor Ambrosius had finished making his "first pass" through the student body for Sunday Afternoon Tea, which meant she could get chosen again for that *honor* at any time, since student's names were chosen at random. It would be just her luck to make the list this Sunday, and how would she be able to sit there and smile nicely and pretend that there was nothing wrong, that Seth and Camilla weren't missing, that Nick hadn't had his mind destroyed?

To top off what was turning out to be a really awful day, Mr. Wallis was in a horrible mood during karate class. Not only did he pick Spirit to come up to the front of the class to demonstrate a new form with, when she screwed up—she *had* only been in the class for a month and a half!—he did a foot-sweep that knocked her sprawling and then spent five minutes shouting at her about what a clumsy useless loser she was. The dojo had an exhibition coming up at the end of the month (for "exhibition" read "competition," even if they were only competing against the other students in the class), he announced—as if he let any of them forget it for an instant—and he was not going to have them all made to look ridiculous by a lazy, un-talented, good-for-nothing, spoiled little princess like her. He made her do forms with the other students for the rest of the class—even when she should have been working on her kendo—and of course Dylan Williams took the opportunity to hit her—and hit *hard*.

By the time the lesson was over, Spirit was bruised, nearly crying from sheer rage, and just about ready to run away from Oakhurst herself. As the other students folded and packed away their kendo equipment in their gym bags, Spirit strode toward her unopened one. It was probably just as well that she didn't have a real sword. She'd probably have beheaded somebody.

"If you'd like, I could do some extra practice with you," Burke said softly.

He'd come up behind her so quietly she hadn't even heard him approach. If she had her magic, she'd have known he was there, Spirit thought, gritting her teeth. Over the last several weeks she'd noticed how all of the other students—even Loch, and that really hurt—seemed to notice whenever one of the others was there. How many times had she seen Muirin trying to sneak up on Addie, or Brendan, or even (she winced mentally) Nicholas, only to have her intended victim spin around just as she reached them? She was the only one who couldn't tell. Spirit White. The loser. The *cripple*.

She was about to tell Burke that she didn't need any more charity, and forced herself to bite back the words unsaid. Burke wasn't offering charity. Burke was her friend. He wanted to keep her from collecting any more bruises from Mr. Wallis. And if she was honest, she'd have to admit she needed the help.

"I don't know when you'd have the time," she said grudgingly. The football team was playing under lights now, and they had practices every afternoon and a game every Saturday. Burke was heading off to football practice now.

"Evenings after dinner," he said promptly. "We can get in an hour or so as often as we can. It'll help."

She straightened up and turned around, heaving the bag of armor and padding up onto her shoulder. If there had been the least scrap of pity or sympathy on Burke's face, she would have refused: she refused to accept pity and she rejected the entire idea that she needed sympathy. But his face showed nothing but kindness, so she nodded. "Okay."

⁂

The horrible session with Mr. Wallis had driven everything else out of Spirit's mind. It was only when she was on her way into the Refectory for dinner that she remembered that Loch had been supposed to be sneaking back into the Infirmary while she'd been collecting a choice set of new bruises. When she saw him sitting at their table, she felt a sharp pang of relief. It would have been unbearable if Loch had vanished, too.

If any of the others had.

Camilla's disappearance and Nick's accident were the main topics of conversation at dinner—apparently everyone had heard that he'd been found and was going to be in the hospital for a long time. Listening to Brendan talking about it with Troy Lang and Eric Robinson, though, Spirit realized that nobody knew Nick was here at Oakhurst right now. Everyone thought that he'd been found in Radial—that much was true—and was still in the hospital there.

The rumor about his accident and Camilla's disappearance having something to do with "drugs" was making the rounds, too. Sarah Ellis and Cadence Morgan were both sticking up for Camilla, but Spirit doubted it would matter much. If she didn't go to Oakhurst and know how impossible it was to get even an unapproved aspirin here—if she hadn't known everyone involved and known that Nick would rather die than touch anything harder than caffeine—it would probably seem like a plausible explanation.

Only Brendan, Troy, and Eric—and Jillian Marshall and Kristi Fuller—*did* go to Oakhurst, and they sounded as if they believed it. That just was such a WTF moment it almost made Spirit's eyes cross.

And then she realized something else; never mind why the other kids believed the bogus story. That didn't matter. The real question was, how did the rumor get started in the first place?

L och didn't say anything at all about Nicholas during dinner, even though Muirin kept giving him Meaningful Looks. Loch pretended not to notice, insisting on talking to Cadence about tonight's basketball game, and Burke about tomorrow's football game. Addie said that the football team played their last game the Saturday after Thanksgiving, and after that, a lot of the other Oakhurst sports took over Saturday afternoons—the swim team, and the fencing team, the gymnastics teams, and (of course) the martial arts club.

"You should take up tennis in the spring," Addie said to Spirit. "And there's a golf course, too."

"Golf?" Loch asked, looking interested.

"Just nine holes," Addie said. "But"—she dropped her voice conspiratorially—"at least we don't have to *compete* at it."

Loch smiled at her, understanding her perfectly. *They want us to compete at everything here,* Spirit thought—not for the first time. *And against each other. It's almost as if somebody's trying to make sure that only a few of us survive to graduate, and that none of us make good friends.*

"Hey, at least the skeet range is open for a few more weeks," Burke said. "You might like that, Loch. You need to do something besides swimming and chess. And shooting's fun."

"I don't like guns," Loch said, his smile fading as he looked away. "I don't think they're fun at all."

"I didn't—" Burke began, looking hurt.

"Archery," Spirit said quickly. "That's outdoors, right? Or—I don't know—just pick something that's going to get snowed under six weeks from now. Then they'll be happy, and you won't have to think about it again until March."

"April, actually," Addie said drily. "There's soccer. Or field hockey—we'd love to have you on our team, Loch."

Loch snorted rudely. Field hockey was one of the few sports at Oakhurst—football was another—that didn't have both a boys and a girls team.

"Croquet," Muirin said instantly.

"Shuffleboard," Spirit said. It was the most ridiculous thing she could think of.

"Hopscotch," Loch said, capping both of them, and the somber mood was broken.

✦

The five of them had gone to the Friday night basketball game as a group every week—at least since Spirit and Loch had arrived at Oakhurst—and by unspoken agreement, they went tonight as well. If you were forming a secret cabal (even if you didn't know what your secret cabal was *for* just yet) the first thing you had to remember was to keep behaving exactly the way you had *before* you'd formed your secret cabal.

But at least they could all sit together at the top of the bleachers without doing anything unusual. And not everyone came to the Friday games—or to the basketball games at all (not like the football games that practically the whole school attended). So they could hide in plain sight—and talk.

Loch sat in the middle, with Spirit on one side of him and Muirin on the other. Addie and Burke sat on the ends. Most of the other kids either didn't want to climb up that high, or wanted to sit at the ends near one or the other of the baskets. All the Oakhurst teams played full-court, and the court was regulation size—94 by 50—so that left plenty of room in the middle for them to have privacy.

"Well?" Muirin demanded, as soon as Mr. Gail had blown the whistle to start the game and the ball was in play. The sound system was blasting a techno mix version of "Oakhurst We Shall Not Forget Thee" (Spirit had nearly died laughing the first time she'd heard it, but she had to admit it kind of grew on you), and everybody was whistling and shouting.

"Okay," Loch said, leaning forward. "I went down to the Infirmary after class, instead of going to the Chess Club—"

"Wow, I bet that took real courage," Muirin said snidely.

"You've been here longer than I have, Muirin—you know they like us to be where we're supposed to be all the time," Loch snapped.

"He's right, Murr," Burke said. "That was a real risk you took," he added, and Loch smiled at the praise.

"So I eavesdropped on Ms. Bradford. You know how everybody was talking at dinner about how Nick's going to be in a hospital for a long time? Well he is, but not in Radial. Ms. Bradford was making the arrangements on the phone with somebody to have an ambulance meet her and him at the train station in Billings."

"When?" Addie asked tensely.

"They're going first thing in the morning," Loch said. "If you're thinking about—about breaking him out, or—or anything—there isn't any point. I tried talking to him."

He sighed, and looked really upset. *But he was laughing and joking all the way through dinner,* Spirit thought. She didn't know whether to be proud of Loch for being able to lie so well—or worried, because if he could lie that well to them about something like this—something they all knew about—what else might he lie about later?

"I had to wait almost an hour for her to leave. Ms. Holland

says that when I'm a full-fledged Shadewalker, I'll be able to fool security cameras into not seeing me, and walk right up to people and have them not see me even if they're looking for me, but right now it's more like they just happen to not look where I am. I didn't dare try to walk past her desk and try to talk to Nick while she was there."

"But she *did* leave," Muirin said impatiently. "And then what happened?"

"They have him strapped into a bed, with an IV in his arm, and one of the bags was just saline, but the other one was really small, and I figured it was some kind of sedative. So I stopped the drip and tried to wake him up, and—stop hitting me, Muirin. I'm going to tell this my own way."

"It'll go faster if you don't try to hurry him, Murr," Burke pointed out.

"I was scared to death," Loch said shakily. "If Ms. Bradford came back, she'd be sure to see me. And Nick wouldn't wake up. He looked so awful—pale, and . . . I don't know how to describe it. Kind of . . . starved." Loch stared off into space for a long moment, and even Muirin didn't try to hurry him this time. "Like he hadn't just been gone for a few hours. Like he'd been gone a really long time. But I remembered something I read in a book once, how to wake somebody up if you really had to, so I pinched his earlobe as hard as I could. And he did wake up—at least a little—and I asked him what had happened to him."

On the floor below, the game had reached the end of the

first quarter. The break in the action meant a drop in the noise level, and Loch stopped talking until the ball was back in play again.

"I don't know if he was really awake. I don't know if he knew I was me," Loch said. "All he'd say—over and over—was: 'the horns—the horns.' I couldn't get him to say anything else—and he started getting louder and louder—and trying to get loose. So I started the IV again and got out of there. Maybe I should have brought Brendan with me to talk to him—his Gift is Animal Communication," Loch added bitterly.

Spirit blinked in surprise; she'd never heard Loch say anything that cruel before, especially about a friend who was hurt. But then she thought about how guilty he must feel at having to leave Nick there. He'd said Nick had been trying to get loose. And he'd sedated him and run.

"You did the right thing," she said firmly, and Loch glanced at her warily. "Hey," she added, forcing a smile. "At least Nick gets to leave Oakhurst, right? Maybe he'll get better in Billings."

"I hear Billings's the garden spot of Montana," Addie drawled.

"I do *not* want to know what the garden spot of Montana could look like," Muirin said feelingly.

"Well, it would have streets and buildings, just for starters," Burke said, and they all made wry faces of agreement.

"So I guess what he said doesn't mean anything to any of you?" Loch asked. And, when they all shook their heads, he added: "Well, we'd better find out what it *does* mean, because Nick ran into something out there that did something to his mind, everybody's covering it up, and I have the feeling that at least some of them already know what did that to him. And if it happened to Nick—it can happen to any of us."

On Monday afternoon, in the hour before dinner, Muirin and Spirit were in the Oakhurst Library trying to follow up on the clue Loch had gotten from Nick. So far it had been slow going: Spirit had been occupied with the surprise paper from Ms. Groves all weekend, and Monday, Wednesday, and Friday were martial arts class, which ate up another hour and a half after regular classes. Muirin had fencing classes in another section of the gym complex that the fencers shared with the gymnasts, and despite her boasts that she was "so advanced" as an Illusion Mage, she still had to practice, and constantly, because the teachers always wanted to see improvement in your spellwork.

Not that Spirit would know anything about that.

In addition to everything else, Spirit was doing her best to squeak out the promised hours to practice with Burke. She'd only managed it once so far—on Sunday afternoon—but she could already tell it had made a difference. Burke was a kind and patient teacher. He didn't expect her to know any of this stuff already, but he had an unswerving belief that she could learn it. And he was willing to demonstrate the basic moves as many times as she needed, gently point out her mistakes, and show her how to fix them.

Spirit thought he'd make a much better teacher than Mr. Wallis.

"I just like people," Burke had said, shrugging. "They're basically good, you know. Or they want to be. Sometimes they get scared, or confused, but underneath that, they're really good."

While Spirit could definitely see what Muirin meant about Burke being *"too good to live,"* she thought his attitude was . . . kind of nice. And even one lesson had made a difference in class that day. She thought if it kept up, she might manage to get through the exhibition at the end of the month with all her limbs intact.

But classes and exhibitions and their "regular" lives at Oakhurst had suddenly become nothing more than an elaborate lie they were telling everyone. Their real lives revolved around solving the mystery of Nicholas Bilderback's last words to Loch.

"The horns—the horns." They could only hope they could figure it out before anyone else vanished.

Their research would have gone much faster online, but as Muirin had pointed out, online research left online traces. And besides, some of the sources they needed were only actual, not virtual. At least it wasn't unusual for them to be in the Library at all hours. Mr. Jackson and Ms. Anderson were the librarians who took care of the collection, and the rest of the work was done by the students.

The five of them had tacitly decided that Nick must have been attacked by magic. If he'd been attacked by someone and drugged, there would have been marks on him—and the hospital would have tested for drugs, and the police in Radial would have had actual *facts* to go on, rather than just a story they really liked. The only thing that really fit the few facts they had—Camilla just vanishing and Nick turning up in the condition he had—was magic.

There were a lot of references to horns in magic and folklore, but so far none of them were very useful. Muirin and Spirit had ruled out the Horn of Gondor, since that was fictional. But that left *Gjallarhorn*, which the Norse God Heimdall would blow to announce Ragnarok; the Amalthean Horn, which some legends said gave forth food and drink and other legends said spewed out demons; the Horn of Roland, which had the power of summoning Arthur's Knights from their enchanted sleep; and a number of references to things like unicorn's horns. None of those things would have *hurt* Nick—at least not without leaving a lot more evidence behind, like a plague of demons or the end of the world.

"This is useless," Spirit said in frustration, closing the latest book. It was about the size of a telephone book and weighed more than all her schoolbooks combined. "How can we figure out what's going on if there isn't any pattern to it?"

Muirin looked up from behind her own pile of books. "Maybe there is." Her green eyes gleamed brightly in the gloom; they'd chosen the darkest, most secluded corner of the Library to work in. "Halloween is one of the four Fire Festivals."

"I know," Spirit said, rolling her eyes. "Halloween, and Imbolc—February second, and Beltane—May first, and

Lammas—August first. And then there are the four Cross-Quarter Days between them, the summer and winter solstices, and the spring and fall equinoxes."

"Ms. Groves would be so proud," Muirin murmured sweetly.

"But so what? Nick wasn't hurt on Halloween. And Seth didn't disappear either on Halloween or on the Autumn Equinox," Spirit pointed out.

"I take it back," Muirin said. "Nick left Halloween night, so he ran into whatever grabbed Camilla. And . . ." She stopped, and stared down at her notepad, and when she continued speaking, it was in a small reluctant voice. "Seth . . . had been talking about leaving for a while. He'd been going to go next summer. During 'Alumni Days,' because, you know, it's *warmer* in June. And he said everybody would be distracted then."

"So he *did* really run away," Spirit said quietly. Muirin had been adamant for weeks that Seth wouldn't have done any such thing.

"He wouldn't have run away in September," Muirin said flatly. "Too cold, no tourists going through he could hitch a ride with, and all his contacts in Radial in school with no reason to go out after dark. Not unless . . . Not unless he thought he had a really good reason."

"Okay," Spirit said. She thought about Murin's first point, how cold September here was, and shivered. "So say he had a really good reason. Then . . . If whatever took Camilla and hurt Nick grabbed him, it did it because he went outside the wards and it knew he was running away. So it's sort of like a watchdog."

"Not one I ever want to meet," Muirin said, hugging herself and staring off into the distance.

🌟

The television in the little lounge had a DVD of *A Midsummer Night's Dream* in it; supposedly they were all studying it, but they all knew the play practically by heart, so it made a good excuse to get together that wouldn't attract anyone else. "But why didn't the—the whatever-we're-looking-for take Nicholas the way we're assuming it took Camilla and Seth?" Addie asked. "He was out at Halloween—it's Halloween—well, *Samhain Night*—from sunset until dawn."

"Because in magic, a day starts at dawn, not at midnight," Loch said. "And it ends at sunset. So the hours between sunset and dawn belong to the Otherworld."

They hadn't been able to get together in one of the lounges to compare notes until after nine. Loch was proctoring a tournament for the Chess Club, and Addie and several of the other Water Witches had magic practice after dinner, because the swim team was using the pool in the afternoon. And none of them dared to make changes to their routine they couldn't explain. At least it gave Spirit and Burke another hour of practice time in the gym while Muirin did some more digging on her own.

"Maybe the *Whatever* couldn't grab Nick," Muirin said, frowning thoughtfully. She waved the spiral notebook she was holding. She'd told the others that they didn't dare keep a single thing on their computers—not even if they were sure they'd saved it to a disk and deleted the copy on their computer—so all their notes were being kept in pencil on paper . . . and carefully hidden. Spirit kept hers between the mattress and the box spring on her bed. "Loch said he heard the cops say they found Nick a little after dawn. Maybe dawn meant the *Whatever* had to stop chasing him."

"But by then the damage had already been done," Burke said grimly.

"Yeah," Muirin said. "I've found something else you aren't going to like. I think I have, anyway. Okay, June is when Graduation is."

"Right," Addie said. "That and Alumni Days. Same week." She glanced toward Spirit and Loch, the newcomers. "Doctor Ambrosius doesn't make a really big thing of graduating, and . . . you know, I don't think I've ever heard anybody talk about what they're planning to do after they leave Oakhurst?" She frowned, wearing the same baffled expression Spirit was starting to become all-too-familiar with—as if thinking about life after Oakhurst was a concept that had never occurred to her before.

Spirit sighed. "Anybody have any idea of about how many alums come to the Alumni Days?" she asked hopefully.

"Twenty? Thirty?" Burke said. None of the three who'd been here for Alumni Days—Burke had been here for four of them, beating out Muirin by one and Addie by two—seemed to know.

"The *point* is," Muirin said determinedly, "that Alumni Days is held during the week of the Summer Solstice—June 21—and that's also the week that the students who take 'early graduation' leave. Surprise. And I've been making a list of all the kids I can remember who've just left—no matter what reason Oakhurst gave—and okay, I didn't exactly keep track of when they went. But it looks like we've got them vanishing at least in the right months for this to have something to do with the Quarter Days and Fire Festivals. Ads, didn't Jimmy Richardson leave last October?"

"He didn't *leave*. He broke his leg the week before the Halloween dance. Down at the stables," Addie said, sounding indignant. "Ms. Wood drove him down to Radial to get it x-rayed."

"He never came back," Muirin said simply, and the five of them looked at each other for a long moment.

"I broke my collarbone in the first game in the spring, when Blake Watson clotheslined me," Burke said, looking stunned. "I made it to the sidelines, and Colin Harrington Healed me right back up. I played the whole second half. Why didn't someone just Heal Jimmy?"

"Maybe there was . . ." Addie said, and stopped. She looked at the others, but Healing was a Fire Gift, and none of them were School of Fire.

"Far as I know," Burke said, after a pause, "the only reason to *not* Heal somebody is if you're afraid you might make it worse—or if you're too tired. 'Too tired' wouldn't be a reason not to Heal Jimmy. And a broken leg isn't that complicated."

Burke wasn't a Healing Mage, but he'd certainly been *Healed* often enough to know things like that.

"So there was something more than a broken leg wrong," Addie said determinedly. "They don't tell us everything. Why should they?"

"So we find out for sure," Loch said. "Muirin said—the other day—that Oakhurst might . . . benefit . . . from people like me—or Addie—dying while we're here. If that happens, you can bet it's going to be investigated by somebody higher up than the cops in a no-horse town. And magic or no magic, everything will go a lot more smoothly with the right paperwork. A place like this has to keep records. It's insured, certified by the County Health Department, has a state license to operate, is accredited at the state and national level—that's a lot of paperwork. You can't just *pretend* you filed all of it. Or maintain an illusion from here to the State Capitol for years."

"So . . . what?" Spirit asked. "We're looking for a book that says 'There's a Portal To Hell In The School Basement' with a list of names in it and the dates the teachers threw them in?"

Loch coughed, unsuccessfully trying to hide a laugh. "More like old files on former students. Maybe even death certificates, if they're admitting that anyone died here. At the very least, a better list of who 'ran away' from Oakhurst."

"Or graduated early," Burke said.

"Whatever that means," Loch muttered.

"Like Tabitha Johnson and Ryan Miller," Muirin added.

Thanksgiving was coming, and Spirit kept thinking about last year, when she'd still had a *family*. She remembered grumbling and griping through the whole day—they'd driven into town to volunteer at the local shelter to serve Thanksgiving dinner to a couple of hundred people, then come home to eat their own with a bunch of Mom and Dad's hippy-dippy friends, all of whom brought weird "organic" casseroles. They hadn't even had a real turkey—because so many of their guests were vegetarians—it had been Tofurky, and Spirit and Phoenix both hated that. And all she'd been able to think about all day was that she wished she had a normal life, with normal parents, where she could eat a normal Thanksgiving dinner, without arguing whether or not something was "ethical," "vegan," or "green," with sugary cranberry sauce and an actual turkey, and pie and ice cream for dessert, and not have to listen to a bunch of people who thought that Woodstock Was Not Dead.

She'd give anything to be able to step back into that life again.

The week seemed to drag on forever. It was boring and terrifying at the same time: they had to behave exactly as they had been—right down to hanging out on IM at night—and they could never even hint to someone outside their group that they suspected there was something going on.

At the same time, they couldn't let Oakhurst notice there was an actual *them*, either. Spirit had started out only suspecting that Oakhurst didn't want you to make good friends—not the kind of friends you'd be drop-dead loyal to—and the more she looked around, the more hints she found that she was right.

Zoey Young and Jillian Marshall were the two girls who'd arrived at Oakhurst before Spirit, and they'd become close friends. Both of them—and Spirit—were in the same afternoon History of Magic class with Ms. Groves. Then Zoey got switched to the morning class, and Ms. Groves announced—in class, so everybody knew—that it was because Zoey was "more advanced." Spirit knew that Jillian was the better magician. Jillian knew it, too. She stopped sitting with Zoey at meals.

When Spirit mentioned that to the others, Addie didn't seem to see anything odd in it, and Spirit wondered if she was being overly paranoid. The truth was that Oakhurst rarely needed to meddle that much to keep all of them at each other's throats. With all the competition going, it was hard to stay friends with someone. On Wednesday in kendo, she'd been sparring against Jenny O'Connell, and when she'd blocked with her *shinai,* it exploded into splinters and ash in her hands. Somebody had carefully burned the bamboo-slat sword to cinders from the inside out. Jenny backed off and let Spirit get another *shinai.*

Spirit had thought Jenny was being nice until she saw her laughing with Andy Hayes about it after class. Andy wasn't taking kendo—but he was a Fire Witch. So much for being nice; Jenny had sabotaged her sparring session.

When Spirit wasn't dealing with her classmates, or trying to be "normal for Oakhurst," she was helping the others try to figure out what was going on. What she was actually figuring out was that this kind of double life left her feeling as drained as those first weeks of rehab had—when she was struggling to reclaim her own body. There were never enough hours in the day, and they weren't much closer to figuring out what the *"Whatever"* was (Muirin's name for it had stuck), either. They were guessing it was something that had to vanish with the dawn, but there were a lot of magical things that did that.

On the other hand, they were starting to develop a scarily long list of missing students.

Oakhurst Academy had opened almost forty years ago, according to Loch. They couldn't exactly ask any of the proctors or the teachers about kids who'd disappeared from Oakhurst before they turned twenty-one, but Burke was well-liked and knew everyone—and he had a good memory. When he sat down and thought about it, he came up with something that startled all of them, even Muirin. At least two kids had left Oakhurst in the weeks around the Fire Festivals and Cross-Quarter Days for as far back as Burke could remember. And if it had been going on for the last four years, well, there was no reason to think it hadn't been going on for the last forty years. They were all orphans. Who'd know—or care—if one of them vanished, so long as everything looked right on the surface? Like Loch said, if the paperwork was all in order . . .

Oh, there were dozens of explanations. Illness, injury, ran away, long-lost relative turned up, transferred to a different boarding school . . . kidnapped by space aliens, for all Spirit knew! The point was, Oakhurst was like a Roach Motel in reverse: kids checked out—and they never checked back in again.

✣

The double life was exhausting and nerve-wracking, and the expected attendance at the football game was pretty much the last straw. As the victorious players trotted from the playing field, Spirit decided her plans for the rest of the afternoon would be curling up with a good book, and . . . curling up with a good book. The football game had just been a reminder that Oakhurst encouraged confrontation and conflict—five players had been carried from the field into the hands of the Healing Mages—as well as a reminder that there was nobody any of them could turn to for protection. And if that wasn't bad enough, it was *cold* out there in the stands.

When she got back to her room, her IM was flashing and chiming with a request for chat. *So not in the mood,* Spirit thought, muting the sound and turning her computer around so she wouldn't have to look at the nagging image on the screen.

✣

How come you weren't answering your IM?" Muirin demanded, practically the moment Spirit settled into her seat in the Refectory. "I was paging you right up until dinner."

Spirit felt a flare of irritation—and an unreasonable wish

172

that she'd sat somewhere else tonight. Couldn't Muirin give her a rest for one afternoon? "I was busy," she said shortly.

She glanced around. The others were all looking at her as if she'd done something wrong—or something particularly stupid—and for just an instant Spirit was tempted to leap to her feet and start shouting: *"Hey! Everyone! Camilla didn't run away! She was kidnapped by the Monster Of The Week! And so was Nicholas! And so was Seth! And so was everybody that you think has left Oakhurst for any reason for the last ten years!"*

"What?" she said instead, knowing she sounded sulky and out of sorts.

"Um, just, I could use some help on this thing I've got to work on, if you've got time after dinner," Loch said, after an awkward pause.

Spirit was about to point out that not only were they not in any of the same classes, Loch was probably a better student than she was. He might have been bounced around among half a dozen private schools (or more), but the ones that weren't just babysitters for the rich and bored were academic pit bulls. And Lachlan Spears, Senior, had probably been the type of father to go for the pit-bull school over the babysitter school. But she didn't. She opened her mouth to say something when she felt a foot settle over hers and press down. Hard.

She glanced up in surprise. Addie was reaching for a roll and looking completely innocent, but Spirit had no doubt as to whose foot it was. "Um, sure. Glad to," Spirit said unconvincingly.

She was grateful when dinner was over. She didn't have a lot of appetite between wondering what the others wanted to talk about and trying to keep up a stream of inane chatter about stupid things. They hadn't seemed quite as stupid when she'd just thought Oakhurst was a perfectly normal orphanage where all the kids happened to have magic powers. (*Will you listen to yourself, Spirit White!*" her inner voice said. *"'A perfectly normal orphanage where all the kids happen to have magic powers'? Is it any wonder you're a few fries short of a Happy Meal these days?"*) But now that she knew it was an orphanage where all the kids had magic powers and some of them were *inexplicably disappearing,* she'd lost any patience with trivialities that she'd had left after her family's deaths. Life wasn't just serious business, it was downright grim. Why didn't everyone else see that?

She was just as glad that Loch's "cover story" of needing her help with a school project meant they could all head over to the Library after dinner instead of going to the gym for the basketball game. It was one more example of how Oakhurst was trying to turn them all against each other.

She really wasn't in the mood.

The School Library occupied the second floor of the East Wing of the original house, and it had more books in it than the piddly little Association Library in Spirit's hometown. Her former hometown. The Library was one long room, about twice the size of the Faculty Lounge where Doctor Ambrosius held his Afternoon Teas. The ceiling was painted dark blue, with a pattern of constellations on it in gold. Above each of the windows there was a half-moon-shaped panel (Loch—of course he'd know—said it was called a "lunette") on which the celestial motif was repeated: there were twelve lunette panels in the library, and each had a painting of one of the signs of the Zodiac on it.

There were oak bookshelves all along all four walls, and if that weren't enough storage space for the Oakhurst Library (and apparently it wasn't) there were also bookshelves jutting out into the room to form "study bays." There were large oak tables in each of the "study bays," at which the students could congregate to work.

Ms. Anderson was behind the checkout desk this evening. You could check out as many books as you liked from the Library, but you could only keep them for seven days, and if you didn't return them on time, you got demerit points, and they were assessed per book, not per you-had-overdue-library-books. And of course they had to be returned in good shape. But aside from that, they didn't care what you read, and it was one of the nicest libraries Spirit had ever been in.

Ms. Anderson looked up as they walked in, nodding briefly before returning to the book she was reading. On a Saturday after dinner, the Library wasn't too crowded, though there were about half a dozen students sitting up near the front, typing away on their laptops, a stack of reference books beside them.

The five of them went back into the stacks, to what had

become Spirit and Muirin's usual study table. There wasn't as much light back here as in the rest of the Library: during the day, the freestanding shelves cut off most of the light from the windows, and at night, they blocked a lot of the light from the chandeliers. Also—by some fluke of the building's construction—laptops in this corner couldn't get a signal to connect to the school intranet.

So it was perfect.

Spirit settled into a seat and waited with ill-concealed impatience while the others collected chairs and settled around the table.

"Okay," Burke said. "So I get back from the game today, and Brendan comes over, because he was going through all his stuff to find all the books he needed to take back to the Library, and he had this."

He reached into his blazer pocket and pulled out a handkerchief. He set it on the table and unfolded it carefully. Inside was a tiny zip-up carrying case with the initials "NB" handpainted on one side in flaming letters.

"What is it?" Spirit asked. She was curious in spite of herself.

"It's an earbud case," Burke said. "Brendan said Nick was studying in his room a few days before the dance. Nick brought his earbuds with him so he could listen to music without bugging Brendan. He was looking all over for it later—and Brendan forgot he'd left it there. So now Brendan doesn't just want to throw it out, and Nick's room's already been emptied. I said I'd take care of it."

Spirit couldn't figure out why the others looked as if this was a really big deal. So Burke had found Nick's earbud case. So?

"It's something Nick handled a lot, and something he cared about," Burke said. "Loch should be able to use his Kenning Gift to trace it back to where anything that has an affinity with it is."

"We know where Nick is—or where he's supposed to be. Billings," Loch pointed out.

"Sure. But his *stuff* isn't in Billings," Addie said. "And they probably didn't just toss it out—because somebody might notice, and wonder why. And if they didn't . . . then maybe it's with other stuff they've got stored."

"And if it is, and I can find where that is, who knows what else I might find?" Loch said, looking excited.

"Well, you're going to have to be careful," Muirin said warningly. "And you're going to need help."

☆

When Muirin said that Loch would need "help," it'd never occurred to Spirit that the help Muirin meant was her.

But as Muirin explained, if Spirit hadn't come into her magic yet, that also meant a magician couldn't sense her by following her magic. So in the event Muirin and Loch were caught, Spirit could get away to warn the others.

Probably.

It'd seemed like a crazy idea after dinner, and it seemed like an even crazier one three hours after Lights Out, when

she, Loch, and Muirin—all dressed in their darkest clothes—
went sneaking down the back stairs of the main building.

Loch was the one who had to do the actual Kenning
spell, and Muirin was coming along at least partly—Spirit
thought—because Muirin could never bear to be left out of
any "adventure," no matter how dangerous, and partly because her ability to cast illusions might give them some protection.

Spirit had never been gladder about Loch's obsession with
local history. The Kenning spell pulled him in a straight
line—as if there were an invisible string stretching between the
object he held and the objects for which it had an "affinity"—
but he wasn't forced to follow it slavishly. He could tell that
it led down, so he led them around the main rooms of the
house, into the classroom wing, down into the basement level
there—and then back toward the house.

"When they added on the new wings, they covered at least
one of the exterior entrances to the cellar," Loch whispered,
shining his penlight over the walls. "This is the main one.
Oakhurst used to be heated by coal."

Spirit wished he'd stop talking. If Oakhurst was a little
creepy during the day sometimes, it was full-on spooky in the
middle of the night. And she wouldn't quite put it past one of
the teachers—or one of the proctors—to follow them and then
jump out shrieking just to give them the fright of their lives.

The door Loch was indicating looked just like any other
door down here, except for the sign that said NO EXIT: KEEP OUT.

It was gray metal and looked grimly institutional. But when Loch tried it, much to Spirit's surprise, it opened.

"What if there are burglar alarms?" she whispered.

"Oh don't be silly, Spirit," Muirin hissed. "Who's going to break in down here?"

"Well . . . us," Loch said inarguably. "Come on."

The basement—cellar, really—was the only part of Oakhurst that Spirit had seen that didn't look shiny new and rolling in money. It was freezing cold and faintly damp, and while Loch's little penlight didn't do much to illuminate it, what she could see was dusty, dirty, and generally unused. The walls were made up of wide-spaced wooden planks, and she could even see cobwebs.

"Hey," Muirin whispered. "Shine that on the floor again." When Loch did, she made a small sound of surprise. "Somebody put down a new cement floor here. Newer than the house, anyway."

"How would you know?" Spirit asked, despite herself.

"Daddy Dearest was a contractor," Muirin said simply. "I spent a *lot* of time on construction sites when I was a kid."

"Do people ever put basements *under* basements?" Loch asked, sounding confused.

It took them a while to find what Loch was looking for. The part of the cellar they'd come in through had contained the old coal bins. From there, they found the (modern) Furnace

Room, where Muirin—over Spirit's protests—grabbed a flashlight to replace Loch's failing penlight.

"We're already going to be in trouble if we're caught down here, what's one little flashlight going to matter?" she said blithely.

Spirit wasn't sure what Loch was expecting to find down here. The basement was cut up into a number of rooms (Loch said that was to provide support for the ground floor above) and it was easily as large as the main house. A lot of it seemed to be devoted to storage: there were shelves of ancient computer equipment, a whole room full of broken wooden furniture and tattered carpet ends, things that had obviously been sent here to die—and other rooms filled with shelves that obviously held quantities of things in current use, everything from fifty-pound sacks of flour to industrial-size boxes of trash bags.

Loch kept circling around as if he were lost, clutching Nick's leather case in one hand. Finally he returned—for the third time—to the Furnace Room.

"It's here," he said, sounding disgusted. He pointed at the floor. "Right there."

"Huh." Muirin looked around the room, shining the flashlight around the walls and the ceiling. Suddenly she darted off and disappeared behind the furnace. "Maybe through this door, geniuses?"

"What?" Loch spoke loudly and Spirit hissed in dismay. "Sorry," he whispered.

The two of them groped through the darkness to where Muirin stood. There was about three feet of space between the back of the furnace and the wall, and in the middle of that space was a door—or, rather, a hatch. It looked like a hatch on a ship, with rounded corners and a raised bottom edge, and it was painted the same color as the wall. Between that and the fact that it was a little smaller than an ordinary door, they hadn't found it before.

"This way through the rabbit hole," Muirin said.

It was also locked with a padlock.

"How are we? . . ." Loch said.

Muirin handed her flashlight to Spirit and dug around in her pocket. While Spirit and Loch were both wearing their school clothes—the dark brown was the perfect shade for sneaking around in, actually—Muirin was wearing black jeans and a black turtleneck sweater. She looked like an elegant cat burglar.

"Trust me when I say I know everything there is to know about smuggling contraband into fancy private schools specializing in 'attitude readjustment,'" Muirin said. She came up with a ring of keys and shook them at the other two. "And about keeping it hidden once you get there. These are skeleton keys. They'll fit most locks. They were Daddy Dearest's. And now—for reasons that don't need explaining at this juncture—they're mine."

Muirin had to try several different keys, but finally one of them turned, and the padlock sprang open. Muirin removed the lock and pushed open the door. It moved silently, but with a ponderousness that made Spirit think it must be heavy. Loch shone the flashlight in through the open door. There was a flight of metal steps leading down into the dark. He flicked the beam around as much as he could. Support beams. Blank walls.

Muirin carefully tucked both the ring of skeleton keys and the open padlock into her pockets. "I'd rather be caught than locked in down there," she said.

"Yeah," Loch said shakily.

The three of them walked carefully down the stairs. Muirin came last, pulling the hatchway door closed behind her. When the beam of the flashlight revealed a light switch on one of the nearer pillars, she skipped over to it and switched it on.

"Hey!" Loch protested.

Strings of bare bulbs strung from an overhanging wire illuminated the room. Series of rooms, actually: this one was large, but Spirit could see doorways leading off of it. The walls, the floor, and the ceiling were all poured concrete.

"We're in the secret sub-subbasement, which—you may have noticed—doesn't have any windows, and if they find us here, we're toast anyway," Muirin said. She looked around, her expression thoughtful. "Somebody's Earth Gift got a workout, I'd say."

"Or something," Loch said, conceding her point. "This way."

The fact that there was a secret sub-subbasement *at all* was bad enough. Some of the other things they found down here were worse. For instance: There were several small rooms set up as cells. In each, there was a bed, a table and chair, a toilet—and a door with a barred window that locked from the outside.

There was a room that looked as if it must be an operating room, or an infirmary of some kind. There were shelves along the wall to hold some kind of supplies, and a sink, and a bed in the middle with a big lamp over it. The bed had heavy leather straps.

"I guess now we know what happens if you collect too many demerit points," Muirin said, looking at it, and Spirit could hear the fear beneath the mockery.

"Here we are," Loch said in relief. *"Finally."*

The room was about as large as the Library upstairs. Spirit had gotten completely turned around while they'd been following the trail, but she thought it might even be directly under it. There was a big oak table in the middle of the room—like the ones upstairs but considerably more battered—and along one wall there was rack after rack of rough wooden shelving containing rows of cardboard boxes. Beyond them were rows of file cabinets.

Loch walked unerringly over to one of the boxes and opened it, dropping the little leather case inside. "Nick's stuff," he said, making a face. "It's labeled. They all are." He walked along the row of boxes, his lips moving silently as he read the labels. "Here's Camilla's stuff. And Seth's. It looks like they're arranged in chronological order." He looked at the wall of boxes. He didn't say anything. He didn't have to.

"Why are they keeping all this stuff?" Spirit asked.

"They're probably planning to ditch it when it's convenient," Muirin said. She walked quickly along the row, obviously looking for something. "Maybe they take it all to a big city dump or an incinerator. Someplace where no one will know any of these kids or care about asking questions. Tabitha Johnson and Ryan Miller," she said in disgust. "Early graduation last June. Not."

Spirit looked at the wall of boxes and swallowed hard. There were more than twenty names between Ryan and Tabitha—and Seth, Camilla, and Nick. She walked over to stand beside Loch. "How can they do this?" she asked plaintively. "How can they just keep doing this?"

"I don't know," Loch said miserably. "It could just be . . . we could just be blowing things up out of proportion. We know why Seth and Camilla and Nick's stuff is here. Maybe there's a good reason for everything else. Maybe it's stuff they didn't want anymore." He walked down to where the boxes marked TABITHA JOHNSON were and lifted one down, bringing it over to the table. He lifted off the lid.

The first thing Spirit saw was a raggedy sweater in Oakhurst gold. Loch lifted it out carefully and set it aside. Beneath it was a two-sided silver frame. In one side was a picture of a smiling dark-haired girl with her arms around the neck of a panting golden retriever. Behind her stood a man and a woman, obviously her parents. In the photo on the other side, a handsome boy teased the same dog with a Frisbee. Brother? Boyfriend? It didn't matter. No matter what, Tabitha Johnson wouldn't have left that behind when she left Oakhurst.

Not if she'd had a choice.

"Hey, kids, look at this," Muirin said. She walked over to the table with a file folder in her hand. "Those file cabinets are all full of files. There must be *hundreds* of them. I looked at some of the dates. They go all the way back to the seventies."

"That's when Oakhurst opened," Loch said. "It's probably just their dead files. You know, former students? They'd have to keep them forever."

Muirin snickered cruelly. "'Dead Files' is right. This is Camilla's. Let's see what the Powers That Be had to say about the trailer trash."

"That's not very nice," Spirit snapped.

"She's gone, what's the harm?" Muirin said. She flipped through the manila folder. "Transcripts, notes from the teachers—huh, she was getting better grades in Art than I am—evaluations from her magic coach—Kissyface Bowman always was too easy on anybody with a flashy Water Gift— Demerits . . ." She stopped suddenly, as she got to the last page, and stared down at the folder in silence.

"What?" Loch said. Muirin simply held the folder out to him mutely.

He took it, and looked down at the last page. Spirit looked over his shoulder. There was just a single page there at the end, something it would be easy to take out and dispose of if for some reason you were going to hand it over to someone. At the

185

top of the page there were several lines of illegible handwriting. The rest of the page was blank.

Except for a large red stamp that said: *"Tithed."*

And the date.

Halloween.

EİGHT

Loch dropped the folder. The papers scattered everywhere. He stepped back quickly, as if the folder contained
something dangerous.

"Tithed," Muirin whispered harshly.

In that split second, the world seemed to lurch danger-
ously, and Spirit remembered the nightmare moment when
she'd felt her parents' car spin out of control—of thinking it
would be bad, then worse-than-bad, then the blind mindless
terror that swallowed up all thought. She'd relived that terror
for weeks afterward, its echo enough to drag her up out of
even heavy sedation.

*It was like a flash, only negative, and before any of them could
react with more than a flinch, there was something in the road—
right in the middle of the road. It was—*

Oh God! It couldn't be— It couldn't be—

And it looked at them and Mom screamed and Dad yanked the wheel sideways—

She'd told herself for months that what she'd seen wasn't real. And now she was at Oakhurst, and she knew it *could* be, that it *was,* that whatever it was, it had come for Camilla Patterson and it had come for Nick Bilderback and it had come for Seth Morris and it would come for her. She had somehow eluded it once. She'd never be able to escape it a second time. Terror turned her insides to liquid.

"We have to— We have to—" Loch stammered in a stunned disbelieving voice.

"Burn this whole place down," Muirin said viciously. "All of it—just burn it!"

"No. Wait." Spirit dragged in a deep gasping breath, clutching her hands into fists to stop them from shaking. She was so terrified that all she wanted to do was burst into tears and hide. And if she did, all that would happen was other kids would end up just like her. And Loch. Burke, Muirin, Addie— and all the kids who'd died here.

She took another deep breath, closing her eyes tightly. *Play hard and think harder.* Mom always said that. "We need to put everything back the way it was. We need to get out of here without anyone noticing. We need to find out what *t-t-tithing* means," she said, stumbling over the horrible word. "Tithed to who? What? And by who? Who put that note in there? Why? Was it supposed to be a warning in case someone came looking into these records?"

"It can't be everybody doing this," Loch said. He sounded better now. Calmer. As if Spirit managing to hold onto things was making it possible for him to do the same. "Not all the teachers. Not for almost forty years."

"Why not?" Muirin demanded. She sounded angry, and almost about to cry. "Look at that!" She pointed an accusing finger at the page, which had landed at her feet. "It was in the file! They *have* to know!"

"You said once that Burke and Spirit aren't anybody, Murr, and even you and I aren't anybody. And you were right. But Addie is heir to Prester-Lake BioCo. She's worth millions. At the very least. She can't be the first super-rich kid to end up here. Doctor Ambrosius probably sold her trustees on what a great safe secure place it would be for her, because if he hadn't, it would be the easiest thing in the world to tie up Conrad Lake's will in court until she was of age."

"'Safe and secure,'" Muirin said bitterly.

"That's the whole point," Loch said eagerly. "Anybody who had proof that it wasn't—that this whole place was something out of Wes Craven land—could just take her out of here and get a lot of money from her trustees for bringing her to safety. They wouldn't even have to break any Magician's Code of Silence. They could leave that part out."

"And nobody's ever done something like that," Spirit said.

"Well, Oakhurst is still here," Loch said. He bent over and began scooping up the scattered papers. "And believe me, my dad worked with people like Conrad Lake. When the really rich want something to go away, it does."

✦

Spirit didn't stop twitching at every sound until she was back in her own room with her door shut. Of course the door didn't lock. None of the doors in the dormitory wings locked: the demerit points you got for stealing were astronomical; almost as high as the ones for being found in the dorm wing of the opposite sex. *Ever.*

But even when she was lying in bed, lights out, right where she was supposed to be and doing (almost) what she was supposed to be doing, Spirit couldn't relax. For the first time in months, cruel recollections of the life and the family she'd lost pushed into the forefront of her mind, and nothing Spirit could do could stop the torture of those memories. She remembered when the first *Pirates of the Caribbean* movie came out: She'd been nine, and wild to see it, and she'd been afraid she wouldn't get to, because the house rule was that any theater movies had to be something both she and Phoenix could go to, and Phoenix was three years younger than she was, and at nine she was *barely* old enough to see some PG-13 movies.

But Dad was crazy about pirates (Mom preferred cowboys), and Spirit's parents had struck a deal, so she and Dad drove an hour to the only theater in the area showing *Pirates of the Caribbean: Curse of the Black Pearl*—just them—and all the way home Dad had talked in a pirate voice while Spirit had yelled and stuffed her fingers in her ears. *"Yarrrr!"* he'd said. *"Yarrrr, me heartie! T'will be our secret, arrh arrh! Three can keep a secret if two of them are dead—arrrrrh!"*

She missed them so much.

And Oakhurst held a horrible secret—and it wasn't the one she'd thought for the last two months that it was. It was bad enough to be drafted into a secret wizard war. It was worse—much worse—to find out that war might have started early, in the place that had been supposed to be *safe*.

And if it wasn't safe, who was the enemy? Spirit stared unseeing at the ceiling.

She thought Loch had to be right: it couldn't be Doctor Ambrosius and all the teachers and staff doing this. Three can keep a secret if two of them are dead. Addie couldn't be the first student at Oakhurst who'd be going back to claim a family fortune when she turned twenty-one. As Loch said, somebody—in all the years Oakhurst had been open—would have taken the quick path to easy money. Even if the rich kids weren't the ones slated to be "Tithed," it wouldn't matter—not if there was evidence that anyone was being . . . taken away. No matter what you saw in summer blockbusters or in books, trustees didn't want heirs disappearing. Things could get tied up in court for decades, the way they always seemed to with money. Just look what had happened when that rich guy Anna Nicole Smith married died!

For the first time since the accident that had killed her parents and her sister, Spirit made herself think about that night on purpose. What had she seen? What had been there in the middle of the road? As hard as she tried, all there was in her mind was too much darkness—and eyes, and teeth, and cold.

She lay in her bed unable to sleep until the sound of music from her laptop told her it was time for her day to begin.

Another happy day at Oakhurst Academy.

✦

The next day was Sunday. Spirit held her breath all through the morning service, but none of them was picked to attend Afternoon Tea. Aside from studying—and magic practice—Sunday really *was* a day of rest at Oakhurst, without any games or competitions or demos scheduled. It made it easier for them to get away to talk. Burke was the one who suggested—at lunch—that they all go for a nice walk.

November was freezing cold in Montana—it was twenty degrees out—and there were already snow flurries. They'd agreed to leave separately and meet down at the train station again, to avoid attracting attention by leaving as a group. Spirit bundled up in her warmest clothes—with an extra sweater for good measure—but the wind still cut like a knife. She walked quickly, hoping the exercise would warm her.

She was the last to arrive. "This is *warm*," Burke said, grinning at her and Loch as they stamped and shivered. "Too bad neither of you has a Fire Gift." Addie shook her head, and Muirin just groaned hollowly. "Come on," Burke said.

"Where?" Loch asked, frowning slightly. "We can't leave the grounds."

"There isn't any out there to go to," Muirin pointed out.

"Yeah, but you know the grounds go a lot further than this," Burke said, pointing. "Come on."

Once they'd crossed over the railroad tracks, it seemed to Spirit as if they couldn't be on the school grounds any longer, but Burke swore they were. There was nothing much around them but green-brown rolling earth, and mountains in the distance—and there was a lot of distance.

"See that stand of trees over there?" Burke said, pointing to a small clump of evergreen trees about a mile away that seemed to have been dropped down out of nowhere. "That marks the northern boundary of the school property. You'll see when we get there."

"Because a two-mile walk in the freezing cold is just how I want to spend my Sunday," Muirin grumbled. But now they had all the privacy they could possibly want, so the three who'd been there—Spirit, Loch, and Muirin—told the two who hadn't been—Addie and Burke—what they'd found in Oakhurst's hidden subbasement.

Addie shook her head, looking troubled. The wind pulled strands of her long black hair out from under the collar of her coat and whipped it around her face. "I don't think— How could they—?" She ducked her chin into her scarf and fell silent.

"We know Doctor Ambrosius said there's some bad people out there," Burke said soothingly. "That's why he brought us here. Not all the Oakhurst Legacies come here, you know. Just the ones with magic. Like us."

Like you, Spirit thought. *Not like me.* She knew that Doctor Ambrosius and Ms. Smith had both said she had magic. But what if they were wrong? Burke said sometimes it showed up late—but how long was she supposed to wait to find out she was a magician? Or to find out she wasn't?

She wondered if she would've liked the place where the nonmagical Oakhurst orphans got sent better. But . . . what if they got Tithed, too? They'd have no idea what was happening and never see it coming.

Burke was chewing on his lower lip and looking thoughtful. "You said Camilla's folder was stamped 'Tithed,' right?"

"Yeah," Loch said unhappily. "It's an old word that means a payment. It used to be a tenth part of whatever you had—like in the Middle Ages, when people tithed a tenth of their harvest to the Church. Who's being paid—or what they're being paid *for*, though . . ." Loch shrugged.

"Yeah," Burke said. "And whatever—whoever—it is, they're probably being Tithed eight times a year, on the dates of the old-time Festivals. It doesn't matter what—or who—you worship: There've been celebrations on those eight days in most places about as far back as anybody can trace things."

"Yeah, yeah, yeah," Muirin said. "Astronomical calculations, tides of Power rising and falling, yadda. So?"

"So," Burke said, "the problem I see right now is that Camilla disappeared right outside the gym. And she was Tithed. But Oakhurst and the grounds are supposed to be completely warded against anything bad getting in. And that means—"

"That someone here at Oakhurst is giving permission for the *Whatever* to pass the defensive wards," Addie finished grimly.

Imagining someone at Oakhurst might be out to kill them was one thing. Having logical proof that they really were—and had outside allies—was another thing entirely. Spirit actually saw the moment that Addie was really, truly convinced: first, a kind of shock, and then a kind of glazed chill. The five of them walked on in silence for a few minutes until they got to the stand of trees.

It was like being in a miniature forest. The pines filled an area about thirty feet by sixty—a long irregular rectangle—and at the outer edge of the long side were a couple of staggered rows of young trees. The oldest trees were easily thirty feet high, and someone had trimmed them while they were growing, because there were no branches growing out of their trunks lower than seven feet above the ground. Spirit wondered why anyone would do that. Ease of bringing a brush-hog in? The ground in the middle of the tiny forest was soft with fallen pine needles, and in here, sheltered from the wind, it seemed warmer.

At the far edge of the forest was a white marble cylinder, about four feet tall. Burke walked over to it and brushed the fallen pine needles off the top. Carved into the flat disk of its surface was the Oakhurst crest, and carved into one side was a large letter "N."

"This marks the northern boundary of the school grounds," Burke said, tapping the top of the cylinder. "The southern boundary marker is set into the stone pillar on the left side of the foot of the driveway up to the school. The eastern one is about three-quarters of a mile past the centerline of the tennis courts—it's a plaque set into a big boulder. The western one is out past the stadium about a mile, dead level with the fifty-yard line."

Loch turned and looked back the other way. While the ground was fairly level, there were too many things in the way to be able to see even the main gates—let alone the drive and the markers at the foot of it. But: "They all line up," he said.

Burke nodded. "A perfect cross—if you could see them from the air. Or a perfect square, if you connected them around the edges. And everything inside that square is warded."

"Or it's supposed to be," Addie said quietly, returning to the earlier conversation.

"Wouldn't Doctor Ambrosius know if the wards failed?" Loch asked curiously.

"He can't be the one responsible for this," Spirit said doubtfully. "I know he was really horrible to us those first couple of days, but then I saw him at the Afternoon Tea, and— Did he seem, well, *different* to you, too, Loch?"

"A little confused," Loch agreed, nodding. "At my tea party, he didn't seem quite sure who I was. He had that dragon with him—you know, his assistant, Ms. Corby—and she had to tell him my name was Lachlan, not Lawrence. If there's a bad guy at Oakhurst, I vote for her."

"Can't be," Muirin said promptly. "Doctor A. would know if the wards went down, but people get permission to cross them all the time—like those cops the other night, or the ambulance that brought Nick up from Radial. All the school staff with magic can manipulate the wards—but *La Corbyissima* doesn't have magic."

"They put them back the way they are afterward," Addie said softly. "It's called Revoking. You'd never be able to tell that someone's been through the wards once their permission's Revoked. But that means somebody inside is cooperating with someone on the outside so they can come through the wards. And that means one of the staff with magic. Which— I don't know how that ties in with someone being 'Tithed' . . ."

"And why 'Tithe' anyone?" Muirin said. "Because—"

"It doesn't matter why," Spirit said harshly.

All of them looked at her in surprise.

"It doesn't," she insisted. "All that matters is stopping it. Don't you see? Don't any of you see? It's going to happen again. It's going to happen on the Winter Solstice—that's less than two months from now. Two more kids are going to die—disappear—go crazy. Doesn't matter. Unless we find out what's doing it and how to make it stop, it's going to keep happening."

*

If her double life had left Spirit feeling worn out and shaky and constantly on the edge of a crying jag during the previous week, it was nothing to what she felt during the days that followed. Now they not only had a deadline—December twenty-first—but they knew that someone here in the school was in league with . . . whoever the enemy was.

Student? Faculty? Staff? It was Loch who pointed out that whichever member of the Oakhurst staff was turning the school from a safe haven into a hunting ground, they weren't their only problem. There were good reasons to suspect everyone. Knowing what they now did, it seemed more likely that the "secret society" that might-or-might-not exist among the Oakhurst students was more likely to be allied with Doctor Ambrosius's enemies and the Whatever than it was to be on the side of the Good Guys. ("Just because they're keeping it a secret?" Addie had demanded indignantly, and Loch had replied: "Yeah. Think about it. We've got a Chess Club, a Tennis Club, a swim team, a Kendo Club, and every other kind of club and team I can think of here at Oakhurst. If there were an Honors Society for wizards—a legitimate one—don't you think they'd tell us about that, too? If only so we could fight over who got in?")

So they didn't just have to find the enemy—they had to do it while they were surrounded by potential spies. And then there was another problem: the Alumni, and the secret society that might (or might not) exist. Were they (and it) Good Guys? Bad Guys? Some of each? Not even Burke remembered who'd visited the Alumni during Alumni Days, so they didn't know who they *definitely* had to avoid. And anyone at all who saw one of them in the wrong place at the wrong time—or saw something they shouldn't, like their research notes on the *Whatever*—could betray them innocently and by accident, just by mentioning it to the wrong person.

Was Angelina Swanson one of the bad guys? She was one

of the proctors, and most of the younger girls didn't really like her: Angie was an Air Mage, and not above using her Gift to raise a wind that would scatter your schoolwork all over your room—or out a window—or make a door slam on your hand. Was Dylan Williams? He had a nasty streak a mile wide, and used his Mage Gift—Dylan was School of Earth; a Jaunting Mage—to make life unpleasant when he could: He'd grab your pencil or your calculator out of your hands in class, and you'd be the one who had to make a disturbance in order to get them back.

Or was it just too simpleminded to think that because someone was a creep they were actually evil? Maybe they should be worrying about the nice people at Oakhurst, like Kelly Langley and Ms. Smith. Only Ms. Smith was just *too* nice to be real.

Wasn't she?

This was all enough to make Spirit want to crawl into a hole and never come out again.

🌟

"We aren't getting anywhere," Spirit said tiredly.

It was a Tuesday evening. Thanksgiving was in just a few days. And more to the point, the last football game of the Oakhurst season was this Saturday, and Saturday evening—instead of a basketball game—the martial arts club was giving an exhibition.

"No, no," Burke said. "You're getting a lot better, Spirit. Honest."

The two of them were down in the gym, wearing their *gis*.

Lately the only time Spirit felt as if she could relax was when she was practicing with Burke, because at least then she was doing something "normal for Oakhurst," and Burke's gentle style of teaching was a relief after the constant high pressure from everyone else at Oakhurst.

"I don't mean this," she said, smiling wanly. "This is great. I mean everything else."

She tilted her head back, trying to work some of the tired stiffness out of her neck muscles. It had been two weeks since she, Loch, and Muirin had made their midnight trip to the sub-basement, and they were all regularly blowing off the "lights out" part of curfew in order to get their schoolwork done, because they were all spending hours in the Library trying to figure out what Nick's last cryptic warning—if it *was* a warning—had meant.

"Oh," Burke said, as if she'd reminded him of something he really wanted to forget. "We're all doing our best, but . . . Muirin wants to go back down there and look for more clues. I don't think that's a good idea."

"God, *no*." As much as she wanted to find answers, the thought of going back there made Spirit shudder with fear.

"But unless we come up with something soon, I'm scared she will," Burke added. "And I'm scared something will happen to her."

"You like her, don't you?" Spirit said impulsively.

"Uh." Burke looked as startled as Spirit had ever seen him. He turned away, fiddling with the hem of his *gi*. "Not that way. I mean," he added, obviously thinking he sounded rude, "she's too smart for me, I guess. Always making jokes and, um, they're not really the kind I like," he finished awkwardly.

"She doesn't mean anything by it," Spirit said. "It's just . . . I don't think she knows any other way to be funny." Muirin's humor was cruel, and her jokes were always at someone else's expense. She rarely had anything nice to say about someone— just as Burke never had anything bad to say about anyone.

"That kind of makes it worse," Burke pointed out quietly. "I think she needs friends. I'm glad that you and Addie and Loch are willing to be her friends. And I don't mind if she insults me. But I know she thinks I'm big and stupid." He shrugged.

"You aren't stupid," Spirit said, because there was no point in denying that Burke was big. He was the kind of guy that, if his life were normal, the spotters would be knocking on his parents' door right now and offering him a full scholarship if he'd come and be a linebacker on their college football team. "It isn't stupid to not want to say mean—"

"*Clever*—" Burke corrected, grinning at her.

"Whatever," Spirit said, waving her hand. "—things all the time," she finished. "Especially around here." But saying that only brought her thoughts back around to where they'd started. "We've got less than a month," she said. "And we're no further along at finding answers than we were two weeks ago."

"Trouble is, Loch's Gift isn't strong enough to get us the

answers we need, and Addie doesn't have the right Water Gift," Burke said.

Spirit bit her lip. She knew what Burke was getting at. Kenning could tell you a lot more than just where something was—it could tell you something's whole history, and even a lot about the people who'd handled it. And one of the Gifts in the School of Water was Scrying—a Scrying Mage could see past, future, and other places in the here-and-now. Some Scrying Mages did it in dreams, some in waking visions, and some even used "focus objects" like the traditional crystal ball.

"We can't bring someone else into this," Spirit said, alarmed. "What would we tell them?"

"That's something to think about after we decide if we're going to risk it," Burke said seriously. "I don't know if I can see any other way, though. It's that or give up—not forever, but before the Winter Solstice for sure. But right now what we have to do is make sure you get through that demo in one piece. C'mon now. No more slacking."

Spirit groaned theatrically, shaking her head, and stepped toward him on the practice mat again.

Without Burke and Loch, she didn't think she could have borne Oakhurst at all.

Thanksgiving was horrible.

There weren't any classes that day, but in the morning there was a concert and in the afternoon (oh joy) there was going to be a play. Naturally Oakhurst had a Choral Society, an Orchestra, and a Drama Society, but you weren't allowed to try out for any of them until you'd been at Oakhurst for at least six months.

So an hour after breakfast, when Spirit would really rather have been watching the Macy's Thanksgiving Day Parade (she knew it was silly and childish, but she still loved it), she was herded into the Theater along with everybody else.

Spirit hadn't been in the Theater before. It was in a part of the main house she hadn't been in yet, and it looked like an actual theater, with velvet seats and a stage with curtains and everything. It was hard to imagine that Arthur Tyniger had actually built it as part of the original house, because there were seats for everyone, and who'd build a theater this large if they never used it?

The decoration was the same kind of "King Tut and Back-To-The-Land vibe in a blender with *Titanic*" design that she'd seen in most of the house: There was a big Egyptian design over the top of the stage, and Deco ornaments down the sides, and then—just to top it all off—there were cartouches all up the walls of the Theater on both sides, and painted inside them were scenes of elks and snow-covered mountains and railroad trains.

"My brain hurts," Loch said very softly, as they walked in.

"You get used to it," Muirin said. "Just keep your eyes closed. Like the guys who painted it did."

Loch made a rude noise of appreciation at the joke and

Spirit just rolled her eyes, much as Addie would have if she'd been there. But Addie was in the choral society, so she was performing this morning.

To Spirit's mild surprise, they were separated in the theater—boys on one side of the center aisle, girls on the other. That was a little odd, considering that the administration didn't make any attempt to keep them apart the rest of the time. She shrugged and took her seat. She wasn't going to worry about it. There were too many things about this day she was trying not to think about already.

But: "First Thanksgiving is rough," Muirin whispered to her when they were seated. "First Thanksgiving, first Christmas, first birthday—they all suck. A lot."

"Yeah," Spirit said. She blinked hard, refusing to give in to the prickle of tears that had welled up in her eyes. *I wish I was home. Even for Tofurky.*

Maybe it was just as well she wasn't watching the parade. She remembered how she and Phoenix made fun of the floats and the has-been stars, and her parents would get indignant and make comments about "rampant commercialism." And everyone would always bitch that after coming all that way, the band kids wouldn't even get thirty seconds on-camera. And Mom or Dad would say, "Well in *my* day, we got to see the whole band routine instead of two minutes of commercials." And—

She started to choke up just thinking about it, and riveted her attention on the curtain and stage. After a few more minutes of shuffling, everybody was seated. Then Mr. Henderson—

Spirit knew he was the Music Teacher, even if she didn't have any classes with him—came out from behind the curtain and announced the morning's program. It sounded horribly boring.

It was.

Something could be done very well and still not be something you wanted to have anything to do with, and "an exciting exploration of nineteenth-century American composers" was really high on Spirit's list. Of course the two-hour concert began and ended with the School Song. Unfortunately, the end version was the orchestra and chorus together, so Spirit had to listen to the words. All *seven verses* of them.

"Okay, now let's go do something mind-rotting that actually belongs to *this* century," Muirin said, bouncing to her feet as the green velvet curtain closed.

"I— I think I just want to be by myself for a while, okay?" Spirit said.

"Yeah, sure," Muirin said. "Don't do anything emo or anything, right?"

"I won't," Spirit said, forcing a smile.

✦

She went back to her room for her coat—and to change from a skirt into slacks—and then went for a walk. Dinner would be served early today, at five instead of six, and because the kitchens would be running flat-out all day, lunch would be a make-your-own sandwich bar. She wouldn't be missed.

She knew she should be seizing this opportunity to plan

with the others, because Burke had been right: one way or another, they either had to take a risk to get more information, or admit they wouldn't be able to do anything when the December "Tithing" came.

Let Muirin go back down into the subbasement to look for information? There were a lot of file cabinets down there, but what they probably held was more files like Camilla's. Whoever was doing this wasn't going to write down all the details of their Secret Plot and then leave them lying around loose.

Recruit another student who could find out what they needed by magic? Suppose they picked the wrong one? Suppose it was somebody who was already a member of the secret society?

Yes, that was what she *should* be doing today. And she was too miserable to even think of it.

✦

"Come on inside, Spirit," Burke said. "You'll freeze, and you know Mr. Wallis won't accept a head cold as an excuse for staying out of the demo Saturday." He shrugged out of his jacket and draped it around her. It was nice and warm, warm like Burke. It even smelled like him, clean, with a hint of nice soap.

"How'd you know where to find me?" she asked. "Magic?" She heard the anger in her voice and winced.

"Nah," he said. "Useless old Combat Mage, remember?

Muirin said you wanted to be alone, and, well, this is where *I* always came to be alone when I first got here."

She blinked up at him. He was holding out his hand to her. She took it. It was warm even through her gloves. He pulled her easily to her feet. "Your coat—" she said.

"Keep it," he said. "I'm tough. Besides, it isn't that far back to the house."

They walked out from under the bleachers. "Yeah," Burke said, glancing back, "it's a good place—you can't be seen, you aren't really that far from the house, you've got shelter from the wind . . ."

"Don't make fun of me!" Spirit said sharply, pulling away.

Burke's face reflected his honest confusion. "I wasn't," he said. "That's why I chose it. I figured that might be why you chose it. Maybe you're a Combat Mage, too. It'd be nice if there was another one here," he said, a little wistfully.

"You're the only one?" Spirit asked in surprise.

"Well, not the only one *ever*," Burke said. "But the only one here in all the time I've been here."

"Maybe I am," Spirit said. "I'd like to be something."

"You'd like to be home with your family," Burke said. "So would everyone here. Even people like Muirin and Loch who didn't really have families. And I'd like to be back with my foster family—right now, right this minute—and it's still awful, even if I know I'll get to see them again in a few years, when I can protect myself *and* them. And I know that makes me luckier than everybody else here. I have a family to go back to."

"I think it would be worse," Spirit said. To have something and not to *have* it would be the worst thing she could imagine. "But at least you write to them, don't you?"

"No," Burke said in a low voice. "No, I don't. It wouldn't be fair. Doctor Ambrosius told me that when I got here. He was right. If I wrote them, the people who—well, they might figure out—" He shrugged. "Hostages."

Spirit slipped her hand back into his. She thought it was a horrible kind of fairness—and what was worse was that Burke had accepted it so completely. "We won't let anything turn us against each other?" she said a little desperately. "Us five? No matter what happens—or what other people tell us? We won't believe them? Promise?"

"I promise, Spirit," Burke said in a low voice. "I'll always believe in you."

Every meal at Oakhurst was formal, and Spirit had actually gotten used to it. But Thanksgiving introduced a new element into Oakhurst's "elegant dining" obstacle course. Place cards.

She'd gone back to her room to try to get warm, having only realized how cold she'd gotten once she got inside. She took a hot shower and stayed under the water until she was on the verge of being late, but she still had to dry her long blonde hair. When she got to the Refectory, half the kids were already seated, and as Spirit headed for her usual table, Angelina grabbed her by the arm.

"Not today, White. You're over there. Don't you read your e-mail?"

"Oh, give her a break, Angie, she's new." Kelly Langley walked over to them. "Seating's semi-alphabetical on Thanksgiving and a few other days: It's in your Orientation Manual. Boy-girl-boy-girl. You're over there: T through Z."

Spirit nodded and walked over to her assigned table. She realized, with faint despair, that she was seated between Dylan Williams and Brendan Wilson. She liked Brendan—but she'd rather have skipped the meal completely than sit beside Dylan.

Blake Watson smiled at her as she passed him on her way to her seat. He was nicknamed "Henry" because he was a Healing Mage, and Henry Blake had been a doctor on an old TV show. *At least if I stab Dylan with a fork there'll be help nearby,* she thought. *Although I ought to be worrying about Dylan stabbing me!*

"T through Z" meant Zoey Young was on the other side of Brendan, and also that Loch and Muirin were a couple of tables away, sitting at the "S" table. Most of the kids at her table were "W"s, except for Alexis Zimmerman and Nadia Vaughn, though there were a handful of "T"s, too: Andrew Tate, Kiara Tyler, Christopher Terry, Mariana Thornton, Noah Turner, and Serenity Thompson (why did parents *always* give their kids such horrible names?). Spirit didn't need the place cards except to find her own seat; she knew everybody at her table by at least their first name, because she'd been here almost three months now. Some of her fellow students she liked, and some of them she didn't know more than to just say "hi" to in the hallways, and some of them (like Dylan) she actively disliked. *But the ones you have to worry about are the ones who are out to kill you,* Spirit reminded herself. *And which ones are those?*

She'd never had a flat-out *bad* meal at Oakhurst, though some of them had been pretty weird. Spirit tried not to think about what Mom had always called "Apology Turkey"—the real-turkey dinner she made sometimes the week after Thanksgiving, though it wasn't an actual Thanksgiving dinner, just turkey. When the servers started going around, Spirit realized this was going to be like Thanksgiving dinner in a movie, with everything clichéd and perfect, from the stuffing and gravy to the cranberry sauce and mashed potatoes to the servers asking everyone if they wanted dark meat or white.

It all tasted like sawdust to her, and after a bite of her turkey, she set her fork down. Fortunately, the one thing they *didn't* do here was nag you about eating if you didn't feel like it. Maybe that was because they knew there wasn't any junk food to eat.

"Hey, if you don't want it, just pass it over here," Dylan said, elbowing her. Under the table, he was pushing his leg against hers, too, but Spirit couldn't work up the energy to care.

"Hey, Dyl." The girl speaking was Kylee Williamson. She was in the martial arts class, but Spirit didn't know much about her beyond that. "Know what an Energy Mage can do?"

"What?" Dylan asked suspiciously.

Kylee favored him with a bright hard smile. "Anything she wants. So if you want to keep enough Gift to be able to Jaunt your toothbrush tonight, lay the hell off. Know how Dylan ended up here, Spirit?" she added.

"Shut *up*," Dylan said. There was as much desperation as anger in his voice.

"I don't really want to—" Spirit said. Whether she wanted to know or not, she knew Dylan would hate her for knowing—rather than just enjoying tormenting her, the way he did now.

"I think you ought to know. Everybody ought to know about Mister Dylan I'm-So-Hot Williams. See, our last names are so close that our files keep getting mixed up, so one day I got ahold of his. Family vacation right? Mom, dad, three kids—"

"Kylee, *shut up*," Dylan hissed.

"You bring the proctors over here and I'm not going to be the one in trouble," Kylee said. She took a big bite of cranberry sauce. "So they ditched him at an amusement park in Florida. Took the police three days to track them down. Found 'em all dead. They'd run off to commit suicide rather than have him around anymore."

"That's a lie! *They were murdered!*" Dylan cried. He was halfway up out of his seat, and all of the silverware on the table was starting to shake.

"Dylan, don't." Spirit grabbed his arm and squeezed. "Don't do it. Don't." If Burke were here, he'd help her. Loch would. Even Addie might. But they were all scattered around the room. And in another few seconds the proctors—or one of the teachers—would notice there was something wrong.

Dylan stared at her, his green eyes wide and unseeing.

"Yeah, stupid, chill," Zoey said from Dylan's other side. "You're a jerk, but you don't have to act like one. And I'm hungry."

After a long tense moment Dylan settled slowly back into his seat and reached for his glass, but his hands were shaking so badly that he would have just tipped it over if Spirit hadn't rescued it. She looked across the table at Kylee. *How could you do something like that? How could you say something so cruel?*

"You try sticking up for somebody else, you'll just both go down when the time comes," Kylee said softly. She picked up her knife and began to butter her roll as if nothing had happened.

❧

The karate and kendo exhibition two days later wasn't a disaster, but about all Spirit really remembered afterward about her own performance was that Mr. Wallis didn't stop things in the middle to scream at her. She wasn't just nervous, she was terrified—and knowing that most (and probably all) of her martial arts club teammates were crazy didn't help at all. She already knew that Jenny O'Connell was happy to sabotage her partners' equipment for fun. Now she knew that Kylee was . . . Spirit wasn't sure what. And Dylan didn't seem grateful for the way she'd stuck up for him at Thanksgiving. Aside from Burke, that left ten other students, and the odds were that every one of them was . . .

Normal for Oakhurst.

But the hours of practice with Burke had helped a lot. She got through her two sections of the demo—sparring hand-to-hand against Nadia, and a sword-*kata* with Kylee—without screwing anything up. Of course, neither Nadia nor Kylee wanted to look bad in the exhibition. In between those parts, she got to kneel on the mat with the other beginners and watch the advanced students' routines. And the showpiece of the whole thing was Mr. Wallis versus Burke, both in karate and kendo.

It was beautiful—like a dance—but it scared her to watch it, because by now Spirit had done enough training to know no punches were being pulled—at least by Mr. Wallis. And Burke had already played a football game—both halves—only a couple of hours before. Blake Watson could Heal him, but Healing didn't take the place of rest.

Watching Burke's part of the exhibition, she remembered what he'd said the first night she'd been at Oakhurst: how it would be *unfair* for him to compete against non-magicians at something in which he had a Mage Gift. She remembered how Muirin had jeered at the thought. But today, Spirit understood it bone-deep, where before it was only something she'd believed to be right.

Mr. Wallis was a master *kendoka* and *karateka*. He'd trained for years to gain his level of skill. Burke said himself he'd only been doing this for a year or so. But he was better at it than Mr. Wallis—better, faster, *superior.*

Burke says it doesn't matter what Gift you have—even if it's

something little like sensing weather patterns, you're generally stron-
ger and healthier and everything *than non-magicians. And . . .*
nobody here wears contact lenses, or glasses, and . . . I haven't even
seen a single zit.

She wondered for the first time if the "enemies" Doctor
Ambrosius talked about really *were* other magicians—or if
maybe they were non-magical people who just hated the fact
that there was another kind of person around that was *better*
than they were?

If it was really true that they were better.

*

The five of them had only had scraps of time to get together as a group since what Muirin had started calling
The Adventure of the Haunted Basement, and none at all to get
together since Spirit had conceded they weren't going to solve
this. Everything would have been so much easier if they could
just have gotten onto IM for ten minutes—or could risk sending an e-mail. But they didn't dare. So there'd only been
enough time to state the problem, not to discuss the solution.
Not until this Sunday. As it was, they had to put that off until
late in the afternoon, because Addie had to go to the Afternoon Tea, and she didn't want to do it before that.

At least there were two full hours before dinner. Plenty of
time to find the most deserted corner of Oakhurst they could
that was indoors, because the weather had now graduated to
being really freezing, and there were patches of snow on the
ground.

"Dearly beloved, we are gathered here together," Muirin said in portentous tones.

"Oh, hush, Murr-cat," Addie said.

The Greenhouse wasn't off-limits, but it wasn't a place most of the kids thought of hanging out in, aside from some of the Green Witches whose magic had a direct involvement with plants and growing things. Even most of them associated it with studying and not free time, though, so on a Sunday afternoon the Greenhouse was deserted.

"We all know what the problem is," Loch said. "The question is, what are we going to do about it?"

"I bet there's more information down in the Haunted Basement," Muirin said darkly.

"Why should there be?" Spirit demanded. "Or—what if there is, and there's a booby trap, too? Then they lock you up in one of those cute little cells we saw and tell everybody you ran away to be with Seth."

Muirin's face sharpened with anger. Spirit knew it was a low blow, but she was scared. And if Muirin got into one of those crazy states where she'd do anything—she might go down there alone, without telling the rest of them.

"I suppose you want to go just telling everybody else about this and seeing if they have any good ideas? Sure! Then we can *all* be down there! Except Ads, of course—*she's* got her trust-fund lawyers looking out for her!" Muirin said viciously.

"Spirit didn't say that, and you know it," Burke said. "She's just worried because she's your friend. But look: does it really make sense that the *Whatever* and whoever's serving it would be stupid?"

"Huh," Loch said, sounding surprised. "We've kind of been assuming that the *Whatever* is working for whoever's on the inside here. But what if you're right, and it's the other way around? Because if kids have been disappearing for forty years, the only one who's been at Oakhurst that long is Doctor Ambrosius."

"We don't know that they have, Loch. That's one of the problems," Addie said. "If—"

"Will you all stop getting sidetracked by unimportant things?" Spirit demanded, trying to keep a leash on her temper. *"It doesn't matter.* Find out what the *Whatever* is and *how we stop it. That's* what matters!"

"Huh," Muirin said speculatively, losing some of that angry spark. "So . . . how do we do that?"

Burke looked at Spirit. She shrugged helplessly.

"We can't follow up Nick's clue; we tried," he said, ticking the points off on his fingers. "Whoever's letting the *Whatever* onto the School Grounds and cleaning up after it probably hasn't left a Monster Manual around with the page conveniently marked for us. We have twenty-four days until the Winter Solstice, and we have to figure out how to stop the *Whatever* once we identify it, or one and probably two more kids will die. We can't ask anyone for help, or we might be asking the wrong people—or they'll tell the wrong people what we asked. So we decide—now—whether to approach somebody else here for help in identifying the *Whatever*—or we have to decide we're okay with a couple more people dying and hope we can figure it out by February."

"Isn't approaching somebody for help in identifying the *Whatever* the same as asking them for help?" Addie asked, after a long moment when nobody said anything.

"Oh. No. *No*," Loch said, sounding as if he'd found the solution. "We can ask someone for help—but we don't have to tell them why they're really helping. Right?"

"I think," Addie said slowly. "I *think* that could work. We get someone with the Scrying Gift, and we ask them to See something for us. Everybody does that all the time. We make it something that seems reasonable—"

"But something that will tell us what we need to know!" Muirin said. Her eyes gleamed avidly.

"They won't be hurt, will they?" Spirit asked doubtfully. She'd studied Scrying, the way she'd studied all the Mage Gifts of all the Elemental Schools, but it still seemed so unlikely. See something somewhere else than where you were, okay—a television camera could do that. But view the past and the future? That was pure science fiction.

"A Scrying Mage just Sees what they're looking for," Addie said. "They don't experience it. It's real, but it's not like it's *right there*." She thought for a moment, chewing on her lower lip. "It's going to be hard to find somebody who's got a strong Gift and stays awake while they use it."

Muirin snorted. "Yeah, because it isn't going to be a lot of use to us if we have to hang around waiting for them to wake up and tell us about it."

Especially, Spirit thought, if just seeing it had the same effect on them as it'd had on Nick Bilderback. But right now, this wasn't just the best idea they had.

It was the only idea they had.

★

NINE

Wednesday was December first. Three weeks from today, either somebody else would be dead, or they would have stopped the *Whatever. No pressure, right?* Spirit thought to herself.

The pop-up calendar app on her desktop told her that the twenty-first wasn't just the Solstice, but a Full Moon. If this were a movie, she could hack into the school's main database and run a search on every student who had ever been here. She could find out which ones had left before the age of twenty-one, and when, and then she could just hack her way out onto the Internet and cross-index that with the Naval Observatory's ephemeris. And then she could find out what lunar phases those dates corresponded with and get all the other information she needed, too. Like complete bios on all the Alums. If she had the complete files on everybody who'd ever

gone to Oakhurst, she'd have all their Social Security numbers, and there were any number of sites on the Internet where
you could find out about people . . .

Great wish list. She was about as likely to get any of it as
she was to find out that she was the last Jedi Knight. Her computer skills were probably good enough to get out of the sand-
box to the system itself, but she doubted she could get past
whatever security Oakhurst had set up around its data files.
And even if she could (because who knows, its security *might*
suck), she *definitely* couldn't do it without getting caught.

Looks like technology's a wash. Better hope magic comes through,
she thought.

❖

"You have *got* to be kidding," Muirin said, her whisper harsh
with disbelief. "Crazy Eddie?"

"Don't whisper, Murr. It makes it sound like you're plotting something," Burke said in a quiet voice.

"Well we are, aren't we?" Muirin demanded reasonably.
"But—oh come on, Ads."

It should have been an idyllic scene, Spirit thought. The
five of them were sitting in front of a crackling fire (a real fire,
not an illusion) in one of the student lounges. Snow sifted
down outside, as fine as powdered sugar. It was so cold that
the snow blew around like dust instead of sticking, and Burke
said it would probably be gone by morning.

There were six student lounges at Oakhurst: three on the
first floor and three on the second. Five of them had sixty-inch

flat-screen DVD players and microwaves. The sixth lounge was less than half the size of the others. It backed on the School Library and the staff didn't want the sound of a movie disturbing the students who were studying. The only people who used it regularly were the Chess Club—who found the library too noisy—but right now the five of them had it to themselves.

"He's a good choice," Addie said stubbornly.

"He's *nuts*," Muirin retorted.

"Hey, uh, time out?" Loch said. "Who's, uh, Eddie?"

"*Edgar Abbott*," Addie began, looking sternly at Muirin, "is a Scrying Mage with an extremely strong Gift. Edgar uses a bowl of water to focus on."

"And he's cra-a-a-a-zy," Muirin sang softly. "Addie, come on! He walks around talking to himself all the time! He's on drugs! Last year he came to breakfast in his underwear—"

"He's had his Full Gift since he was five years old," Addie said forcefully. "Full—and completely uncontrolled. He'd have a Scrying episode whenever he saw water, or anything that glittered or sparkled. His visions were as real to him as what was actually around him and nobody understood that he wasn't crazy. The 'drugs' he's on is just Ativan, and he doesn't take it all the time."

There was something niggling at the back of Spirit's mind. Finally she teased it loose. "But—if he's here—he's a Legacy, right? Wouldn't his parents have . . ."

She stopped as something abruptly occurred to her. She remembered the day she'd found out about Oakhurst, traveling on the private jet with Loch, seeing the "Welcome to

Oakhurst" video. And she remembered what Ms. Corby had said:

"Certainly you must be curious about the reasons your parents had for arranging for Oakhurst to become your guardian . . . the reason is simple . . . you are a Legacy . . . what this means is that your parents, one or both of them, was also raised at Oakhurst."

I'm here because I'm a Legacy, Spirit thought. She'd been too stunned on the plane to think of this, and afterward there'd been too many new things to take in. *So either Mom or Dad—or both—were here. But that would mean they were magicians. . . .*

"He could be a Legacy without his parents having gone here," Burke said. He smiled at her, as if he guessed her thoughts. "There's that Other Oakhurst out there somewhere, the one where all the kids are normal."

"You mean there's *two* places that look like this in the world?" Muirin said. "Now *that's* scary. But Eddie's still crazy."

Addie set her jaw and looked stubborn.

"Look," Burke said. "There's no point in fighting. Addie had a good reason for picking Eddie. Why don't we listen to it?"

Loch smiled brilliantly at Burke. "Yeah. Because . . . I can't even imagine what it would have been like just to get Kenning when I was a little kid, and Scrying's got to be even rougher, right?"

"Yes." Addie smiled at Loch gratefully. "Edgar's got one of the strongest Scrying Gifts here. He's the only strong one who works while he's awake. We could ask Emily Davis or Cassandra Moore—they're strong, too—but both of them work in trance."

"Which, uh? . . ." Loch prompted.

"Which means they wouldn't be able to tell us anything they Saw until they came out of trance—and then they might decide not to. Edgar can tell us what he's Seeing as he Sees it," Addie said. She shrugged. "And he'll do it if I ask him."

"Okay," Loch said, blowing out a long breath. "I'm in. Let's do it."

"Me, too," Burke said. "Spirit?"

"Yeah." She didn't like it much, but it was this or let someone die whose death they could prevent.

"And we know Addie's in, Muirin, so that leaves you," Burke said. "Because it has to be unanimous."

Muirin was frowning, her mouth set in a thin angry line. She said nothing.

"Muirin—if Edgar had his Scrying Gift since he was five—and he wouldn't be here if he wasn't an orphan—what if he Saw what was going to happen to his parents, and couldn't tell them?" Spirit said softly. "Or what if they didn't believe him? I think—I think I might be a little crazy, too. But that doesn't mean what he Sees can't be trusted."

"Oh, sure," Muirin finally said offhandedly. "I think it's stupid, but—what's the fun of playing it safe?"

Spirit heaved a sigh of—not relief, exactly, but at least the decision had been made. "So what do we ask him to do?" she asked.

But just as she asked the question, six kids came in, two of them carrying chessboards, and the chance to speak privately was gone.

✦

So much for Wednesday. For the rest of the week—in every private moment they could grab—the five of them argued over what to tell Edgar Abbott that would protect both him and them from the enemy inside Oakhurst who might be working with the *Whatever*. It was Muirin who finally came up with a story that all of them thought would work: asking Edgar where Seth was and if he was all right.

It made more sense than asking about Nick. None of them knew Nick that well, and either Edgar would just See him in a hospital in Billings, which would be pretty useless, or he'd look backward and See Nick being brain-fried, and while Addie said nothing someone Saw while Scrying really affected them, the others weren't as sure.

But Muirin had a logical reason to ask about Seth, and if Seth had been taken by whatever was making Oakhurst kids vanish, Edgar would See what it was. And they'd probably have enough warning from listening to the things he said to interrupt his Scrying before he got to anything that might actually *hurt* him.

✦

Addie had already talked to Edgar during the week, telling him as little as possible, but enough that she was able to tell the others that he'd agreed to See for Muirin. They decided that Sunday would be the best time—Sundays were the days when nobody expected them to be anywhere or do anything, unless one of them who hadn't gone got picked to

224

attend Afternoon Tea. They chose to do it in the Greenhouse, because if they tried to drag Edgar off somewhere *really* secluded, he'd probably pitch a fit (and besides, it was snowing), and agreed that they'd do it right after lunch whether they could all be there or not, because Sunday was already December fifth, and they were running out of time.

But they were lucky enough that none of them was picked for the "honor" of Afternoon Tea this Sunday, so once lunch was over, they went off one by one to the Greenhouse.

Spirit arrived after Loch and Muirin; Burke got there soon afterward. It was nearly another half hour before Addie arrived with Edgar Abbott.

It was only when she saw him that Spirit realized that everybody else at Oakhurst Academy really *did* look kind of perfect. It didn't matter whether they were tall or short— or even fat or skinny—all the students at Oakhurst looked vibrantly *alive.*

Spirit wasn't sure how to describe it. It wasn't that everyone at Oakhurst was happy, because, just, no. Or even energetic (again, no), or cover-model gorgeous. And it *really* wasn't their clothes, because the dress code made everybody look like robot zombie escapees from a weird religious cult. But whatever it was, Edgar didn't have it.

His hair was light brown, and he had a good haircut, because there was an in-school salon where you could go get your hair cut if you wanted—and where you *had* to go get your hair cut if you were a guy, because boys' hair length was part of the dress code, just like not dying it *blue* (whether you were a boy or a girl) was. But Edgar's was messy and un-combed and sticking up all over the place. His clothes were a mess, too—not dirty, but rumpled, as if he'd just pulled them on and then never bothered to make sure his sweater lay flat or his shirt was tucked in. Worst of all, his hands flapped while he walked, and he twitched and stumbled along—not like he was a *spaz*, but as if he was constantly being dis-tracted by sights and sounds that nobody else noticed but him.

"Oh boy," Muirin said. "Here comes Freakazoid."

"Do I even need to tell you how rotten saying something like that is?" Loch asked her in a perfectly pleasant voice.

"Why, no," Muirin said, smiling a big false smile. "I can get there on my own." She took a step forward as Addie and Ed-gar approached, since this was supposed to be her idea.

"Hi, Eddie," she said unenthusiastically.

It seemed to take Edgar a moment to notice her. "You're really pretty for a dead girl," he told her. His voice was high pitched, like a child's, though Spirit would have guessed he was about Addie's age.

Muirin grimaced. "Yeah. I like you, too."

"You didn't say there were going to be a lot of, a lot of people here, Addie," Edgar said. He had his book bag slung precariously over one shoulder, and he clutched at the strap as if it were a kind of security blanket.

"Remember, I said Muirin's friends wanted to know, too?" Addie said. "This is everybody, Edgar. You know Burke. And this is Spirit White and Lachlan Spears. They came here in September."

"Hi, Edgar," Loch said.

"Hi," Edgar said. He looked at Spirit. "You don't have a crown," he said, sounding disappointed.

Spirit blinked. She had no idea how to answer, since *"I'm sorry"* seemed kind of tacky. She was trying to remember if she'd ever had a dress-up princess outfit as a child—since it didn't seem likely she was going to be crowned Queen of England any time in the future—when Addie took charge of matters.

"Come on over here, Edgar," Addie said. "Then we can get started."

Edgar smiled at her, and Spirit thought suddenly that Edgar wanted to reassure Addie as much as Addie was trying to reassure him. "It's okay. We're near the water," he said.

Spirit heard Muirin growl faintly under her breath.

Edgar reached into his book bag and pulled out a battered metal bowl. It looked as if it was handmade—although Spirit couldn't tell what the metal was, because it had been painted over thickly with black enamel.

"I use the, uh, the same bowl every time," Edgar said shyly, glancing up from beneath his lashes. "I don't have to. I just do. Ms. Smith, she says the fewer things you have to think about, the easier it is, and, and, and so your focus should be something familiar."

"That makes sense," Loch said, as if this were the most

reasonable thing in the world to be discussing. "I wish my Gift worked that way, but it doesn't. Mine's Kenning."

"Oh, oh, oh then you, you won't want to touch my bowl, no. I've had it since before I came here, and, no. You wouldn't want to touch it. No," Edgar said, shaking his head and clutching the battered bowl to his chest. But not as if he was protecting it from Loch. As if he was protecting Loch from *it*. "No."

"Okay," Loch said, still sounding just as agreeable.

There were folded canvas drop cloths in the tool shed at the back end of the Greenhouse, and they'd brought one out to sit on. Burke seemed to know just about everything about the day-to-day running of Oakhurst. He said they used them when they wanted to move a plant from one of the raised beds to a flowerpot. Some plants "wintered" in the Greenhouse and were replanted in the flower beds every spring. The five of them arranged themselves in a semicircle on the drop cloth facing Edgar, and Edgar set the empty bowl down in front of himself. Addie picked up a nearby watering can, preparing to fill it—though she could just as easily have Called the water out of the can into the bowl with her Gift.

"First I should— Muirin wanted to ask me to See something, right Addie?" Edgar said.

"That's right," Addie said. "She—"

"I want you to See Seth, okay, Eddie?" Muirin said brusquely. "You know him—he has red hair and Pathfinder Gift."

"He ran away," Edgar said slowly. "In September. I don't know why he'd do that."

"I don't know, either," Muirin said, her voice deadly even.

"And I don't know where he is now. And he said he'd send me a message."

"You mean, by, by, by someone like me? Because they wouldn't let you have his letters, you know," Edgar said seriously.

"He'd send it *somehow,*" Muirin said. "So could you look for him? I just want to know where he is and if he's okay, okay?"

"Sure, Muirin," Edgar said. "I like doing things for my friends."

He looked toward Addie and nodded, and she lifted the watering can and poured the water into the bowl. She kept the spout purposefully low, but Spirit could see how Edgar's gaze followed the flowing water, and as the bowl between his knees filled, he became more and more intent upon it.

"Hi, Seth," he said, as conversationally as if Seth were in the Greenhouse with them. "Oh, no. Don't go out there. It's dark, and you don't have a jacket. You'll be cold. Go back to Oakhurst. Nobody will know you ran away if you go back now."

Spirit looked at Loch in confusion. The other three might be familiar with Scrying and seeing magic done, but neither of them were. Spirit couldn't tell if what Edgar was doing was normal, and from Loch's expression, neither could he.

"It's cold. It's dark. He's walking. He's been this way before, many times." Edgar's normal speaking voice was high and stammering, but his voice while in trance was deep and resonant. Spirit saw Muirin nod to herself at Edgar's words. It was obvious to all of them that Edgar was Seeing the past.

229

"He hears howling in the distance. It sounds like wolves. A whole bunch of them."

Spirit saw Loch frown and hesitate, on the verge of saying something, then shake his head and change his mind.

"He looks around. He starts to run." Edgar stopped, staring down into his bowl. "Now he's stopped. Listening. What does he hear? Engines? Maybe. They don't sound right. They shouldn't be out here. He starts to run again. I'm getting scared."

Despite that last statement, Edgar's voice didn't change its calm even timbre. Addie shifted forward on her knees, obviously intending to interrupt Edgar's Seeing, but Muirin shook her head violently and reached out her arm to block Addie.

"He's running as fast as he can now. There are a lot of engines, but it's dark. He sees a boxcar ahead. He can hide there and, and—*no! Too late! Cold! So . . . cold! The riders have found him! They're here! The dark! The hunters of the night! The hunt! The horns! The horns! THE HORNS! Nooooo—!*"

It happened so fast that not even Addie—already primed to stop Edgar from Seeing more—could interrupt in time. One moment he was narrating a confusing description of Seth running from engine noises, and the next he was talking faster and faster, his voice getting higher and higher until he was kneeling upright and screaming out the same words that Nick Bilderback had said in the infirmary.

Burke grabbed for him, but it was too late. Edgar's final words blended into a wordless wail as his body arched back-

230

ward. He kicked over his Scrying Bowl as his body arched, jerking as if electrical current were running through it. A few seconds later he went limp.

"Is he dead?" Muirin asked after a moment.

"No," Burke said after another moment, kneeling beside Edgar and feeling for the pulse at his neck. "Just had a seizure." He bent down and picked Edgar up in his arms, getting to his feet as easily as if the other boy weighed nothing. "I'm going to take him to the Infirmary."

"Hey, no, wait, you can't do that," Muirin said, sounding rattled. "What are you going to tell Ms. Bradford?"

"Half the truth," Burke said grimly. "That's why we came up with the story, right? You asked him to See where Seth is now. He had a seizure. He didn't say anything."

He turned away before Muirin could protest further, and Loch scrambled to his feet and ran ahead in order to open the Greenhouse door for Burke.

"I don't want to be involved," Muirin said. "I didn't want to have anything to do with this."

"Too late now," Addie said callously. "You agreed. You're in." She reached over to pick up Edgar's bowl, then pointed. At first Spirit thought she meant the two of them to look at something, but then she saw all the spilled water literally crawling across the surface of the drop cloth and back into the watering can.

"Yeah, but—" Muirin said.

"We should put this thing away and get out of here," Loch

said, coming back. He looked at Muirin. "I'm sorry, Muirin. You were right. Seth *would* have written to you from outside. Now let's get what killed him."

Muirin Shae was a green-eyed redhead, with the skim-milk pale skin to match. As Spirit watched, rage made Muirin turn even paler, until her eyes seemed as brilliantly green as a cat's. She nodded sharply. "I *was* right. And we will."

Spirit felt a twinge of unease. No one could say that Muirin's buttons weren't both highly visible and easy to push—but she wasn't sure that pushing them this way was the best idea that Loch had ever had. Even if it did get Muirin back on board, it also focused Muirin on revenge—maybe even to the exclusion of her own safety.

⸙

They all felt too guilty to do what would have been the logical thing if they'd been innocent, which was to go to the Infirmary and see if Edgar was okay. At least Spirit did, and none of the others suggested it.

"But what does it *mean*?" Addie asked, sounding lost. "What did Edgar *see*? Nothing should have . . . Nothing could have . . ." She faltered to a stop and looked despairing.

"At least we know more than we did before," Loch said quietly. "Even if we don't know much."

"Yeah," Muirin said. "Riddle me this, campers: what hunts at night and drives you insane if you run into it?"

The other three looked at her, and none of them had an answer.

✦

Muirin's question was the clue that let them finally give the *Whatever* its true name, but before that happened, they all got another unwanted lesson in just how far someone—or something—at Oakhurst would go to protect its secrets.

Once they'd cleaned up the Greenhouse, they weren't really sure what to do or where to go. By mutual agreement they split up, and Spirit spent the afternoon waiting for a summons—by whom and to where she wasn't sure—that never came. When she saw the other four sitting at their table at dinner, it just showed Spirit how scared she'd been that one or more of them wouldn't be there, and that just made her angry. She hated being scared all the time. She hated being afraid of her teachers, of her classmates, of the entire *school*. She hated the thought that there wasn't anybody she could go to for help. She hated the thought of having to live this way for years.

And the fact that everyone else at the table was bubbling over with anticipation for the upcoming whole week of no classes with the Winter Dance right in the middle of it—on the twenty-second, a Wednesday—and talking about the big tree that would be brought in next Sunday to decorate the Main Entry just made everything worse. Spirit didn't want to think about Christmas at all, let alone her first Christmas without her parents and her baby sister.

"What?" Spirit said, suddenly aware that one of the others had asked her something.

"I said, do you want to get in another hour or so of practice tonight?" Burke repeated. "I know we don't have another demo until March, but it doesn't hurt to keep in practice. Um, I mean—"

"Ooooh, can we watch?" Muirin purred.

"No, Muirin, you can't watch," Burke said, in long-suffering tones. "If you want to take karate, go see Mr. Wallis."

"Sorry! Busy being a brilliant fencer!" Muirin chirped brightly.

Loch smiled at her. "You can come and be brilliant in the Library then. It's dark back in the stacks," he said.

Addie groaned appreciatively at the joke and Muirin made a face. Spirit just stared at her plate. Loch's ability to, well, *pretend* still bothered her in a way she couldn't quite explain.

*

Burke, do you wonder about Loch?" Spirit asked.

It was an hour later, and they'd both changed to their workout clothes and were down in the gym. While it wasn't empty—there were two pick-up basketball games going on, one at each end of the court—nobody was paying any attention to them.

"Spirit, I have wondered about more things in the three months since the two of you got here than in the four years before," Burke said. "Wonder what in particular?"

"I don't know," she said, frustrated. "It's just . . . it doesn't seem to matter how awful something is. He can just laugh and pretend it doesn't matter to him at all. Do you think it really doesn't?"

"Don't know," Burke said. "Get your feet wider. Bend your knees more. Yeah. Like you're going to sit. Good. But if it helps any, Addie's the same way, really. She just gets all quiet and polite. But maybe that's just how rich folks are. Not supposed to let anybody know what they're thinking."

"That would be hor— Ow! You pushed me." In the middle of her sentence, Burke had reached out and shoved at her shoulder. It had taken Spirit off guard.

"And if I could push you over, your stance still wasn't good enough," Burke said reasonably. "Come on, let's try that again."

"I wouldn't have fallen over if you'd warned me," Spirit grumbled, taking his hand and letting him pull her to her feet.

"Oh, yeah, the way Mr. Wallis always does?" Burke said, and Spirit had to laugh. It felt good.

They spent another half hour working on what Burke called "first principles"—he freely admitted he'd skipped all this stuff when he'd been working with her to get her ready for the demo because these were the things that could take months of work to get right (if you weren't a Combat Mage). Standing. Balance.

"You don't stand low enough," Burke told her. "I know you're short, and you think you want to be at eye-level with your opponent, but you don't. You want to stand in your center, so all your movements come from your center and return to your center. If you do that, you'll spend a lot less time looking *up* at your opponent from the floor."

Spirit nodded. What Burke was saying made sense. And telling her why she should do it—and why she was constantly making the same mistake—was a lot more helpful that Mr. Wallis yelling at her. "So then I'll be able to throw you over my shoulder?"

Burke shook his head, smiling. "Too much difference in height between us for you to do *Ippon Seoinage*—and that's judo, anyway, not karate. But, oh, in a couple of years you could probably do a hip throw, sure. I mean, if we were doing judo."

"And if you let me," she said.

"Yeah," he agreed.

Spirit hadn't wanted to ask about Edgar at all. She didn't really want to hear the worst—if there was a worst. But she knew that was being cowardly, because whatever had happened to him today, she was partly responsible. So when Burke said they'd had enough lesson for the night, she took a deep mental breath and said:

"Burke, what happened today when you took Edgar to the infirmary? He's okay, right?"

Burke shrugged, looking uncomfortable. "I hope so. I ran in there with him and Ms. Bradford asked me what happened, and I said he'd had a cat-fit, and she said to put him down on a bed and go out in the hall and wait. So I did. And about fifteen minutes later she came out and wanted the whole story. So I told her Muirin had been really down in the dumps since Seth ran away, and she wanted to know how he was, so we all came up with the idea of getting someone to See for her, and Edgar was the best choice because maybe Seth was somewhere that one of the deep-trance Scrying Mages wouldn't want to tell Muirin about. And I said he looked into his bowl, and let out a scream, and went rigid and shook for about half a minute and passed out, and I brought him right to her. And she said I did the right thing and she hoped Muirin wasn't too upset, and I said I didn't know because I hadn't stayed to find out. And she said Edgar would be fine and I should run along, and I thought that was a really good idea."

"Me, too," Spirit said quietly.

★

It had become habit for Spirit to check her e-mail first thing in the morning. In addition to several other pieces of the Oakhurst equivalent of spam (a request for students to review their "wish lists" and submit their first, second, and third choices to the Office no later than December fourteenth; a terse e-mail from the dance committee saying that it was almost New Years and the voting ballot for next year's dance committee had to be *final* by January third; a long incoherent rant about a missing hairdryer from Madison Harris, who seemed incapable of figuring out how *not* to send her private e-mails to the entire school) there was a memo from "Staff" notifying "Oakhurst Students" that "Staff" was sure they would all regret to learn that Edgar Abbot had been taken ill Sunday afternoon and had been sent to Billings for treatment, and that "Staff" joined "Oakhurst Students" in wishing Mr. Abbot a speedy recovery and return to Oakhurst.

Spirit shuddered and closed her e-mail. She wondered if Edgar would be put in the same room as Nick.

She wondered if he'd be there for the same reason.

The rest of Monday was a "normal for Oakhurst" day: English Comp, Bio, Math, and Art in the morning; Humanities, PE, Art Class, and History of Magic after lunch, and Martial Arts Class after that. All of them except PE and Art came with hefty homework assignments, and at that, Spirit was carrying a light courseload, because she didn't have magic labs, and she was only doing one sport. Spirit didn't know how people like Addie—with magic labs, Choral Society, swim team, dance committee, and (for most of the year) field hockey—managed to get it all done. That kind of schedule didn't leave much room for free time at all.

But that's the whole point, isn't it? Spirit thought. *Set us all up with crazy schedules and more work than we'd have in college, make us all see each other as competition instead of friends, make sure none of us has time to think about how crazy this place is, how the reason we're learning all this stuff is that there are people out there waiting to kill us when we leave—or maybe something even worse . . .*

She wondered how she'd managed to escape that particular trap.

And how long it would take someone in authority to notice.

That evening the five of them met briefly in one of the lounges to compare notes. Briefly, because Loch and Muirin both reported being teased about having a "gang"—which meant that despite their best efforts, they were drawing attention to themselves—and Addie had a virtual meeting of the dance committee, because the Winter Dance was a little over two weeks away and the committee *still* hadn't settled on a music program. "And of course we can't just recycle the one from the Halloween Dance—even though nobody heard most of it—because that would be too easy," Addie said tartly. "At least I can get a lot of homework done while Kristi and Madison scream at each other in IM and Andy says we should include more Metal. You should get on it for next year, Spirit. It'd be nice to have somebody *sane* for a change." She waved distractedly as she hurried off.

"I guess that leaves . . . huh," Loch said, looking around. Muirin was already gone. "That illusion thing is pretty cool," he said, sounding faintly puzzled.

"That 'illusion thing' is going to get the Murr-cat into real trouble one of these days," Burke said.

"Or save her neck," Loch said. "Anyway, this is a good chance for me to get in some practice time. Piano," he explained, when the other two looked curious. He flexed his fingers theatrically. "Every good junior plutocrat gets music lessons. Although considering everything, I wish I'd studied something more portable."

"There's always the harmonica," Burke said, and Loch grinned.

"Another karate lesson?" Spirit asked reluctantly, once Loch had left.

Burke shook his head. "We had class today. How about a walk?"

"In the snow?" Spirit asked in disbelief.

"Sure," Burke said, smiling. "Get your coat. I'll meet you at the terrace doors in fifteen."

✦

One thing you could say for Oakhurst, it didn't stint its students on any of the basic necessities. At the beginning of November, Spirit had been sent a GIF-filled e-mail with winter wardrobe choices: snow boots and down filled waterproof mittens and high-tech fabric glove liners and heavy wool pants (with the notation that these were not to be considered classroom wear under any circumstances) and long johns and heavy wool hats and thicker scarves than the one she already had (with an appliqué of the school crest on the ends, in her choice of the three school colors) and her choice of heavy winter coat in two lengths. The fact that she already had a warm coat and hat and scarf and was being issued a warmer coat and enough extra gear to outfit an expedition to the North Pole had been a depressing forewarning of how cold winter here in Montana was going to get.

But it meant that once she bundled up and stepped outside with Burke, Spirit wasn't cold at all.

The walkway lights were on, illuminating the snow falling from the sky. It was light—almost like dust—but it had been falling steadily for several days, and the ground was white as far as Spirit could see. She was used to heavy snow in Indiana, of course, but not to it starting this early—or to being out in the middle of nowhere when it did. The snow muffled even the ordinary sounds she expected to hear, making everything seem even more than ordinarily silent. Even without moonlight, the lamplight and the light from the house windows scattered across the snowfield and reflected back from the low clouds, illuminating the featureless whiteness for miles.

"Winter's when most of the Elemental Schools—not mine—get a real workout," Burke said as they walked across the terrace. "Come on. You'll see."

The terrace was completely clear of snow, and the brick walkways were wide dark lines crisscrossing the whiteness beyond. Spirit followed Burke cautiously down the fieldstone steps onto the bricks, but there wasn't a trace of ice. Just as the Air Mages swept away the autumn leaves, they swept away the snow.

"Too cold?" Burke asked, when Spirit shivered.

"No," she answered. "It's just . . . I don't think I'm cut out for all this . . . sneaking and plotting." She kept her voice carefully low, even though they seemed to be the only ones going for an evening walk.

"I hate it," Burke said. Spirit glanced at him in surprise. It was the first time she'd ever heard him say anything so negative. "I hate lying. I hate going to bed at night knowing I'm keeping secrets from Doctor Ambrosius. I hate thinking I'm planning to do bad things to someone—even if they might be bad and might even deserve it. I don't . . . I don't want to be that guy, Spirit."

Impulsively, she put her hand on his arm. Her heavy mitten made a pillowy plopping sound, and she saw him smile a little ruefully. "At least we're warm, right? And just wait until there's a few more feet of snow. Then we can really have fun."

"A few more . . . feet?" Spirit asked in disbelief.

"Sure," Burke said. "Average snowfall over the winter here's about sixty inches. We get enough snow on the ground, and the Fire Mages and the Ice Mages'll have enough to work with to build us a great skating rink. Block of ice about a foot thick and as big as the football field. It's great. If you don't skate, I can teach you."

"It's been a while," Spirit said. Winters in Indiana were cold, but they weren't *that* cold.

Burke smiled at her. "I know what you mean. This makes Indianapolis feel downright balmy." He sighed. "I sure miss Thirty Days in May."

Spirit blinked, more homesick than she would have thought at hearing the local nickname for the Indianapolis 500. "Don't tell me you're a racing fan?" she said.

"Oh heck yeah," Burke said. "My folks' house is right on the Speedway. They rent the lawn, the driveway, and the backyard out every year for people to camp in. It was always a great way to make new friends."

Spirit thought it probably was. She thought Burke had probably never met anyone in his whole life he hadn't liked.

"Here we are," he said. "Look."

He pointed off to the side of the path. Spirit turned to look—and gasped in wonder.

The snowfield was filled with sculptures. Clear as crystal, delicate as gossamer, abstract designs whose closest resemblance was to those high-speed photographs where the photographer manages to capture the exact moment when a drop of water shatters against the ground. They glittered in the lamplight as if they were on fire.

"Ohhhh. . . ." she breathed. "They're beautiful. . . ."

"Ice and Air and Fire Mages having some fun out here," Burke said. He sounded pleased at her reaction. "They won't be here by morning—wind'll shatter 'em, they're so delicate. See? Over there? Some of them are already broken." He pointed, and when Spirit looked closely, she could see broken shards of ice lying on the surface of the snow. "I wanted you to see them, though."

"I'm glad," Spirit said simply.

They turned to walk back toward the school, and Spirit was surprised to see how far they'd come.

"If there's enough snow vacation week—and there usually is—we do a whole Winter Carnival thing," Burke said offhandedly. "You know: full-scale ice sculptures and all that. I think you'll really enjoy it. If, uh, we're all still alive by then," he added in belated realization.

The reminder brought Spirit back down to earth with a thump. "What do you think Edgar Saw?" she asked cautiously. "I know he Saw . . . whatever took Seth, but . . ." *But whatever it was he Saw, he didn't tell us the details, and we really need to know.*

"At least we know more than we did. It's something that

243

hunts at night. Something that—we know because of Nick—disappears at dawn. Something that drives you mad if you even see it. Hunters, riders, horns—both Nick and Edgar mentioned horns . . ." Burke said.

"Something that needs to be Tithed," Spirit added grimly.

"Yeah," Burke said unhappily. "That should be enough. We just have to put it all together."

Neither of them spoke the rest of the way back to the house, each lost in their own thoughts.

The Wild Hunt," Muirin said with fierce satisfaction.

Muirin said at breakfast Tuesday that she'd found their answer, so the five of them were risking a meeting. They were meeting that evening at the swimming pool. And Muirin was casting an illusion to make the indoor pool area look as if it were empty, so maybe nobody would come and wonder why they were here in the first place.

"That's the *Whatever*?" Burke asked. "But the Wild Hunt's English."

"It's found in Germany, Ireland, Great Britain, Denmark, Sweden, Norway, France, and there are similar legends in parts of North America," Muirin recited in bored tones.

Addie was making waterspouts in the center of the pool. First one, then two, then three, drawing them up thinner and finer until they towered twenty feet in the air and the level of water in the pool itself had dropped several feet.

"The details vary a little bit from place to place, but they're consistent enough that this really seems to be what we're looking for," Loch said.

"Okay," Spirit said, trying to ignore the dancing water-spouts. "But what *is* it?"

"Aside from—apparently—real?" Muirin said. "Which is a little something Ms. Groves has conveniently forgotten to mention in her really long and boring History of Toads, Newts, and Bats?"

Between the two of them, Loch and Muirin managed to deliver a concise and disturbing lecture—which was even scarier for what they *didn't* know.

The Wild Hunt appeared in legends all across Europe. The basics were always the same: a supernatural group of hunters, mounted on things from horses to goats to other people and accompanied by hunting hounds, chasing across the sky or across the ground in wild pursuit of . . . something. Depending on which story it was, the hunters were the Fair Folk, or ghosts, or the souls of the damned, or outright demons. The leader of the Hunt was the demon Hellequin, or Herne the Hunter, or Odin, or just whoever'd been unlucky enough to encounter the Hunt as it rode out, because anyone who saw the Wild Hunt might be driven mad by the sight, or hunted down by it and never seen again, or forced to join it—and according to the tales, any attempt to leave again resulted in instant death.

"—and all the sources Muirin and I could find said that the Hunt appears 'mostly' in the fall and winter, but, uh, obviously 'mostly' isn't 'always,' because the rest of this fits so

well that this has got to be what we're looking for," Loch finished.

"But are they elves or ghosts or demons?" Addie asked.
The waterspouts all collapsed at once, but before any of them
could get splashed, all the water in the pool curled up and in,
until it was a large round glob of water sitting in the middle of
the pool like a loaf of bread in a pan. Addie looked at the rest
of them. "You know as well as I do that what works against
one of those isn't going to work on the other two."

"I guess we're going to have to go prepared for all three, in
that case," Burke said.

"Gosh, gang, more research!" Muirin said, opening her
eyes very wide. "Just what I was looking forward to!"

Amazingly, Burke snorted with amusement. "If you don't
know at least three ways to get rid of a ghost by now, Muirin,
you haven't been paying attention in class. You leave the
ghosts to me. It's if this Hunt is elves or demons I'm worried
about."

"But—" Spirit said. It was bad enough having to seriously
think about there even being demons or elves (*What's next?* her
inner voice demanded, *Vampires?*), and worse to think about
having to *fight* them. But worst of all was having to think
about the details of how to *do* it, because if the Wild Hunt was
riding out on the Winter Solstice, it would be riding in search
of its Tithe, and Spirit was almost certain that none of the five
of them would be it, so how? . . .

"Time's up," Loch said, glancing at his wristwatch. "We'd
all better go pretend we don't know each other."

246

Everyone got to his or her feet. Loch slipped out first—his Shadewalking ability would provide him with at least some ability to evade curious observers—and Burke and Muirin went together. Burke hadn't walked more than half a dozen steps before he vanished, to be replaced by a duplicate of Muirin. Anybody who saw Muirin with "herself" would just assume she was practicing her mirror illusions again.

Having come to watch Addie practice was innocent enough, so Spirit walked out with Addie. But her final question remained both unasked and unanswered.

How were they going to make sure that the Wild Hunt came after them, instead of claiming whoever had been chosen as the latest innocent victim?

✝ЕΠ

In Wednesday's Martial Arts Class, Dylan broke Kylee's arm while the two of them were sparring.

Spirit was paired up with Nadia for the free-form sparring because, although Mr. Wallis was a maniac, he actually did his best to match them with opponents close to their own skill level for the free-form stuff. It was a ninety-minute class, and overall they covered four different elements. There was drill and free-sparring in karate, and drill and *katas* (in pairs) in kendo. One of the four elements was dropped each session so that they could do half an hour each on the other three. Of the four elements, the sparring was the one in which you could get into the most trouble, because there was no set pattern to follow.

Since Thanksgiving, Dylan had been quiet in the classes he

and Spirit shared—that was only Math and Martial Arts—and Spirit had been just as glad, since she'd had a lot of other things on her mind, and trying to defend herself from Dylan Williams and his brutal form of teasing would have been the last straw. She doubted he'd forgotten who'd been at the table that day. She'd just hoped he'd decided to make someone else his target.

And as it turned out, he had.

Nadia gasped in surprise just as Spirit heard the choked scream from behind her. Spirit's immediate reaction was to step out of range, fearing some trick on Nadia's part, before turning to look over her shoulder. Kylee was down on her knees, rocking back and forth in agony, cradling her arm against her stomach and crying.

"Not such a big mouth on you now, huh?" Dylan said in a low vicious voice.

"He punched her," Nadia whispered in disbelief. "She tapped out, and he just . . . *punched* her."

"She should have expected it," Spirit heard herself say. "You were at our table at Thanksgiving. What did she expect?"

The moment the words were out of her mouth, she felt sick. Sick at herself. Sick at what she had just said. She should have been horrified, and instead she'd been . . . cold. *What is Oakhurst turning me into?* she thought wildly. *And how can I stop it?*

Burke showed up at Kylee's side half a step before Mr. Wallis did. From the expression on Burke's face, Spirit knew he'd guessed the truth of what had just happened, but when—in response to Mr. Wallis's brusque question—Dylan said it had been "an accident," Kylee didn't contradict him. Neither did anyone else in the class, though at least a few of them must have seen it happen besides Nadia.

Fortunately one of the students in the class was a Healing Mage. Burke helped Kylee over to the bleachers, and Claire Grissom followed them over. The moment she placed her hands on Kylee's arm, Kylee's pain-filled gasping eased.

"What are you all standing around gawking for?" Mr. Wallis barked. "This isn't a rest period! Back to work—unless you'd rather be running laps for the rest of the lesson?"

※

"Why didn't you say anything?" Spirit asked quietly.

They were all in the Girls' Locker Room. Most of them didn't shower at the end of class, since it was only a short walk back to their rooms where they could shower in privacy, but everybody changed back into their regular clothes. There was no actual rule about wandering around in your *gi* outside of class, but the minute someone did it, there probably would be.

Kylee looked up, her expression guarded. "Because nothing happened." She studied Spirit's face for a moment, then sighed. "Look, Spirit. A little advice. You don't get the teachers involved, ever. No matter what. You do that, and you'll be looking over your shoulder for the Gatekeepers."

What Gatekeepers? What's a Gatekeeper? Spirit wanted to ask. But she was too late. Even as she was forming the words,

Kylee hefted her bag of equipment onto her shoulder and turned and walked out, leaving Spirit staring after her.

But figuring out Kylee's cryptic comment was the least of her worries. This was December eighth. They had less than two weeks to figure out not one, but *three* plans of attack, and figure out how to use them.

✦

"Slow, Spirit. We're going half-speed. Let's walk that block through one more time. And blessed salt will banish a wandering spirit," Burke said reassuringly. "That's in pretty much every tradition I've found. So that takes care of any possible ghosts."

They couldn't risk being seen together as a group anymore. With the winter break coming up, everybody at Oakhurst was excited and on edge—and some of the excitement was playful, and some of it was malicious, and it wouldn't really matter either way if it made the teachers notice the five of them and decide to do something to break them up. But pairs didn't come up as high on the Oakhurst radar as a group of five would. So Addie and Muirin were researching the best way to destroy the Wild Hunt if it was composed of elves, and Spirit and Loch were looking for a good way to banish a demonic force. Fortunately at Oakhurst, neither research project looked at all out of the ordinary to anyone who might notice it. They might even be able to use what they found for an extra-credit paper when this was over. Right now, though, an extra-credit paper was the last thing on Spirit's mind, because even now none of them could stop doing everything they were officially supposed to be doing. And that meant homework, and extracurricular activities, and going to the Friday night basketball games. Spirit had begun to cherish the few hours a week she got to spend practicing her martial arts with Burke; it was starting to seem like the only chance she got to actually relax.

At least when she wasn't worrying about how they were going to destroy the Wild Hunt.

"But I— Burke, how are you going to get anything like *that?*" she asked, trying to keep her voice from rising in a wail of despair. "You can't go into Radial. And I don't think that Doctor Ambrosius is an actual minister. Even if he'd—"

Burke shook his head at her, smiling gently. "Anyone who believes can bless salt, so long as they're acting with respect and mean to do good with it. And I guess keeping folks from being murdered—and letting some poor spirits find their rest—counts as good."

"I guess," Spirit echoed, confused. Burke was the last person in the world she would have imagined to be a devout Christian—he certainly didn't spend his time either quoting Bible verses at the drop of a hat or ranting about the evil of "witches" and "magic." *I suppose that wouldn't go down too well at a school for magicians,* she thought irreverently. And apparently Burke had read the "other" Bible, the one that contained such verses as: *Thou shalt not avenge, nor bear any grudge against the children of thy people, but thou shalt love thy neighbour as thyself . . .*

How had he managed to keep Oakhurst from poisoning him? He'd been here longer than any of them.

"Penny for your thoughts?" Burke asked.

"Oh, nothing," Spirit said, and grimaced. "I just hope taking out the elves will be as simple. Walk me through the block again?"

After a solid week of research—more *search* than *research*, as Addie said to Spirit one evening when Addie and Spirit were studying in Spirit's room—Addie and Muirin had settled on iron ("cold iron" as it was called in all the folklore databases) to get rid of the Wild Hunt if it turned out to be composed of elves. As Addie explained (sounding more than a little frustrated, but if Oakhurst's graduates were expected to deal with supernatural creatures, they hadn't been given any hint of it yet), there were a number of different ways to simply *protect* yourself from elves, but that wasn't what they were going to need. What they needed was a form of *attack*—something that would make elves go away—and for obvious reasons, there wasn't much reliable information about things like that available. People in the past—especially non-magicians—had been more interested in protecting themselves from the powerful magical creatures than doing something that might make them angry.

"We found other methods that might work, but they either involve things we can't get, or we couldn't find clear enough information to risk using them," Addie said, propping her chin on her hand. "So it's too much of a risk."

"Like what?" Spirit asked curiously.

Addie smiled briefly. "Well, there's St. John's Wort—you know, that stuff that comes in pills that's supposed to cure just about everything? That's supposed to work. Like garlic with a vampire. Only it's not like we could get a truckload of it shipped in here in a week. And I'm not sure if it has to be fresh or dried or what. And then there's bread."

"Bread?" Spirit asked in disbelief.

Addie nodded vigorously. "Stale bread. I know! It seems ridiculous, but just about all the books and folklore databases say 'stale bread.' Only the only kind of bread we can get is out of the kitchens, and the books don't say what kind or how much—and what if what we've got is the wrong kind? Nope. I'm sticking to iron. Now all we have to do is get enough of it," Addie said, looking down at the pile of books. "And figure out what to do with it, because I'm pretty sure that just *having* it won't be enough. But Murr says she's got some ideas."

"I hope so," Spirit said in a low voice. She tried as much as possible not to think about what they were going to do; if getting yelled at by Mr. Wallis in martial arts class scared her, how was she ever going to go off and actually fight something *for real*?

"So how are you and Loch coming along?" Addie asked. "You've got demons."

Spirit had managed to stop being startled by hearing sentences like that, although she still couldn't decide whether they were funny or bizarre. "Loch says demons are the worst," she said slowly, "because they're powerful and evil by definition. But he says the good thing about demons—"

"Assuming there *is* anything good about demons," Addie interjected, and Spirit smiled ruefully.

"—is that they're also really vulnerable, if you can hit them just right."

"You mean like with a spell?" Addie asked.

"Or something," Spirit sighed. She was pretty sure that when she found out what the "or something" Loch would come up with was, she wasn't going to like it.

I can't do that!" she hissed at Loch. Spirit was keeping her voice low by habit—and a good thing, too, because she could get together with Addie in her dorm room, and with Burke in the gym, but the only place she could meet with Loch was either the Library or one of the student lounges, and the Library offered slightly more privacy.

"You have to," Loch said simply. "You're the key to making all of this work." He tapped the cover of the very large, very dusty book. He'd spent the last several days copying drawings and paragraphs of text out of it—and then double-checking them everywhere else he could. "We don't know which demon-or-demons we're dealing with, or if there are any demons at all. If we *did* know, it would be a lot easier. But whatever the Wild Hunt is, if it's demons, this should work. It's sort of a General Purpose Dismissing Spell, and what it will do is send a demon back to Hell. It comes in two parts: a spell-trap, and a spell. Once the demon-or-demons is inside the spell-trap, the spell has to be read out, and that will make the spell-trap send whatever's in it back to Hell. So one of us has to be ready to decoy the demon-or-demons into the spell-trap . . . and the other one has to be ready to work the spell."

"I— But— Why me?" Spirit demanded, starting to get angry. "You know damned well I don't have any magic!"

"I know *damned* well you do—or you wouldn't be here at Oakhurst," Loch retorted just as hotly. "And we'd just better hope your Mage Gift doesn't show up in the next week, or we are really, *really* in trouble. Look. Based on everything I've researched, a demon will sense magic, so it will sense me. That makes me the logical one to be bait. It-or-they will chase me to the spell-trap, and the spell-trap will hold it-or-them for a few seconds all by itself. That's where you come in. I'll set the spell-trap up in that little stand of woods up by the boundary stone. There's less chance of somebody else coming across it ahead of time. Then—that night, when the Wild Hunt comes—you have to wait by the spell-trap for the demon-or-demons to enter it, and as soon as it-or-they're caught, you do the spell. It-or-they won't know you're there, because your Mage Gift hasn't shown up yet. That's why it has to be you, and why it can only be you."

"But Ms. Groves always says that the reason spells don't work most of the time is because non-magicians do them," Spirit blurted out, feeling more than a little trapped and desperate. "If ordinary people can't make spells work, what makes you think *I* can?"

"Because you're a magician," Loch repeated patiently. "The power is in you. There's no such thing as a false positive for magical power, okay? Just trust me. You can do it, Spirit. But you'll need to learn it by heart—and every word has to be *exactly right.*"

Oh my God, no pressure, right? Spirit thought for the ten thousandth time since she'd come to Oakhurst. What if Loch was wrong? What if *she* did something wrong?

That was too unbearable to even think about. If there *were* demons— If they followed Loch— If she did something wrong—

Then both she and Loch were dead.

But did she have a choice?

"Okay," she said, resigned. "Give it to me." She was going to say she'd try, but then stopped herself.

If they turned out to really need this spell—and she screwed it up—it wouldn't just be her and Loch who'd be dead. Once the demons got through with her and Loch, they'd be mad, and they'd go hunting, and they'd find whoever was out that night.

They'd *all* be dead.

＊

The next several days passed in a blur for Spirit. Fortunately she had a good excuse when Ms. Smith took her aside after Math Class and asked her if she was feeling okay. Spirit forced a smile and said she was feeling a little down because of the holidays. It hurt to use her parents' memories like that—as part of a lie—but she knew they'd have understood. Especially Mom. Mom had always agreed with Davy Crockett: "Be sure you're right, then go ahead." Mom had always had a saying for every situation. Spirit wondered which one she would have used this time, and knowing that she'd never know—that she'd never know what saying Mom would have applied in any situation *for the rest of her life* made Spirit want to lie down and howl.

But she was too busy.

The spell Loch needed her to learn was long. And it wasn't in English. Most of it was Latin—which was okay, since she had Latin three days a week now—but a lot of the words in it weren't even Latin.

And it wasn't as if she had any more free time than she did before. She actually had less. The Christmas tree had been brought into the Main Entry on the twelfth, and the whole enormous room—including the balcony—was garlanded in pine boughs. There'd been a lottery to see who'd get to decorate the tree and the garlands, and of course it had been Spirit's bad luck to be chosen, so there went more precious free time, because this was Oakhurst, and it wasn't as if you could just hang a couple plastic balls around and throw on some tinsel and call it done. Most of the ornaments were glass, and looked as old as the house, and each of them was probably worth more than the White family's entire decorated tree.

In addition, everyone in the school was learning Christmas carols, because they'd be singing them every Sunday from here to Christmas, and on the twenty-fourth, too, when presents from Oakhurst were handed out. There'd be a few other presents, too; because while they weren't allowed to shop on the Internet even if they had money, there was no rule against making gifts for their friends, so Spirit had been making book covers and matching bookmarks, since they did a lot of crafts in Art Class and Ms. Holland was willing to let them have stuff for special projects. Some of the other girls had seen her working and offered to trade for some to give as gifts, so Spirit was doing that, too, since it would look odd if she didn't.

She didn't dare do anything that would look odd.

The most frustrating thing about the so-called vacation was that everyone got extra-heavy homework assignments and "special projects" to do during their week off, just as if they weren't already snowed under with homework all the rest of the year. *That* at least Spirit could ignore—there'd be time enough after the twenty-first to do it. Memorizing this spell was more important. Because if she didn't memorize it perfectly, it wouldn't matter whether she'd done her homework or not.

And Oakhurst seemed determined to present her with the whitest of White Christmases; because it hadn't stopped snowing once in the past seven days.

How are we going to get out of the school without being noticed? Spirit thought, staring out her window in anguish. She thought she knew now why so many kids preferred second floor rooms—the windblown snow had already drifted as high as her windowsill. Even if they could manage to walk through it, they'd leave footprints that would be visible for miles.

Someone else is going to have to come up with a solution for that one. I've got enough to do with this, she thought grimly. Jaw set, she reached under her mattress and pulled out the sheet of paper that held the written-out spell.

Today was December eighteenth.

She had three more days.

⁂

From the end of the day on Friday—when classes were over for an entire week—the entire student body took to the great (and cold) outdoors. Even kids who'd loudly complained about the weather from the fall of the first snowflake spoke excitedly of their plans. And no wonder: winter at a school for magicians was a whole different season from winter anywhere else.

The first inkling Spirit had of that fact was when she looked up from her study of the spell on Saturday to discover that the snowdrift outside her window had vanished.

It hadn't melted. It had been removed. The snow looked as if someone had come along with a giant ice-cream scoop and just scooped it all away. *What the heck?*

Maybe the snow's demonic, she thought, faintly dazed. She'd certainly been doing the Spell of Dismissal enough times to banish every demon in the entire state of Montana. But there wasn't any time to really ponder the question. It was nearly lunchtime, and she couldn't skip going to the Refectory, no matter how little she felt like eating. It wasn't that anybody would actually *care* if she skipped a meal, but Kelly would be sure to ask her if anything was wrong, and . . . Spirit wasn't sure she could survive anybody being nice to her. Not right now.

It was just as well she did decide on lunch in the Refectory, because she received her answer to the puzzle of the missing snowdrift.

"—not enough snow yet to make a proper rink," Burke was saying to Loch as she arrived, "but everyone's impatient, so the Jaunting Mages are grabbing it from everywhere."

"You wouldn't think you'd need any Ice Mages in this weather," Loch said. His skin was red with cold. *He must have been outside all morning,* Spirit thought, and repressed a flash of irritation. *Why shouldn't he goof off? Loch doesn't have a whole spell to learn by heart!*

"But the water just won't freeze fast enough—no matter how cold it is out there," Addie said. "So the Jaunting Mages help the Air Mages pile up a big snowdrift, and the Fire Witches turn it into water. Then a Water Witch—or two— holds it steady until an Ice Mage can turn it into ice."

"Presto—instant skating rink!" Loch said. "Wow, that's some trick!"

"Not quite 'presto,' Loch," Addie said, smiling. "But they built the rim for the rink this morning and filled in a lot of it. Once there's a solid block of ice, it won't matter if it warms up outside—and a Fire Mage can just melt the top when the surface gets too cut up."

"Better than a Zamboni," Burke added lamely.

"Not that I'd call fifteen below zero warm," Muirin muttered, shivering ostentatiously. She darted a questioning look at Spirit.

"Me, either," Spirit said unconvincingly. How could they all sit here and talk about ice skating rinks when in a few days they'd all be . . . well, be facing *something* horrible. Or . . . Addie looked cool, as usual. And Loch . . . gah, she just wanted to strangle him! *And* Muirin.

At least Burke didn't look as if he didn't have a single worry on his mind. He just looked like he was doing his very best to pretend he didn't. She remembered what he'd said the night he'd taken her out to see the ice sculptures: *"I hate it. I hate lying. I hate going to bed at night knowing I'm keeping secrets from Doctor Ambrosius."*

And it would be nice to think it would be over soon, but it wouldn't be. This was only the beginning.

❧

The morning of the Winter Solstice dawned bright and clear. Spirit watched the sun rise from a chair looking out her window. She'd been completely unable to sleep.

Full Moon tonight. Plenty of light. Chris Terry was a Weather Mage, and he'd said on Monday it would be clear for the next few days, to the disappointment of everyone who wanted more snow for the skating rink, and the Winter Carnival, and all the other things that were utterly meaningless to Spirit right now. Chris's Gift wasn't accurate past seventy-two hours, but that made him more accurate than the National Weather Service. And Spirit didn't need to know what the weather would be like on Christmas. Just tonight.

It's going to be a beautiful day, she thought, and felt like bursting into tears. As she got to her feet, she heard the crackle of paper from the pocket of her robe. *The spell. Maybe I should?* . . .

But no. If she hadn't learned it by now, she wasn't going to. She carried the incriminating sheet of paper into the bathroom, tore it into tiny scraps, and flushed it down the toilet.

✷

At breakfast everyone in the Refectory was so noisy the proctors actually had to stand up and ask them to quiet down a couple of times. Spirit had managed to forget the Winter Dance was tomorrow until Brendan asked her who she was going with.

"To the dance? The Winter Dance?" he asked in disbelief as she just stared blankly.

"Oh, Spirit's going with *Burke!*" Muirin announced, bursting into a peal of mocking laughter. "Spirit *likes* having her feet stepped on!"

Spirit just stared down at her plate and shoved her eggs around with a piece of toast. While she was grateful to Muirin for the quick save, she did wish Muirin had been less cruel about it.

"It's okay," Burke said quietly. "You don't have to."

"I'd love to," Spirit said defiantly. She liked Burke a lot. At least with Burke she didn't have to watch her back—like she did with most of the Oakhurst boys—or try to figure out what he meant by anything—the way she did with the other ones. Even Loch. She trusted Loch, more or less, but she didn't understand him at all.

Once breakfast was over, Spirit wasn't sure whether to spend time with the others or avoid them. She was too nervous about tonight to read or to work on any of her homework assignments, and too irritable to go outside and take "advantage" of their vacation time the way the other students were. Instead, she wandered around indoors for a while and then ended up back in her room. Only that turned out not to be a good choice either, as Kristi and Madison both came and asked if they could use her room to stash presents in until Christmas, and then Sarah Ellis came looking for Kristi because they were going to go skating, and by that time Spirit gave up and went and hid in the back of the Library until lunch.

At lunch everybody was talking about how Claire Grissom had fallen while she was out skating and broken her ankle. Mr. Bridges had driven her to the hospital in Radial.

Or had he?

"When Kylee broke her arm in karate a couple of weeks ago, she didn't have to go to Radial," Spirit said carefully. "In fact, Claire Healed her."

"No," Loch said slowly. "She didn't, did she? And Claire's

not the only Healing Mage here." His expression was grim, and Spirit knew that he was thinking the same thing she was: Claire was tonight's Tithe to the Wild Hunt.

"But that was different," Addie countered. Spirit couldn't tell whether Addie was speaking for Spirit's benefit—or for the benefit of whatever unseen listeners they might have. "Claire's a Healing Mage. It's a lot harder to Heal a Healing Mage than it is to Heal a regular person. And if their Healing Gift is strong enough, it's impossible."

"Sucks, huh?" Muirin said, reaching for her cup.

"In a word," Loch agreed.

During lunch Loch complained about the lack of proper winter sports equipment, saying that this was the perfect weather for cross-country skiing, and Muirin pointed out that you couldn't ski very far before you were off the grounds, and Addie said she was tired of listening to the two of them squabble. When lunch was over, Burke said he was going to go practice, and nobody even asked what he was going to practice, since Burke did just about every sport Oakhurst had to offer.

If Spirit had been restless in the morning, she was even more restless in the afternoon—but she felt as confined being indoors now as she'd been unwilling to venture out earlier. She went back to her room and changed into her heaviest outdoor clothes. Maybe a walk would clear her head.

❧

The brick walkways were clear as always—in fact, right now they radiated heat, as the Fire Witches had heated them to turn some stubborn ice into water that the Water Witches could whisk away. Which sure beat the heck out of having to shovel them, even if she did still think it was a little creepy. There hadn't been a lot of sunny days lately—and when there had been, she'd been stuck inside studying—and the combination of bright blue sky and sunlight on white snow was dazzling. Despite the fact that the hours were ticking inexorably away until the time the Wild Hunt rode out, Spirit felt her mood lighten. For a little while she could almost pretend that tonight wasn't going to come, because she'd spent the last four months learning about all the bad ways life was different at Oakhurst, but today seemed determined to show her there were good ways, too. She spent a solid fifteen minutes watching two groups of Air Mages having a snowball fight—only the way *they* did it, the snowballs hovered in mid-air between the two teams, buffeted back and forth on gusts of wind, until they finally fell apart.

When she got tired of watching them, Spirit walked on, to where another group of kids were standing around a mound of snow. Bare patches on the ground and a couple of discarded snow shovels showed where the snow had come from. But why? . . .

Suddenly the snow mound began collapsing inward, melting down into water, but before it could trickle away, it swirled upward. First into a column, and then making a lightning transformation through a dozen different shapes: tree, dancing figure, rearing horse, bird in flight, leaping tiger. Each shape was shimmering and transparent like the water it was composed of, and as realistic as if it were the living thing it was modeled after. Each new shape was greeted with laughter and cheering until at last the water took the form of a dragon with spread wings and arched neck. Amid whistles and applause, the glistening water of the draconic form silvered over as it was turned to glittering ice.

But Spirit had only a moment to admire the ice dragon before the unbalanced weight of its own form fragmented it. The delicate outstretched wings snapped off and shattered, the head broke from the slender coiled neck, and the whole sculpture lurched to one side, toppled, and shattered. Its fall was greeted by groans of disappointment from the onlookers, then the Fire Witches began melting the ice so they could begin the game again.

Of course, not everyone who was enjoying the winter holiday was using magic to get pleasure from it. There were ordinary snowball fights going on, and Spirit even saw a couple of snowmen, looking a little odd decked out in Oakhurst caps and scarves. But she didn't want to get into a snowball fight with anyone, and the snowmen only reminded her of building snowmen with Phoenix. She walked quickly past them, staring straight ahead.

Spirit was a little surprised to find that she'd walked all the way down to the train station. Surprised—and cold. But it was interesting to see that the tracks were completely clear of snow, just as the walkways were. She glanced back over her shoulder at the house, then along the tracks. *Even if there is a full moon tonight, if someone took the path down to the train station, and then followed the tracks as far as they could before heading out into the snow, I bet their tracks wouldn't be visible from the house. . . .*

🌟

Spirit had reason to be grateful for that forethought not too many hours later, as the four of them crept out of the classroom wing of the main building. Muirin had passed her a note at dinner, telling her to be ready to go at eleven. Dorm curfew was at ten, lights out was at eleven . . . but somehow Spirit suspected nobody would look too closely at anyone sneaking out on a night that the Tithe to the Wild Hunt had to be paid.

We're only hoping it's just one teacher who's working for the Bad Guys. It could be two, or three, or half a dozen. And it isn't as if we even know what their Mage Gifts are!

But she could worry about that later. If she worried about it now, she'd make mistakes she couldn't afford to make. *"Never borrow trouble,"* Dad always said. *"The world gives enough of it away free."*

Oh, God, she just wanted to go *home.*

But you don't have a home anymore, remember? Spirit told herself viciously. *The Bad Guys took it away from you. They sent a monster to kill you, and all they managed to do was kill your whole family instead. And someday you'll be able to pay them back. But you have to survive Oakhurst first.*

So she was waiting in her room, dressed and ready to go, when Muirin came to get her.

⁂

To Spirit's surprise, they didn't go directly out of the building, but into the classroom wing and then down to the basement. Muirin opened the door to one of the practice rooms. Addie was already there, and so was Burke.

Spirit was distracted from wondering where Loch was by the sight of Burke, because he had a shotgun under one arm and he looked as if he certainly knew how to use it. "I, uh, what?" she said.

"Skeet shooting," Burke explained. "There's a whole room full of shotguns and rifles here. It wasn't too hard to get in and borrow one, especially since I'm on the rifle team and the skeet-shooting team during the season. Talking Muirin out of her skeleton keys—twice—now *that* was the hard part, but I figured I was going to need it." He pulled a shotgun shell out of his pocket and held it up. "They're filled with salt," he explained simply. "Blessed salt. I've been making them all week. Should have enough to take out a whole army of ghosts without having to get too close."

"Technically you 'lay' a ghost," Addie said pedantically. She picked up her own "weapon" from the table and brandished it. "Meanwhile, this should take care of any elves we meet."

"Say hello to my little friend," Muirin said, and snickered.

Spirit blinked in perplexity at Addie's choice of armament: It was a large green-and-silver plastic thing that looked like a sci-fi movie ray gun. She wondered where Addie could have gotten it on such short notice.

"A Super Soaker with a modified pressure relief valve, increased aperture, and a four-liter reservoir. It has maybe a fifteen-yard range, but fortunately I'm not limited to *its* range—and there are enough iron filings in the water to send any elf, fay, or fairy I hit with it straight back to the Hollow Hills with its tail tucked between its legs. It's a good thing Oakhurst has a metal shop," Addie said. "Believe it or not, this is actually something I borrowed from the lab. There are times when it's *good* to be a Water Witch."

"Me, I'm going with a slingshot and some iron balls. They used to be glass marbles, but . . . I've got connections." Muirin smirked. "Too bad illusions won't be much use tonight."

"Okay, we're all here, let's go," Burke said, ignoring Muirin's last comment. "Spirit, maybe you could carry that? Loch told me he was going to need it."

He gestured at the table. There was still a leaf blower sitting on it, one of the self-contained gas-powered kind. "But . . . where is he?" Spirit asked. "Aren't we waiting for him?"

"He's already up there," Burke said grimly. "He's been sneaking up there for days to work on the spell-trap, but he said he wanted to put the finishing touches on it tonight."

Spirit felt horribly exposed as she walked out of the building with the others. What if someone saw them carrying all this stuff? The moon was full and bright, and there were still lights on in the main building.

"Don't you get it yet?" Muirin said, seeing her expression. "Nobody's going to stop us. There are eight nights of the year that somebody on this campus is sure to make it *easy* for any-one who wants to go out of bounds. Why not? I bet an extra Tithe or two only makes things better for whoever's doing this."

Spirit swallowed hard. Muirin was right. She wondered where Claire Grissom was right now. Out there somewhere shivering with fear and cold and pain? Unconscious? She couldn't be dead: If there was one thing that Spirit had picked up from all the lore about the Wild Hunt, it was that it ignored dead things.

They followed the brick walkways down to the little pri-vate train station, then walked along the tracks for about half a mile. This far away from everything, the wind cut like a knife, and even in her warm clothes, Spirit shivered con-stantly. She was surprised—and grateful—to find, when they finally had to abandon the tracks to head for the stand of pines, that the snow was only a few inches deep.

"The wind blows it and scours it off the open plain. It piles up around the buildings, because the buildings are the only things out here to stop it," Burke said, when she exclaimed in surprise. "It shouldn't be too deep out here for a few weeks yet."

At least something's going right tonight, Spirit thought. She did her best to smother the thought, hoping it wouldn't jinx everything else that was going to happen.

❧

Loch was waiting for them in the tiny pine forest. The moonlight was bright enough that even under the trees he was plainly visible. "Oh, good," he said, taking the leaf blower from Spirit. "You brought it."

"No," Muirin said. "We thought we'd just leave it behind and ruin your plans."

"Fun-*nee*," Loch said, deadpan. He set the leaf blower carefully behind a tree. Spirit looked around, but she couldn't see anything anywhere that looked like the drawing of the spell-trap she'd seen in Loch's notes.

Loch looked at the others. "Okay. I guess we're ready."

"Except for . . . how do we make sure the Hunt comes after us—and not after somebody else?" Addie asked.

This is a fine time to wonder that! Spirit thought, even as she realized that hadn't occurred to her, either. What if they just *missed* them?

"North," Loch said with certainty, glancing toward the white pillar that marked the edge of the school bounds. "Just head north and keep heading north. The Hunt should show up pretty quick as soon as we're off the school grounds—and outside the wards."

Burke nodded, and pulled off his heavy gloves, exposing the thin glove liners underneath them. He stuffed a hand into his pocket and pulled out two shells, dropping them into the barrels of the shotgun he held. When he slammed it shut, the sound echoed through the trees with a terrible finality.

With Burke in the lead, they stepped from beneath the shadow of the trees and began walking north.

ELEVEN

Spirit knew it was probably her imagination that made the night suddenly seem colder the moment the five of them passed the boundary stone. The wards were impalpable, intangible spell barriers that only served to keep baneful creatures and uninvited guests outside them. Magicians would experience a ward as a barrier as real and solid as a stone wall. Normal non-magical people would simply choose not to go through a ward—and their minds would come up with a dozen different reasons why. They'd forget where they were going, or get lost, or think of something they suddenly needed to do somewhere else, or even get sick and need to leave.

All that aside, there was no way any Oakhurst student would actually be affected by them. The wards weren't designed to keep anyone *in*, nor were they designed to keep the

Oakhurst students *out*. No, thinking she could feel them was only nerves.

Their boots crunched over the frozen surface of the snow as they walked, and the night air was so utterly still that the sound of their footsteps was the loudest sound there was. The full moon was almost directly overhead, and the stars were brilliant in the clear night sky. They were so far from any city that the Milky Way was even visible.

When they'd gone about a hundred yards from the trees, Muirin stopped, reached into her pocket, and made a tossing motion.

"What's that?" Spirit asked, her voice barely a whisper. She'd seen *something* leave Muirin's hand, and heard a faint pattering sound as something hit the icy unbroken crust of the snow, but she wasn't sure what Muirin had thrown. She knew she didn't have to whisper out here—no one from Oakhurst could hear them, and whatever else was out here was something they *wanted* to hear them, but in the utter silence she couldn't help it.

"Shoeing nails," Muirin said, and Spirit noticed that Muirin was whispering, too. "You know, like for shoeing horses? Soft iron, and the lore mentions horseshoe nails—specifically—a lot. There's a whole big keg of them down in the stable. They won't miss a few."

Muirin stopped to scatter them again when they'd walked on for a few more minutes. "We're going to feel pretty stupid if all that happens is we end up walking all the way to Radial," she said.

She was about to keep walking when Spirit grabbed her arm. "Wait," she said. "Listen. Do you hear it? Horns." The sound was so faint she could barely hear it, even in the silence: a mellow sweet sound that reminded her of French horns. It was so beautiful that she took a step toward it, wanting to hear it better.

"There aren't any roads out here," Muirin said, suddenly sounding rattled.

"Not car horns," Burke replied grimly. "Hunting horns."

"I don't hear anything," Addie said nervously.

"Doesn't matter," Burke answered bleakly. "I do. And so does Spirit."

Suddenly Spirit felt the first faint breath of wind touch her cheek. The horns sounded again—louder, closer—and abruptly she felt a wild stab of panic. They were doing this all wrong! They'd never stopped to think—if just meeting up with the Wild Hunt drove you insane, how were they supposed to destroy it?

"Only the Wild Hunt's actual victims can hear the horns of the Hunt," Loch said. He didn't just sound nervous, Spirit realized with another pang of fear, he sounded terrified. "I never counted on one of *us* hearing—being—" He gulped. "Look. We might be in real trouble here. We'd better—"

"Listen!" Muirin cried, her voice cracking.

In the distance they could hear the sound of engines.

A lot of them.

We need to get back to the trees!" Loch cried frantically.

The current of air Spirit had felt earlier wasn't just a faint breeze now. It was an actual wind, ice cold and skin-numbing, blowing straight from the north. She glanced at Burke. He looked grimly determined.

"No," she said quickly, hating the way her voice shook. "If we turn and run, we're doing just what they want. If we run, we'll panic, and if we panic, we'll forget what we have to do. We can't give in to fear. We have to—" She broke off as a chorus of howls filled the night, momentarily drowning out the sound of engines. The howls seemed to echo inside her skull, half wolf-howls, half too-human screams of agony. "We have to see what they are," she finished in a shaking whisper. But inside, it felt like everything was turning into cold water. *They know about us. They're coming for us.*

Only Burke stood still. Loch was edging back the way they'd come and so was Muirin. Even Addie looked as if she was going to drop her Super Soaker at any moment.

If they broke and ran—

Every horror movie she'd ever seen told her what would happen. *Separate and run and everyone dies.* She dug deep inside herself and found one tiny crumb of courage. *Maybe I'm going to die, but I won't let them get the others!*

"Come on!" Spirit shouted at the top of her lungs, turning to face the other three. "We came here to do this! We have to! Loch! *The wards aren't going to protect us!* Not tonight!"

It was as if her shouting broke the spell of fear the approach of the Hunt had cast over them. Spirit saw Addie draw a deep breath and take a firmer grip on her squirt gun. Loch nodded. And suddenly Muirin screamed—a high wavering fingernails-on-a-blackboard sound—and pointed.

The Hunt was here.

Spirit turned back just in time to see them appear. "Appear" was the word for it: One moment there was nothing on the endless white moonlit snowfield, and the next moment there was a line of vehicles heading right for them. They left no tire tracks in the snow, and they were running without lights.

As the vehicles got closer, the five of them could see they— Jeeps, SUVs, a couple of pickup trucks—were all rusted, burned, and half-wrecked, as if they'd come from some supernatural junkyard. Their windshields were shattered, their tires were flat—and some had no tires at all. Lashed to every grille or hood was a set of antlers: deer, elk, even moose. And every set of antlers was garlanded with a withered wreath of evergreen.

But that wasn't the most terrifying thing about them. Because each vehicle held passengers.

Some leaned out the sides of doorless roofless SUVs. Some stood in the passenger seats of roofless Jeeps. Some stood in the beds of pickup trucks, whooping and hollering and urging the drivers onward. All of them were dressed in the ragged remains of hunting clothes—hunter's orange and red-and-black buffalo plaids and woodland camo—and every single one of them was dead. Skeletal hands gripped roll bars and steering wheels and door frames. Eyeless skulls covered in tatters of rotting flesh gazed avidly toward their prey. All of them were carrying shotguns or rifles.

Suddenly all the headlights of the Hunt's vehicles came on at once. For a handful of seconds the five teenagers stood petrified in the glare as the Wild Hunt raced closer.

Then Burke raised his shotgun to his shoulder and fired.

The sound of the gunshot was loud enough to shock them out of their terrified stupor. Even through the dazzle of the headlights, Spirit could see Burke's first shot had taken the driver of one of the Jeeps square in the chest. The hunter had dissolved into smoke, but the Jeep seemed capable of acting on its own. Burke fired again—at the Jeep itself this time—but his second shot had no effect.

"It's not a ghost! Run!" he shouted.

But Addie had already raised her Super Soaker. She'd said its maximum range was fifteen yards—but Addie was a Water Witch. It didn't matter that she was firing into the wind; when she pumped the trigger, the jets of water flew from the nozzle and kept going, as if they were arrows—or bullets. When the jets of iron-laden water struck the same Jeep Burke had ineffectually fired at, there was another ear-splitting howl—like an animal in pain—and the Jeep suddenly reared up on its back wheels and sank beneath the snow. It vanished without leaving any trace behind it—aside from its undead occupants, now sprawled in the snow. They scrambled to their feet and ran to one of the trucks, climbing aboard quickly, and left no footprints behind them.

Burke had already reloaded. He didn't bother to shoot at

the vehicles now; he aimed only for their occupants. When he hit them, they vanished. Banished.

The wind was almost a gale now, chilling them even through their warm coats and boots, numbing exposed flesh, making it hard to hear anything other than the howls of the Wild Hunt. As soon as they'd begun fighting back, the Wild Hunt had changed its tactics. It wasn't approaching them at a slow stately pace any longer. Now the remaining vehicles were speeding up, driving back and forth, trying to confuse them.

Trying to surround them.

"Run!" Burke shouted again, but it was already too late. Now they were in the center of a ring of trucks and Jeeps and SUVs, and any time he or Addie fired at one of them, their target would simply dodge out of the circle so that their shot went wild. Soon they would have used up all their ammunition.

They'd be helpless.

"Fish in a barrel!" Muirin snarled, brandishing her slingshot. "Come on, Ads! Let's give these losers a run for their money!"

"Glad to!" Addie shouted back. She and Muirin both targeted the same vehicle. The SUV swung out of the circle. Muirin's iron missile whistled harmlessly past it . . . and Addie's jet of water made a right-angle turn in mid-flight, spraying the unsuspecting truck behind it.

Once again, her target screamed and sank beneath the snow, bolting for the Hollow Hills and leaving its skeletal passengers afoot. The pickup truck behind it swerved to avoid running them over, and Burke took advantage of the moments that the hunters were afoot and vulnerable to empty both barrels into them. The shotgun shells filled with blessed salt did their work, and the ghostly huntsmen vanished.

Then, for an instant, there was a gap in the line. Loch grabbed Spirit and dragged her through it. She was running with him before she realized what she was doing. "What—? We— We *can't!*" she gasped.

"Ghosts— Elves—" Loch panted. "Have to lead them— Back over Muirin's— Traps—"

The nails in the snow! Would they work if the elf-trucks just drove over them? Were they even touching the ground? Could the others get away, too? She ran beside Loch, back along the footprints they'd left in the snow, and didn't dare stop to look back. *Ohgodohgod, we left them, we left them . . .* Behind her she heard Burke fire again and again, the sound loud even over the wail of the wind and the engines and the howling of the hunters. Tears of relief mingled with those of terror as Spirit heard running footsteps crunching and skidding in the snow behind the two of them—she was certain on an instinctive level that the Wild Huntsmen didn't make those sounds.

She thought she was running as fast as she could, but Muirin passed her and Loch—and then, incredibly, skidded to a stop. Muirin slid to her knees in the snow and didn't bother to get to her feet as she readied her slingshot again.

Spirit hesitated, but Loch grabbed her arm again and

yanked her onward so violently she slipped and nearly fell before she could recover her balance. Her throat was raw and burning with cold, and her chest ached as if she'd been punched. If she hadn't survived the accident that had killed her family, if she hadn't undergone months of painful grueling physical therapy to learn to walk again, she could never have kept up the pace that Loch set. But pain was an old friend to Spirit White. It was the one thing she wasn't afraid of. This wasn't any worse than the hospital. This wasn't any worse than waking up, knowing her whole family was dead, so broken that there weren't enough drugs in the world to keep her from feeling the pain of broken limbs and a broken heart.

Behind her Spirit heard another eldritch shriek as another of the not-trucks was sent back to the Hollow Hills. She heard Burke fire again—two shots, then he had to stop to reload—she heard Addie shout for Muirin to *come on, come on*—

"Okay, okay," Loch said, gasping for breath and slowing to a staggering walk. He waved behind him, obviously wanting to convey information but too winded to do it. Spirit stopped, leaning over, hands pressed against her thighs, breath whistling in her throat, coughing and choking as she sucked in great lungfuls of the bitterly cold dry air. She reeled, staggering as she finally turned to look behind her, squinting as she was painfully buffeted by the storm-wind the Hunt had summoned.

There were only five vehicles now instead of the dozen there'd been at the beginning. The Wild Hunt could have overtaken them in seconds if it had wanted to, Spirit thought, but the vehicles were moving forward at a speed no faster than a slow walk. Her friends were running away—but so slowly! And they were staggering as if they were sick or hurt.

"Come on, come on," Loch muttered.

Then Addie fell. The Super Soaker skittered out of her hands, spinning out of reach across the surface of the snow. She lunged for it, but Burke hauled her to her feet and dragged her onward.

"What's—?" Spirit gasped, still panting for breath. *What's wrong with them?*

Then she felt it. A wave of abyssal cold, rolling toward her through the wind as if somebody had just opened a giant freezer. It made the bone-chilling temperature of a moment ago seem balmy by comparison. Too cold to breathe, too cold to do anything but lie down and . . .

"Come on," Loch said, but this time he was speaking to her. "We have to . . . get out of . . . range."

Out of range of the spell, Spirit supplied mentally. But for a moment she couldn't move. She was staring at the driver of the single surviving SUV. The *rider,* rather, because he was standing on the front seat staring at them intently. Though he was dressed like his hunters in ragged hunting clothes, he had antlers—either attached to his cap or growing directly from his skull—and beneath the shadow of the cap's brim, his eyes glowed with a baleful crimson light.

"—demon—" Spirit gasped breathlessly. Not just ghosts.

Not just elves. There was a demon as well. They'd need Loch's spell-trap. And they'd need her spell. *But I don't remember the words!*

For the first time since that terrible night when she'd lost her family, Spirit believed—she *knew*—she was going to die. They were *all* going to die. Banish the ghosts, banish the elves, none of it would matter, because the demon would call up more for its Hunt.

But first—now, tonight—it was going to kill all of them.

Once more she and Loch began their nightmare flight across the snow. It was agony to Spirit to turn her back on her friends—on Burke!—but Loch wouldn't let her go. Tears froze on Spirit's cheeks as she staggered across the snow, every muscle aching with cold. The trees were just ahead, and with them the school boundaries, but there was no safety there. *I'm sorry, I'm so sorry, I didn't want to leave you, it wasn't supposed to happen this way* . . . She didn't have enough breath to tell Loch it was useless, all of this was useless—she didn't remember the spell, there was no point in luring the demon into the spell-trap, *she didn't remember the spell* . . .

She was so convinced she'd abandoned her friends to death that Muirin's whoop of triumph took her by surprise. "Keep going," Loch said as she hesitated. "Trees. Hide. Wait."

Spirit staggered on as fast as she could—alone now, because Loch was staying behind. She could see the trees shaking, tossing in the wind so violently they were shaking off all the snow on their branches. At the edge of the stand of pines, despite herself, Spirit turned back to look. Addie was slogging determinedly onward, staggering with exhaustion, but Muirin and Burke—and Loch—were just standing in the snow. Waiting for the Hunt—for the demon—to come within range. As Burke raised his shotgun again, the five remaining vehicles revved their engines and leaped forward. Burke fired methodically, reloaded, and fired again, and Spirit sobbed aloud in despair. She was going to have to watch them die, and she couldn't bear it!

As she watched, she saw Muirin get off a couple of shots with her slingshot, saw another of the Jeeps let out one of those bone-chilling screams before it sank down through the snow, but then Muirin threw her only weapon aside. Spirit knew without needing to see it that the intense cold had made the elastic snap.

And there were still four of the vehicles left: an SUV, two Jeeps, and a pickup truck.

Muirin and Burke both turned and ran, but Loch—much closer to safety—didn't move. Three of the vehicles followed—including the SUV with the demonic Hunt Lord in it—but the truck had circled back to pick up the hunters who'd been set afoot by the destruction of their eldritch vehicle. The other three sped toward them—

—and struck the scattering of horseshoe nails Muirin had strewn across the snow.

This time the mingled wails of agony were loud enough to make Spirit want to cover her ears. The three vehicles reared back and twisted and vanished beneath the snow.

Now the Hunt Lord was afoot, along with perhaps a dozen

ghosts. He gestured imperiously, and the last remaining vehicle zoomed forward at full speed, intent on running Burke and Muirin down. It crossed the second scattering of iron nails just as Burke turned back and fired. This time he'd loaded his shotgun with some of Muirin's iron balls as well as his own blessed-salt shells. The salt struck the eerie forms crowding the front seat and the iron balls buried themselves in the seat behind them. The truck shrieked in agony and fled back to the Hollow Hills. Spirit didn't know how many of its passengers Burke had also dispatched with those two shots, but as the rest of the ghosts ran across the snow toward him, Burke calmly reloaded, fired, reloaded, and fired again.

Run, Burke! You have to run! Spirit thought desperately, pressing her hands over her mouth to muffle her sobs. With every second Burke spent destroying the ghostly members of the Wild Hunt, its demonic Hunt Lord came closer. And closer.

And Loch still stood unmoving.

"Spirit! Hide!" Addie gasped, reaching the edge of the trees.

"But— Loch— Burke—"

"Loch has to lure him in—Burke has to kill the rest of them," Addie said, dragging Spirit back into the false safety of the trees. Their branches were still shaking, showering the ground below with snow.

A moment later Muirin joined them. "Where do we— What do we— How can we—" she babbled frantically. Addie simply grabbed her and hauled her—silently—to the far edge of the little woods.

Everyone had told Spirit to hide, but nobody had told her where. She didn't even know where the spell-trap *was*. They'd been spending so much time staying away from each other that they hadn't done all the planning they needed to. *Next time we set out to kill some demons we're going to plan things better,* she thought wildly. *Only there won't be a next time! I'm sorry—I'm sorry—I'm sorry—I wasn't good enough to do what you needed me to do—I'm sorry—*

The only place she could think of to hide was behind the tree where Loch had propped the leaf blower. She clung to it and rested her forehead against the trunk, trying to slow her breathing and stop crying. When Loch got the Lord of the Wild Hunt into the spell-trap, she was supposed to say the spell she was supposed to have memorized. And she couldn't remember the words!

A moment later Burke came running past her, staggering with weariness. She wanted to call out to him, to ask him where Loch was. *But I know where Loch is. He told me where he'd be. He's still out there luring that . . . thing . . . in here. That's why the others haven't just run for home. It would just follow their magic the way it's following Loch's.*

But it can't see me at all.

They'd only been guessing about that. She could only hope they'd guessed right.

It was quiet. It was too quiet. It was taking too long. *It got him.* The certainty of it settled on her like lead. Everything they had planned had fallen apart. Everything they had done was for nothing. Loch was dead—that *thing* had gotten him, and it was going to come and take the rest of them because the whole plan depended on her and she couldn't do what she was supposed to do. She blinked back tears. It was so cold out here they were freezing on her eyelashes.

It was so cold . . . .

Suddenly Loch came stumbling and staggering into the clearing. He grabbed the leaf blower and slung the carrying strap over his shoulder. He scrabbled for the starter cord, but he couldn't grip it in his heavy gloves. He pulled them off and flung them aside, then yanked at the starter cord over and over.

But nothing happened.

Spirit looked back the way they'd come. The Lord of the Hunt was only a few yards away from the edge of the stand of pines now, walking toward them with a slow measured tread. With each step he took, his appearance changed. Tattered hunting clothes became a long fur cloak over armor. Battered work boots became high black boots with jeweled spurs. A bill cap and deer horns became a helmet with stag's antlers. Only the glowing red eyes were the same. She was shaking so hard with fear and shame that if she hadn't been holding onto the tree, Spirit would simply have fallen to the ground. *All for nothing. It's all been for nothing. . . .*

As the Hunt Lord walked into the grove, the temperature dropped so sharply that Spirit heard the trees crack and groan as they froze. Loch was still working with single-minded determination at the little engine of the leaf blower as the demon lord silently paced toward him.

And—finally—the little engine caught.

The demon was so close Spirit ached with cold. So close every breath she took was like breathing liquid fire. It was too cold for anyone to be able to smell anything, but despite knowing that, Spirit had the relentless sense that she could smell some horrible combination of sun-heated decaying garbage and burnt rubber and rotten eggs. And though she knew the only sounds in the pine grove were the sounds of the wind in the branches and of the leaf blower's two-stroke engine, she had the conviction she could hear screaming—as if the sound of something in terrible pain was stuck in her head like one of those earworm songs you just couldn't shake.

And there was one more thing she knew: When the demon Huntsman touched Loch, Loch would be dead. She knew Loch knew it, too, but Loch didn't move. He just stood there like some maniac groundskeeper as the demon stepped closer, and closer . . .

And then, just as it reached out its hand to touch him, Loch swept the leaf blower down toward the ground.

Pine needles blew upward, skirling everywhere, and beneath them, Spirit could see the ground had been scraped down to bare earth, and then carved, carefully and elaborately, with the lines of the spell-trap, and the lines of the carving filled in with a mixture of charcoal and sulfur and saltpeter. She knew that was what Loch had used, because those were the materials the spell-trap had to be drawn in if you were drawing it on a bare floor. He must have used water to bind it all together and hold the mixture to the ground—frozen— when he blew the leaves away.

The demon looked down at the intricate design beneath its feet, and as it did, all the marks flared blue, burning with a literally unearthly light. It hissed—the first sound Spirit had heard it make—and when it tried to step out of the design again, it couldn't.

Loch shut down the leaf blower. "Gotcha," he whispered into the sudden silence.

Spirit stared at the tableau before her, her mind utterly blank, knowing that Loch was waiting for her to do her part. The lines of the spell-trap were already dimmer than they had been a moment before. When they went dark, the demon would be free. She closed her eyes, knowing she'd failed them all.

I— Can't—

"Spirit?" Loch said, and she heard the confused fear in his voice. "Spirit, why? . . ."

"*'Can't' isn't in our vocabulary, Spirit.*" The words in her mother's voice cut through the cold, through her paralysis.

Suddenly she felt an uprush of heat through her entire body, as intense as if she, not the spell-trap, was aflame. She took a deep breath and began to speak, her mind automatically translating the Latin into English as she went.

"*Hear me, ancient Abomination, firstborn of Creation, you who have rejected your birthright to reign over the charnel-houses of the Uncreated: I cast you forth from this place! I revoke your license to trespass here, in the name of those who have kept faith: in the name of those who have kept faith, I take from you the name you have been given in this place and name you outcast! I cast you out, to* reign in the place of skulls! I cast you out, to reign on the field of blood! I cast you out, to reign over the Uncreated! You have no dominion here!

I charge you to go from this place! By the power of this seal and this covenant: I charge you to go forth from this place! By the power of this ancient spell and working: I charge you to go forth from this place! By the power of your true name, to be spoken upon the day of reckoning: I charge you to go forth from this place! Come here no longer—stay here no longer—return here no more! I take your name—I take your form—I send you forth! Begone! Begone! Begone!"

By the time she'd reached the end of the Spell of Dismissal, Spirit was shouting as loud as she could. And as she reached the last syllable of the dismissal, suddenly the spell-trap flared up even more brightly than before.

It was as if the carved design on the ground and the demon huntsman were both just water in a bathtub and somebody had suddenly opened the drain. The edges of the spell-trap started to draw inward—sliding across the ground just as if the entire design were a puddle of water being sucked down a drain—and the demon trapped inside began to sink down beneath the earth, its body stretching and narrowing as if it were being sucked down a straw. In moments both it and the spell-trap were gone completely, and there was nothing left behind but bare earth.

At the instant the demon vanished, the air went completely still. Spirit staggered out from her hiding place on unsteady legs, feeling as if the air were not only warmer, but *cleaner* than it had been a moment before. Loch stared at her, the expression on his face slowly moving through baffled confusion to realization toward joy. He raised a hand and took a step toward her—

And suddenly Spirit was seized and lifted off her feet and spun around in a rib-cracking hug as Burke reached her.

"You did it! Spirit! You did it!" he cried. He set her down a moment later, but only so he could reach out an arm to hug Loch, too.

"We *all* did it," Muirin complained, coming back into the woods. But her voice still shook, and Spirit could tell that her heart wasn't in her usual griping.

"That we did, Murr-kitty," Burke said, his own voice giddy with relief. Spirit hugged him very hard. She'd almost lost him—lost all of them—tonight. And she didn't think she could bear losing anyone else. Not now. Not ever again.

"Oh my God," Loch said, laughing. "We won. We did it. I don't believe it."

"Well, you better believe it," Burke said. "With Spirit here on our side, how can we lose?" As if realizing he'd been holding her too close for too long, Burke let go and both he and Loch reluctantly stepped away from her.

"Oh but I—" *I don't have any magic.* Spirit had been about to make her habitual protest, when suddenly she stopped. Loch said there were no "false positives" in magic, and . . . if she didn't have her magic *yet,* then just what *had* she felt when she'd spoken the spell that sent the Lord of the Wild Hunt back to Hell? She knew she'd felt *something*. Something new. Something strange. She just wasn't sure what yet.

"—are a good person to have on our side, no matter what," Loch finished for her. "I'm sorry I doubted you, even for a moment."

"I never did," Addie said firmly, walking up to Spirit and hugging her very hard. "I'm so glad we're all still alive!" she added.

"So am I," Spirit said. "Oh, Addie—Muirin—Loch—all of you—"

"Hey," Muirin said shakily. "Don't get all emo. We've still got to sneak back into the dorms. And we'd better hurry. I'm freezing!"

"Not to mention putting back what we borrowed," Burke said.

Addie snorted. "If anyone thinks I'm going after that Super Soaker, they can think again."

"Come *on,*" Muirin said impatiently.

But the shocks and impossibilities of the night weren't over yet. When they walked from the little grove of trees—Loch carrying the leaf blower and Burke carrying the shotgun— they saw . . .

"Uh . . . Guys, isn't that the sun coming up over there?" Muirin asked, sounding baffled. "You know? In the east?"

"That's where it usually comes up—okay, more to the south this time of year, but—" Loch broke off as he glanced at his watch. "It's stopped. Burke?"

"Mine, too," Burke said, confused.

Muirin wasn't wearing a watch, and when she checked, Addie discovered she'd lost hers some time during the night. Spirit checked hers, and found it had stopped as well. When she and Burke and Loch compared notes, they found that their watches had all stopped at exactly the same time: 12:46 A.M. Or . . . probably just about the time she'd first heard the horns of the Wild Hunt. Despite herself, Spirit shuddered. As if she needed something else to have nightmares about!

"But I know we haven't been out here this long," Burke said in bewilderment. "We left at eleven p.m., and okay, it's been maybe—what? Three hours?" He looked at them. Spirit nodded—that felt about right to her.

"Maybe four at the outside," Loch said. Addie and Muirin just shrugged.

"Okay," Burke said. "But that is *definitely* dawn over there. And sunrise is at 7:48 on December twenty-second. And this is December twenty-second . . ." His voice trailed off as if he wasn't quite sure.

"We're busted," Muirin said gloomily.

"It was the elves!" Addie said abruptly. "Spend a few minutes—or an hour—with the Fair Folk, and when you get home, months or . . . years . . . have passed."

"It can't have been that long!" Loch said in horror. "It's still winter! It *is*!"

"It might be winter *again*, Loch," Burke said with a frightening gentleness. "We'd better get back—take our lumps—and find out how long we've really been gone."

It isn't fair! Spirit thought angrily. A moment before, they'd all been so happy. They'd won. The Wild Hunt was gone. Nobody else was going to have to die. And now . . . who knew *what* they'd find when they got back?

※

But what they found—as they neared Oakhurst—was their fellow students. The sun had just been rising as they left the forest, so by now it was about eight-thirty in the morning. Breakfast had been over for half an hour, and cold as it was, a lot of kids were already outdoors.

Kristi and Cadence were the first ones to spot them. They came running over and then simply stopped and stared.

"Oh my God, Burke, is that a *gun*?" Kristi said, her blue eyes very wide. "Addie, I was trying to IM you all last night and all this morning! The dance is tonight! You can't just go running off like that the night before the Winter Dance! Oh my God!"

"I'm really sorry," Addie said, and Spirit resisted the urge to break down in hysterical giggles, because this was just so ridiculous. *I'm so sorry I couldn't stick around to deal with your emo pain! I was busy saving the world. . . .*

"Oh, Addie, you are in so much trouble," Cadence added. "*All* of you are. Where have you *been*? You are in so much trouble," she repeated. "You just—they didn't make an announcement or anything, but everybody *knows*."

"Well isn't that *special*?" Muirin snarled.

"Hey, uh, Claire. Is she back yet?" Burke asked hopefully.

"Sure." Cadence stared at him as if he'd grown an extra

head. "They kept her overnight down in Radial because they had to do surgery to fix her ankle, she said, but she's back now. And she's excused from all of her sports for the next three months," she added, a little enviously.

Burke glanced at Spirit and smiled, and she smiled back. *This is why we did it,* she thought. *The rest really doesn't matter.*

By now the five of them had attracted everyone's attention. Their fellow students were standing around them, staring at them as if they'd just come back from the dead—although of course none of them could possibly realize how right they were. Everyone was talking at once, asking the same questions over and over. Some of the questions were utterly inane (yes, Burke *really did* realize he was carrying a shotgun) and some of them were questions none of the five of them intended to answer—like where they'd been and what they'd been doing—because answering those questions would just get everyone, including them, into a lot more trouble. It was almost a relief when Angelina Swanson and Gareth Stevenson showed up from the house.

"Okay you guys, break it up, nothing to see here," Gareth said with kindly ruthlessness. "You guys don't want to get points, you know. The dance is tonight." Amid groans of disappointment, the students began moving away. Standing beside Gareth, Angelina simply regarded the five of them coldly. "All of you. Inside. Now," she said, when the last of the other kids had moved away.

At least we know it hasn't been seven months or seven years or, or, or something like that, Spirit told herself reassuringly. *The*

Hunt is gone, Claire wasn't Tithed to it, and we're back more or less the same day.

Gareth took charge of Burke's (long since empty) shotgun, and the two proctors brought the five of them inside to the Entry Hall. Angelina told them to wait right there at the foot of the staircase as she went off to inform someone in authority that they were back, but Gareth didn't protest when they all walked over to the enormous fireplace and stood in front of its roaring heat.

"I will never be warm again," Loch said solemnly, setting the leaf blower down at a careful distance from the heat and walking right up to the edge of the hearth.

"Thought you liked winter sports," Burke said teasingly.

"From now on, the only winter sports I like are the ones you can do indoors," Loch answered with feeling.

"I think you were very brave out there, Loch," Addie said softly.

"No," Loch said, after a moment's startled hesitation. "Burke was brave. He stood and fought back. All I did was run. I'm good at that."

"That's *not* what you did!" Spirit said fiercely. "You let that . . . thing . . . walk right up to you so you could trap it. You were brave. As brave as Burke was. Or Addie. Or Muirin—oh, Muirin, I couldn't believe it when I heard you call them 'losers.'"

"Yeah, well, they were, weren't they?" Muirin said, staring at the ground. "They lost, anyway."

"We were all brave," Burke said firmly. "I'd just rather not have to be that brave again," he added softly.

Spirit bit her lip. They were already in trouble. She wasn't going to make it worse by mentioning that their troubles were far from over, no matter what else happened today.

They'd just gotten warm enough to unbutton their coats and take off their hats and gloves and scarves when the tik-tik-tik of high heels on the tiled floor alerted them to someone's approach. To nobody's particular surprise, it was Ms. Corby. Despite her festive scarlet business suit and the glittering enamel holly-wreath brooch pinned at its collar, she was nobody's idea of a jolly Christmas elf. Instead, Doctor Ambrosius's personal assistant seemed a lot more like the elves they'd spent most of last night dealing with. She looked more than angry. She looked enraged.

"Doctor Ambrosius is taking time out of his very busy schedule to deal with all of you," she said, her words clipped and precise. "He expects a full explanation of your behavior. And so do I."

Asking isn't getting . . . Now, instead of Mom's voice or even Dad's, it was Phoenix's voice Spirit heard in her mind, in the bratty sing-song Fee used to put on when she wanted to drive Spirit absolutely crazy. *Ask-ing is-n't get-ing, ask-ing is-n't get-ing . . .*

Ms. Corby followed them into Doctor Ambrosius's office, instead of just ushering them in and shutting the door this time, as she had the day Spirit and Loch had come to Oakhurst. Spirit glanced quickly at the others, but Loch was the only one who looked unsettled by her presence.

There was no question of them being permitted to sit,

even if there'd been enough chairs here for the five of them. In fact, today there were no guest chairs in the study at all. The five of them stood in front of the desk like errant children as Ms. Corby walked around behind the desk and stood beside Doctor Ambrosius.

"I've brought the five missing students, Doctor," Ms. Corby said. "They walked right back in at dawn, after being gone all night."

Doctor Ambrosius was sitting at his desk, looking over a folder of paperwork. It was nearly a minute before he looked up from the folder. His blue eyes were as piercing as they'd been that first day, and Spirit shivered as he locked eyes with her, but despite herself, she couldn't look away.

"You have all disappointed me greatly," he said at last. "Mr. Hallows, I had hoped for great things from you. Miss Lake, you were doing so very well in your studies. And you, Miss Shae. You had shown such great improvement. As for you, Mr. Spears, Miss White, certainly one's transition to the larger reality represented by Oakhurst is a great shock, following as it necessarily does the loss of one's family. But I had not yet been dissatisfied in either of you."

There was another long silence as he continued to study them.

"I suppose you have an explanation for your behavior?" he said at last. "Miss White, you may begin."

"I, um, I—" Spirit was utterly flustered at the thinly veiled demand that she explain her—explain *their*—actions. She saw Doctor Ambrosius frown at her panicked stammering, and a combination of anger and determination made her take a deep steadying breath. *I faced down ghosts and killer elves and a demon tonight. I can face down one headmaster.*

Who also happened to be a magician.

"It began when we realized that whatever had happened to Seth Morris, Camilla Patterson, and Nick Bilderback was related, and was magical in nature," she said carefully.

It took the five of them over an hour to tell the story of the Wild Hunt. Of coming to realize that the Wild Hunt was riding through the hills around Oakhurst during the eight ancient Festivals, of researching its probable elements, of seeking out suitable weapons, of going out to stop it. Doctor Ambrosius let them tell the story in their own words and their own ways, only speaking when one of them hadn't made something clear enough, or when he wanted to hear a portion of the story from someone else.

The one thing they all avoided, just as if they'd rehearsed what they were going to say ahead of time, was any mention of an "insider" at Oakhurst working with the Hunt. Ms. Corby was standing right there, and while she didn't have any magic of her own, that was no proof she wasn't working with someone who did.

Their story was plausible enough without bringing up the trip to the subbasement and their discovery of Camilla Patterson's file. Loch told of sneaking in to visit Nick in the Infirmary, and Muirin confessed to manipulating Eddie Abbott into Scrying for her because she suspected Seth had been a victim of the same attacker. And as for Camilla's disappearance . . .

well, they only had Nick's word to go on that she'd been on the grounds when she vanished.

"So you see, sir, we weren't really sure whether the Hunt would come at all," Loch said earnestly. "If it didn't, well, we'd just hope to get back to our rooms with nobody being the wiser. And if it did, well, we just didn't want anybody else to die."

"I . . . see," Doctor Ambrosius said. There was a long tense moment, then he smiled. "Miss Corby, I have to say that these five young persons have acted in the finest tradition of Oakhurst. Wouldn't you agree?"

Ms. Corby looked as if her face was about to crack, but she smiled anyway. "Yes, Doctor Ambrosius. The finest tradition."

"And certainly there will be no demerits for any of you," Doctor Ambrosius continued, still smiling and nodding benignly. "Quite the contrary. Commendations all around, I should say. Yes indeed. Commendations. Splendid work. Excellent work. Now run along and enjoy your day. Oh, and I'm sure you'll be wanting nice hot breakfasts after that long cold night outdoors. Miss Corby, do see to it that the young people are provided with everything they need."

"Of course, Doctor Ambrosius," Ms. Corby said. She gestured toward the doors of the study and they began to move toward it.

"Oh, and just one last thing," Doctor Ambrosius said.

Everyone froze.

"I'm sure I don't need to tell you not to gossip about this," Doctor Ambrosius said. "It would only upset your classmates. We wish them to think of Oakhurst as a place of safety. Of

301

refuge. If you five have been forced to discover far too soon how fragile a refuge that is . . . I can only hope that strengthens your resolve to defend it on behalf of your friends. The day is coming, my young warriors, when you will be called to a greater battlefield."

His voice had become deeper and more sonorous as he spoke, and even though they were exhausted, all of them stood straighter upon hearing it.

"Yes, sir," Burke said proudly. "You can count on us, sir. We won't fail you."

"I know you won't, Mr. Hallows," Doctor Ambrosius said. "I know some day you—all of you—will make me proud. But today, please enjoy yourselves. You've earned your rest."

Ms. Corby gestured them toward the door once more.

The interview was over.

✦

Ms. Corby was her regular self: cold, formal, and pissy. Spirit thought it was really hard to cast her in the mental role of Secret Mastermind of the Evil Plot Behind The Wild Hunt.

"Do any of you need to visit the Infirmary?" she asked, gazing at all of them clinically. "No? Then I suggest that you go back to your rooms and change into clothing that looks less as if you've been rolling around on the ground in it all night, and present yourselves in the Refectory in thirty minutes."

✦

I t was only when the door to her room closed behind her that Spirit could feel as if it were all—finally—really truly over. Her dorm room looked strange, at the same time unfamiliar and exactly as she'd left it. *But I never expected to see it again,* she thought. *Not really.*

She would have liked to linger in a long hot shower, but now that the danger was over, her stomach was telling her forcefully that nerves had kept her from eating much yesterday and—according to the clock on her desktop—it was nearly three hours past her normal breakfast time, and on top of everything else, she'd been up all night. That shower would have to wait.

She pulled off her coat and tossed it on the love seat, then sat down in the chair to drag off her heavy snow boots. Doing that made her aware of aches and bruises she hadn't noticed until now—and Ms. Corby had been right; her clothes really *did* look as if she'd been rolling around in the dirt all night. She pulled out a set of clean ones and struggled quickly into them, only then noticing the state of her hair. She'd started the night with it in a long braid down her back under her coat, but somewhere along the way it had come undone, and now it was a mass of tangles.

As she stood beside her bed, muttering crossly as she dragged her hairbrush hastily through her hair, Spirit suddenly remembered what Kristi had said before they'd all come inside.

"*The dance is tonight! You can't just go running off like that the night before the Winter Dance!*"

"The dance is tonight—and I don't have a single thing to wear!" Spirit announced to the empty room. She sat down on the edge of her bed and laughed until her ribs hurt.

EPİLOGUE

I just hope this dance goes better than the last one," Loch said wryly.

"Well it couldn't go much worse," Muirin shot back, cutting in front of him deftly and snagging a Coke from the snacks table.

"Oh, hush, Murr-cat." Addie said. She glanced back at Spirit and Burke. "You'll jinx things."

"Never borrow trouble," Spirit said. "The world gives enough of it away free."

Burke chuckled ruefully in agreement. "That's the honest truth."

The gym had been decorated for the dance, not with a Christmas theme—as Spirit had half expected—but with an entirely nondenominational "winter" theme in silver, white, and blue. That meant giant glittering snowflakes hung from the rafters, streamers of white and blue crepe, and a lot of helium-filled balloons in the dance's signature colors clustering up near the ceiling. This time, the theatrical backdrops were painted with scenes of fantastic winter landscapes— some containing unicorns and fairy-tale castles—and all (as far as Spirit could tell) serving as an excuse for glitter. A lot of glitter. Of course, if the decorations made no concession to the holiday, the playlist certainly did. Practically every third song was an updated techno rap trance rock version of a familiar Christmas carol.

It was hard to believe that the five of them had stood in this very place just about six weeks ago, Spirit mused, and—and the most important thing on her mind was whether Loch or Burke would ask her to dance with them, and what she'd say if they did. So much had changed.

She'd changed.

It wasn't knowing about magic, because she'd known about that the day she came to Oakhurst. It wasn't just knowing that the safety she'd been promised here at the school didn't really exist, either, because since the night her parents had been killed, Spirit hadn't really believed in safety.

No.

Part of it was knowing that when danger came, she wasn't helpless. She could fight back. It might not look as if she could win, but she could still fight.

But the other part was knowing that the danger was much bigger than anything she could ever have imagined.

"You want some, uh, some punch or anything, Spirit?" Burke asked her.

"No, moron," Muirin said. "She wants to dance with you. You're supposed to be her date, remember?"

"Smooth, Muirin," Loch murmured. "Real smooth."

"Why yes, Muirin, I'd love to dance with Burke," Spirit said, her voice dripping with irony as she turned to face him. Burke was actually blushing. "I really would," she added more quietly, taking pity on him.

"Good," he said, gulping. "That's . . . good." Belatedly remembering his manners, he held out his arm to her. "Shall we dance?"

Spirit took his arm. She was so glad that—for reasons known only to Muirin—she'd all but pounced on Spirit as Spirit was dressing for the dance this evening and demanded that Spirit take—and open—her Christmas gift early. It had been one of those rayon "broomstick" skirts in a gorgeous sky blue, and while Spirit was stammering out her embarrassed thanks, because a handmade book cover really didn't seem to be in the same league, Muirin relented and said it wasn't just from her, but from her and Addie. The skirt went beautifully with the remade top that Spirit never really had the chance to show off at Halloween, and was a lot "dressier" than her blue jeans.

A slow dance was playing as they moved out onto the dance floor. Burke put his arms around her as if Spirit were made out of spun glass—red-hot spun glass. "This time last night I would have laid long odds against . . ." Burke's voice trailed off.

"I know," Spirit said, moving easily with him in time to the beat of the music. *May your days be merry and bright,* the singer crooned, but theirs weren't going to be, would they? This was Oakhurst.

"We still don't know who summoned up the Wild Hunt in the first place, do we?" she asked. "Or what they really wanted to use it for. I know Doctor Ambrosius says we—magicians—have enemies, but . . ."

"But if they know where we are, why haven't they done something about us—about him—a long time ago?" Burke wondered.

"Maybe they are," Spirit said. "And I think . . . that's what we're going to have to find out." *But not tonight,* she told herself. *Not tonight.*

Tonight she could dance with Burke and pretend that her life was still ordinary.

TURN THE PAGE
FOR A SNEAK PEEK
AT THE NEXT BOOK IN
THE SHADOW GRAIL SERIES.

There were about a hundred kids here at Oakhurst. It seemed like a lot when you thought about the fact that they were going to be your nearest and dearest until you left Oakhurst at twenty-one. *Or got sacrificed to demons, hey, anything to get out of SATs, right?* Spirit thought. It didn't seem like many when they were all gathered in the Main Hall and the place still echoed.

They'd all filed into the Main Hall by alphabetical order, but once they were there, Burke beckoned to Spirit, and she saw Loch and Addie were standing with him. Muirin joined them a few minutes later, looking—as usual—as if she were getting away with something. Conversation was kept to a subdued murmur.

That conversation died out completely with the entrance of Doctor Ambrosius. He was flanked by his assistants, Ms. Corby and Mr. Devon. Doctor Ambrosius looked like a venerable, old college professor, white beard, flowing white hair, tweed jacket with leather elbow patches, and all. Ms. Corby and Mr. Devon looked—well, like bodyguards. Bored bodyguards. Doctor Ambrosius gazed out at them for a moment, then cleared his throat meaningfully. Absolute silence descended.

"We are here to celebrate the end of another calendar year here at Oakhurst," he said, in a voice as smooth and reassuring as some documentary narrator on Discovery Channel. "Some of you haven't been with us long and some are extended residents, but all of you are part of the Oakhurst family. Indeed, following the deaths of your parents, Oakhurst *is* your family now."

He beamed at all of them, but the moment his gaze had gone to another part of the room, Loch leaned over to whisper in Spirit's ear. "Does he practice being that tactless, or does it come naturally?"

"So, as the old year ends and the new one begins, we pause for a time of remembrance. Remember—always—that it is your responsibility to live up to the high standards that other members of your Oakhurst family have set. An Oakhurst graduate who is merely average is one who has failed. An Oakhurst graduate soars where others plod. And an Oakhurst student can never rest on his accomplishments, for while he is resting, others are overtaking him."

He paused, and Ms. Corby signaled what was expected of them by initiating a patter of light applause.

"Now, in the generous spirit of the season and your family,"

Doctor Ambrosius concluded, beaming on them all again, "let us commence the distribution of gifts."

While Ms. Corby and Mr. Devon handed out gifts, Spirit stood there feeling a kind of bemused horror. When the kids had disappeared, Oakhurst had covered things up with lies that were meant to be reassuring. And maybe they'd had a good reason at the time, but now that she and the others had defeated the Wild Hunt, Spirit had expected some kind of announcement. Wasn't the Wild Hunt a part of what they were being trained to defend themselves against? Didn't its appearance mean they should all be warned to be extra careful? Oakhurst wasn't safe. The enemies Doctor Ambrosius had talked about the day she'd arrived weren't out there. They were in here. They had to start figuring out what was going on. *Now,* before whoever it was that had been behind the Wild Hunt came up with a new way to kill them.

She was so lost in her thoughts that it wasn't until Loch nudged her sharply in the ribs that Spirit noticed Ms. Corby standing in front of her with a look of impatience on her face. She was holding two small boxes wrapped in gold paper with a cream and brown design on it. Spirit reached for the gifts. Ms. Corby held onto them, staring at her meaningfully.

"Thank you, Ms. Corby," Spirit said, flushing angrily. Ms. Corby smiled in triumph and handed Spirit the boxes. Spirit looked around at the others. Addie had a long flat box about the size and shape of a board game under one arm. Burke was holding a large square box about twelve inches on a side. Muirin had a small box about three by three by ten.

And Loch had two boxes identical to Spirit's in every way. He brandished the larger of the two boxes.

"iPod?" Spirit mouthed.

Loch was about to answer, but Mr. Devon had stepped in front of the fireplace.

"Every winner—and you're all winners here at Oakhurst—knows that one of the sweetest fruits of victory is the chance to kick back and enjoy what they've won. All of you have worked hard this year. Now is the time to enjoy yourselves. A dessert buffet is set up in the Refectory. Enjoy!" he added, clapping his hands together and smiling brightly. Spirit thought it was the creepiest thing she'd ever seen—at least in the last few days.

When Doctor Ambrosius and his two assistants had gone, everyone began to head in the direction of the Refectory. Muirin was off like a flash, of course. Unlimited sugar.

"Yup. iPod," Loch said aloud, unwrapping the larger of the two boxes. "It's the Gift du Jour."

The "Gift du Jour" was brown, with the Oakhurst crest engraved on the back, and his name: *Lachlan Galen Spears*. Loch made a face and Spirit winced back in sympathy. It was awful to have a dorky name.

"They come in gold and cream, too, of course," Addie said kindly. "If you don't have one when you get here, you're pretty much guaranteed to get one for your first Christmas."

"Huh," Loch said, sounding surprised. "It's charged. And preloaded."

There was no real point in trying to push through the mob

of students heading for the Refectory, and one thing Spirit could say for Oakhurst was that when it decided to let them fall off the healthy diet bandwagon, it didn't stint on the junk food. There was no need to hurry, there'd be more sugar and chocolate than all of them could eat in a week.

Bread and circuses. For a moment she could hear her Mom's voice in her head. Mom had—*used to have*—a saying for every occasion. In Ancient Rome, the emperors used to keep the people from making trouble by giving them free food and free entertainment. Bread and circuses.

That's what we get, Spirit thought. *Every few weeks there's another school dance, and a lot of candy, and most of the kids don't look past that, to all the things that are wrong with this place. . . .*

"What color is yours?" Loch asked. With a feeling of resignation, Spirit unwrapped the larger of the two boxes. Her iPod was cream-colored. Same crest cut into the back, and her name: *Spirit Victory White.* She didn't bother to complain, even mentally, that now everyone at Oakhurst would know her middle name. She woke her iPod and looked at the preloaded playlist.

"Ah, I recognize this," she said mockingly, scanning the start of the list of titles. "This is next semester's Music History stuff."

"Heaven forbid we should actually use these for recreation," Addie said, her voice dripping with irony. "That would be frivolous. How ever could we expect to excel?"

"Ah, but you forget. We're all already winners here at Oakhurst," Loch replied, deadpan.

"Come on," Burke said. "It's cleared out a little, and we

should go find the Murr-cat and stop her from eating herself into sugar shock."

"Fat chance of that," Addie answered.

✦

The Refectory was full, but not crowded. Most of the crowd was around the dessert buffet, and Spirit had to admit it looked pretty. There were cakes on stands, plates of brownies, pyramids of perfectly round scoops of ice cream frozen so hard that it would take them at least half an hour to melt, and—because this was a school full of teenagers—stacked cases of soda.

The four of them, by mutual consent, took one of the empty tables at the opposite end of the room from the buffet table. Muirin saw them, waved, and came over carrying two plates heaped high with desserts—obviously one for herself, and one for all of them.

"I don't see how you can eat all that," Addie said as Muirin plopped down at the table opposite her.

"Practice," Muirin answered. She pushed the second plate toward them. It was stacked with brownies of various kinds.

Spirit picked up the top one and bit into it. She didn't have much of an appetite, but hey: chocolate. *Bread and circuses,* her mother's voice whispered in her mind.

"So, come on, open your other one!" Muirin urged around a mouthful of fudge and ice cream.

Spirit had almost forgotten about the second box. Why had she and Loch both gotten two when no one else had? She tore the paper off quickly. Inside it was a pasteboard box, and inside that was a tiny wooden jewelry box—a ring box—with the Oakhurst crest (what a shock) laser-cut into the top.

She opened it.

Inside, on a bed of black velvet, was what looked like . . . a class ring. She lifted it out of its box and inspected it curiously. It was gold—when she looked inside the band, she saw it was stamped 24K—and felt heavy, very heavy. On the sides of the band were the broken sword and the inverted cup from the Oakhurst coat of arms. The bezel of the ring said: *absolutum dominium.*

"Absolute dominion," Loch translated. He'd opened his own box and was looking at his ring curiously.

With everything else about the ring being so lavish, Spirit would have expected the stone to be something she recognized. But to her surprise, it looked like something "lab created." It was opaque like an opal; a strange glittery sort of opalescent blue, the kind of thing that made you think there were other colors in it, only no matter how hard you looked, you couldn't see them. . . .

Spirit tore her eyes away with an effort and stuffed the ring back into the box. It made her uneasy for reasons she couldn't quite understand. She saw Loch slip his on—of course it fit perfectly—and bit back the impulse to cry a warning. Against what?

"Oh, they gave you your rings," Muirin said offhandedly.

"Our rings?" Loch repeated, staring at his hand as if he were fascinated.

"Class rings. We all get them at some point in our first year at Oakhurst," Burke said.

"Why don't you wear them, then?" Loch wanted to know.

"Because they're dorky," Muirin said with contempt. "I mean, come *on*. Class rings? That's so fifties!"

"But—"

"Come on, Murr-cat," Addie said decisively. "You guys guard Murr's sugar-horde. We'll be right back."

Muirin rolled her eyes but followed Addie out of the room, while Burke continued. "You don't have to wear them, except for a couple of times a year—like Alumni Days, when we're doing the full School Uniform thing, with the blazer and scarf and everything, like we were—"

"—on the playing fields of Eton," Loch finished for him, in a broad fake English accent. Burke grinned at him.

"Some people wear them all the time, some don't," Burke continued. "The point about them is that they're . . . kind of magic. The stone changes color until it matches your school of magic."

Great. A wizardly mood ring, Spirit thought.

"It does?" Loch stared at his hand again. "Try yours, Spirit," he urged.

Reluctantly, she reopened the box and slipped it on. It felt cold and heavy against her hand—much colder and heavier than she thought it should.

A few minutes later, Muirin and Addie returned; Muirin thrust her hand under Spirit's nose and wiggled her fingers. Her ring was identical to Spirit's, except for the fact that the stone